the
Whole
Bright
Year

Debra Oswald is a two-time winner of the NSW Premier's Literary Award and the creator/head writer of the first five seasons of the TV series *Offspring*. Her stage plays have been performed around the world and are published by Currency Press. *Gary's House*, *Sweet Road* and *The Peach Season* were all shortlisted for the NSW Premier's Literary Award. Debra has also written four plays for young audiences – *Dags*, *Skate*, *Stories in the Dark* and *House on Fire*. Her television credits include *Police Rescue*, *Palace of Dreams*, *The Secret Life of Us*, *Sweet and Sour* and *Bananas in Pyjamas*. Debra has written three Aussie Bite books for kids and six children's novels, including *The Redback Leftovers* and *Getting Air*. Her first adult novel, *Useful*, was published in 2015.

the Whole Bright Year

DEBRA OSWALD

VIKING
an imprint of
PENGUIN BOOKS

VIKING

UK | USA | Canada | Ireland | Australia
India | New Zealand | South Africa | China

Penguin Books is part of the Penguin Random House group of companies
whose addresses can be found at global.penguinrandomhouse.com.

Penguin
Random House
Australia

First published by Penguin Random House Australia Pty Ltd, 2018

1 3 5 7 9 10 8 6 4 2

Text copyright © Debra Oswald 2018

The moral right of the author has been asserted.

Cover design by Alex Ross © Penguin Random House Australia Pty Ltd
Cover photograph by Shutterstock
Typeset in Adobe Garamond Pro by Midland Typesetters, Australia
Colour separation by Splitting Image Colour Studio, Clayton, Victoria
Printed and bound in Australia by Griffin Press, an accredited ISO AS/NZS 14001
Environmental Management Systems printer

 A catalogue record for this
book is available from the
National Library of Australia

ISBN 978 0 14378 825 6

penguin.com.au

For Lynne Downes

I begin to sing of rich-haired Demeter, reverend goddess,
Of her and her trim-ankled daughter . . .

Homeric Hymn to Demeter

PART ONE

PART ONE

ONE

The trees were loaded with fruit, and the peaches were colouring up well. Pallets of packing boxes waited in the shed, the coolroom scrubbed out, everything ready to go. But where Roza should have been able to see four or more pickers working in the orchard, there were just two people slogging away.

The regular picking team had failed to show. The team boss, Roy, was usually reliable – even if that man's breath was sour enough to pickle your eyeballs – but already it had been three days with no pickers. And so, Celia and Zoe, mother and daughter, were bringing in some of the peaches until things were sorted out.

The two of them had been working since five a.m. and now, mid-afternoon, the sun was fierce and their shirts were soaked with sweat, shoulders slumped from the weight of the picking bags.

Roza's job as fruit packer meant she could take refuge in the luxurious shade of the packing shed. This was just as well – she was in her seventies now and although she accepted her status as a wrinkled crone, it was better that the sun didn't shrivel her up any further, like an over-dried prune.

This was mid-December, at the tail end of 1976. The events Roza was about to witness were – well, maybe they weren't inevitable. She had always endeavoured not to judge other people's behaviour. She tried instead to observe with clear eyes, to imagine why a person would do this or that thing, to decipher what might be going on in their mind and in their body (yes, of course the body too, because so many beautiful and dangerous impulses arise there). Roza didn't always succeed in her attempt to suspend judgement – especially when it came to certain individuals in this story – but mostly what she observed was people doing their best, flailing about, trying to avoid the necessary losses.

From inside the shed, Roza had to squint against the glare outside to see Celia and Zoe in the orchard. She was often struck by the physical resemblance between the two – a similarity not obvious to some stranger who might wander past. Celia, the mother, was forty-two, with springy dark curls and olive skin. Zoe – sixteen now – had fine blonde hair and a complexion so pale that if she was upset or excited about something, the veins became faintly visible under the skin. Even her eyelashes were fair. When she was little, Roza used to call her Our Milk Princess.

Celia had always been vigilant about hats and sun-creams for her fair-skinned daughter. Wise, if you considered the desiccated faces of so many of the adults in this country, faces crusted with scabs where doctors had burned off their dangerous blotches.

But even if Zoe had inherited the colouring of the father, her mannerisms, her eyes, her strong jawline, were all the mother. And if an observant person watched them working there side by side, and saw the way they moved their limbs in the swing of the task, the rhythm of their bodies, that person would acknowledge the resemblance.

Roza had always thought Celia's farm was one of the most beautiful properties in the district. The orchard radiated out from the packing-shed yard like chunky slices of a pie, bordered by wind-break rows of conifers. The gravel road continued from the shed for another two hundred yards up to Celia's small weatherboard house with its deep verandahs, chicken coop and vegie garden all tucked in, almost hidden, inside a boundary of hedges and old, generously proportioned trees. The ground fell away behind the house pad-dock, sloping down to a pretty creek that ran strongly even in the driest summer.

At this time of the year, the comic-book green foliage of the fruit trees came from a different colour palette to the muted olive green of the surrounding wedges of bushland and the hazy grey–blue shape of the hills beyond that. Some people might think this mix of colours was incongruous or unnatural, but Roza found it lovely.

When Roza looked out into the orchard again, she saw that Celia and Zoe were emptying their picking bags into the bins on the trailer and climbing onto the small tractor they used to ferry the fruit. Celia drove along the track that looped around to the far end of the orchard, where there would be some blessed shade by this time of the day. Leaving Zoe down there to keep picking, Celia then brought the tractor up to the packing shed.

'How are you going in here, Roza?' asked Celia. She scooped up a peach from the bin and inhaled its scent. 'The Red Havens are perfect. A day over, if anything.'

Red Havens were always the first variety of the season on this farm and, as it happened, Roza's favourite.

The strident ring of the telephone made Roza wince, as it always did, the sound bouncing around the tin walls of the shed. In the corner, a wooden desk and a small filing cabinet served as the farm office. Celia had run an extension line down here from her home phone, with a robust ringer aimed out into the orchard so she wouldn't miss important calls.

As soon as Celia picked up the phone, Roza could tell from her tone, without needing to hear the words, that the news was disappointing. Celia covered the receiver with her hand to explain, 'Roy's in hospital. Poor guy cracked a couple of vertebrae.'

This was why Roy and his pickers had failed to turn up as promised. And according to the series of phone calls Celia then made, it seemed the whole team of workers had scattered, leaving her without anyone to pull in the Red Havens.

'Can you believe this? Best season for five years and the bloody fruit's going to rot on the trees.' Celia made an effort to laugh, even though Roza could see she was worried.

She flipped through the exercise book on the desk, looking for more phone numbers, and muttered half to herself and half to Roza, 'I could maybe hire some students through the teachers' college. But it'd take a few days to arrange that. Which doesn't help with the fruit that won't last until . . . Shit, shit, shit! Santino's not answering his phone. I should try ringing the guy down at the . . . Not to worry, not to worry. We'll be fine.'

Celia stuck at it, making call after call to dredge up experienced pickers from somewhere. She had installed an extra-long cord on the handset so she could move around, getting other tasks done whenever she was on the phone. Meanwhile, Roza got on with the job of packing the peaches from the bins.

Sometimes people expressed surprise that Roza, at the age of

seventy-two, was still working in the packing shed for her neighbour. In fact, many growers preferred to have the older women
working in the sheds because they were steady and careful with the
stone fruit. But it would be fair to say Roza was one of the oldest
packers, and it would be true to say she allowed herself to be a little
bit vain about that.

People were also surprised that Roza's accent was still strong,
considering she left Hungary before the war and came to Australia
decades ago. But because she had always spoken Hungarian with
her husband Sandor when they were home together, the old accent
got itself cemented in.

For days in the packing shed, Roza twisted her long hair up
into a bun to keep her neck cool. She wore comfortable sneakers
under her favourite Indian skirt – a flowing ankle-length garment
made from red, gold and purple fabric with tiny mirrors sewn
onto it. There would be people who considered this skirt too fancy
and overdressed for the packing shed, but Roza wasn't fussed. The
Indian skirt was snug but not too tight on the belly and offered
good airflow around the haunches on a hot day. She saw no reason not to combine comfort with bright colours. There was plenty
of misery in the world – why not wear something bright with tiny
mirrors sewn onto it if there was no one to stop you?

It was half an hour later when Celia and Roza heard a vehicle on
the gravel and both headed outside. Hit by the full sun of the yard
after the deep shade of the packing shed, they could not immediately
make out the occupants of the Holden pulling up next to the trailer.

'Hello!' Celia called out as Joe swung open the driver's door,
rolling up the sleeves of his business shirt.

Even adjusting for her bias as his mother, Roza had no doubt
her son Josef was a good-looking man. From his father, there were

cheekbones, broad shoulders and an abundance of lovely wavy hair. So it counted as even more of a shame that Josef had allowed himself to accumulate a little pudge around his middle. Roza would have liked to blame Heather, the wife. But in fact it was Josef's drinking that had lodged itself round his belly. Then again, he drank too much because he wasn't happy with the woman he was married to – even if he himself was refusing to face that – so Roza decided she could in fact blame her son's belly on Heather.

'Do you want a cold beer on this stinking day?' Celia asked him.

'Nah, I'm fine, thanks.'

'Of course he's fine,' said Roza. 'All he's done is drive here in his air-conditioned car from his air-conditioned office.' Josef worked as a solicitor, with his own practice in town. *A safe but very boring job*, Roza would have said, if anyone were to ask for her opinion of this career choice.

Joe leaned down to kiss his mother on both cheeks, sliding his face away from her questioning gaze. 'How are you, Mum?'

'Why do you come out here to check on me? I'm okay.'

'No checking going on. I'm here to do Celia a favour, hopefully. I tried to ring, but the line was busy.'

'Yeah, sorry,' said Celia. 'I've been giving the phone a walloping. Trawling for pickers.'

'Well, I might have found you some. These guys had a bit of car trouble just outside town.'

Joe turned round and noticed that his two passengers had not followed him from the car. He signalled *up here* to the young woman, who was hanging back, waiting for permission. The woman pressed her mouth into an awkward smile of greeting as she approached.

Roza watched Celia assessing the new arrival. She was only in her twenties but appeared to have done a lot of mileage. Small, sinewy, with too much dark eyeliner and long hair dyed too harshly black for her pale, freckled complexion. She wore a black tank top over tight jeans and bristled with metallic jewellery – several ear studs, rings on every finger and silver bangles lining her forearms like armour. This one was a spiky creature, ready to defend herself against whatever the world might throw in her face.

Celia smiled warmly and offered her hand. 'G'day. I'm Celia.'

'Oh – right – Sheena.' She darted forward to shake Celia's hand.

The other newcomer, the young man, had wandered towards the row of peach trees that grew close to the yard. He was reaching up to touch the spot where the fruit attached to the branch, enchanted by the sight. Roza glanced at Celia to see if she also was wondering whether this young man might be damaged in his head.

Sheena hissed to him, 'Kieran!' and he swung round with a smile so huge and vibrant, it was like some natural power source. He then slapped himself in the head with jokey self-reproach, aware that he wasn't where he was supposed to be.

Kieran bounded up towards the shed. He was tall, with long loose limbs, wearing board shorts, a singlet and sneakers without socks. Down his right arm, dragons and sea animals and tendrils of vegetation curled together in a tattoo that enveloped his arm – well, it would have enveloped it if the process had not been left unfinished, leaving gaps in the design and the bodies of some creatures only half formed. His hair must once have been cut in a mohawk with shaved sections and a longer strip on the top but it had been left to grow out so now it looked like a lopsided mistake. Even so, he was still beautiful in the way well-proportioned young bodies can shine no matter what ill-advised and ridiculous things have been inflicted upon them.

Roza assumed Celia would be uneasy about this strange couple arriving at her door. Then again, you could never be sure how a person might respond. And the young man, this Kieran, was undeniably winning in his handsome puppy-dog way.

'Hi! You must be Celia! This place is mad. The trees right down to the road – they're all yours?'

'Oh . . . yes.'

'Dead-set? All this excellent fruit!'

He grinned at her with such unguarded and exuberant good-will, Celia couldn't help but smile back. But her cautious brain was still ticking away and she was flustered for a moment. 'Uh – oh, excuse me, I should introduce – this is Roza. Joe's mum.'

Kieran swung his body around to offer Roza a flamboyant salute of greeting.

'She helps with the fruit grading and packing for us at this time of year,' Celia explained.

'An old lady with the sharpest eyes and the softest hands in the fruit bowl of New South Wales,' said Roza, dancing her hands in the air.

Kieran barked a laugh, delighted by this idea.

The woman, Sheena, was abrupt as she asked Celia, 'I heard you could have some work going – is that right?'

'Yeah,' said Celia, but there was a cautious thread in her voice. 'Any experience picking stone fruit?'

Sheena shook her head.

'Any kind of fruit?'

'None.'

Celia nodded slowly. 'Okay. I guess . . . that's teachable. And you guys have your own car?'

'Yeah, except it's stuffed. We had to leave it with the mechanic.'

'But when the car's fixed, you'll have transport out here from town every day?'

'Well, no . . . We can't get the car back till we earn the money to pay for the parts.'

'Oh, right,' Celia said. 'We're not set up to have pickers stay on-site.'

She was about to send these two away when the phone rang, relayed to the large bell on the corrugated-iron wall, a sound so sudden and piercing it made the young woman jerk with fright.

Joe followed Celia inside and waited while she took the call. When she hung up, she puffed out a weary breath. 'Bugger. Santino can't spare me any of his guys either.'

'Is there a chance these two could camp on your place?' asked Joe.

'I decided years ago not to go that way.' From the start, Celia had employed pickers who lived off-site, not liking the idea of strangers staying on the farm. 'And the thing is, Joe, you don't know these people.'

'That's true,' he conceded. He had only met them a couple of hours before, when he'd arranged for their car to be towed into the garage. 'They seemed a bit desperate, and I knew you were looking for people and I thought —'

'Oh, I know and I really am grateful, Joe. Thank you. But, y'know . . .'

'But you feel uncomfortable. I get that. Why don't I just give them a lift back into town.'

'I'm sure they're perfectly decent people,' said Celia, pressing the palm of one hand against her temple as if shoving thoughts back into her skull. 'I mean, I don't want to be some suspicious, purse-lipped, anxious creature . . .'

Sheena stepped forward to peer into the dimness of the packing shed. 'Look, um, if it's all a big hassle, don't worry.'

'Oh, Sheena, sorry —' Celia began, off-balance. 'It's just a question of —'

'We'll piss off. So, don't worry about it.'

'No, you know what? Don't piss off.' Celia gathered herself and walked back out into the bright yard. 'I've got twenty thousand peaches that have to be picked before they rot. I need hard workers in a hurry.'

'We need a few hundred bucks in a hurry.'

Celia pointed out the fibro cabin down the slope, in a clearing where the orchard split into two of its slices. The shack had been built as living quarters for pickers, back in the time before Celia owned the farm. Zoe had made it her cubby when she was little and then later, Celia and Zoe had happily camped there together for a few weeks while the roof of the main house was repaired. 'You could stay there. No electricity though. It's a bit primitive.'

Sheena shrugged. 'Primitive is okay.'

'And it's grubby. But we can clean it up. Why don't we go and find what we need to make the place decent, yeah?'

'Sure. Thanks,' said Sheena, then she turned to see that Kieran had wandered to the far end of the yard and was enjoying a curious poke around the fruit bins and the picking bags. 'Kieran!' she snapped at him. 'Stop fiddling with the people's stuff!'

'It's okay. Really,' Celia reassured her. 'In fact, Kieran, why don't you stay here and Roza can show you how that gear works.'

He grinned. 'I'm up for that.'

Sheena fixed the young man with a stern look. 'Kieran. Remember. Don't be a dickhead.'

He nodded resolutely, as if this were a necessary and particular instruction. Only then did Sheena seem willing to leave him on his own and head off with Celia and Joe to the main house.

Roza beckoned Kieran over to her. 'That contraption you're fiddling with is a picking bag.'

He marched across the yard and handed her the canvas bag. Roza ran her eyes over his upper body, calculating the length of his torso. 'You're tall. So I need to adjust this part to fit you.'

She tugged at the buckle on the webbing neck strap, cursing in whispered Hungarian when the thing proved to be jammed.

'Is it hard picking peaches?' asked Kieran.

'If you want to make the good money – pretty hard, yes.'

'I mean hard, like, difficult.'

Roza flapped her hand. 'You'll be okay.'

'This is such a beautiful place,' said Kieran, his bright gaze scanning the orchard. 'And you got peaches on tap! Oh – I guess you guys get sick of eating peaches.'

'Not so much. Because the season ends and by the time it comes around again you think, *Oh, peaches would be nice.*'

'Right. Right. I get you.'

Roza pointed to a bin of leftover peaches. 'Try one of the Red Havens.'

Kieran reached down to take one but then jerked his hand back like a kid caught stealing sweets. 'Oh – we really allowed to eat them?'

'Most of those fellows have a split. So, you might as well.'

He picked up a peach, and when he bit into the red and golden skin he gasped, miming the euphoric rush of a drug. But a moment later he grinned, surprised, sincere, his mouth full of the yellow flesh, and he blurted out, 'This is . . . far out . . . this is – how come I never tasted anything like this in my life before?'

'Because you only ever ate those green bullety excuses for peaches they sell in the supermarkets,' Roza explained. 'You never had a Red Haven fresh from the tree.'

Kieran devoured two more peaches with messy enthusiasm, juice all over his face and hands. Roza was smiling as she watched him and then she called out in a singsong voice, 'Are you going to hide over there and spy on us all afternoon?'

Kieran was confused. 'What?' He spun around with exaggerated paranoia, like a cartoon character. 'Is there really someone spying on us? Or are you some kind of a mental old lady?'

Both Kieran and Roza heard the laughter, and a moment later Zoe wandered out from behind the windbreak of conifers on the other side of the yard.

'So, missy, are you agreeing with this gentleman that I'm a "mental old lady"?' asked Roza.

Zoe waggled her head and smiled, peeling the hat off her hair, which was matted with sweat.

'This is our Zoe,' Roza explained to the young man.

'Oh. Right. Hi. Hi. Kieran. I'm Kieran.' He leapt forward and offered Zoe his hand to shake.

Zoe took his hand, but then quickly withdrew. 'Oh – sticky.'

'Sorry! Peach juice.' He started to lick the juice off his hand and Zoe laughed with surprise.

At that moment, Sheena returned from the main house, arms full of cleaning gear, just in time to see Kieran licking his hand like an overexcited dog. 'For fuck's sake, Kieran. Are you acting like a head case and giving this lady the shits?'

'Oh . . . well, maybe . . .' He turned to Roza. 'Am I giving you the shits?'

'No. You're okay,' said Roza.

Kieran smiled. 'I guess Zoe might think I'm a head case. Sheena – meet Zoe.'

Sheena offered a brusque wave in greeting, then dragged Kieran aside, whispering to him sternly. The young man listened to her, nodding, but Roza saw him sneak looks at Zoe in between those obedient nods.

Celia and Joe walked back together from the house, carrying two foam mattresses and a pile of bedding.

Celia was surprised to see Zoe in the yard. 'Hello, lovely. Have you finished that section down the back?'

'Poor Zoe,' said Joe. 'I guess, because it's school holidays, your mum can work you seven days a week.'

'Like a slave,' agreed Zoe.

'Hey, Celia!' Kieran called out. 'I tasted a sample of your peaches. Brilliant, dead-set amazing, best single item I ever ate in my life!'

'Well, thanks. Good to hear.'

Joe was frowning as he checked his watch. 'I'd better head back. Mum, I'll drop by later this week. So, if there's anything you want from town —'

'I say again: you don't have to come out here and check on me all the time,' Roza insisted, then she turned to Kieran and Sheena with a stage whisper. 'He would do better to be checking on his marriage.'

At that moment, on cue, the phone rang.

'Hello? Heather. Hi,' said Celia. After exchanging some pleasantries with Heather, she passed the phone to Joe, unfurling the long cord. He took the receiver and retreated into the shed to conduct his conversation.

'That's her, the wife, Heather,' Roza explained to the newcomers. 'Heather is the mean-spirited harpy who trapped my son in a marriage with no joy. And who has turned his two children into little snobs who don't respect their own father.'

Celia and Zoe both flashed Roza firm looks – *stop it*. So, she dropped her volume a little as she shared more of her analysis with Kieran and Sheena. 'Josef and Heather – they don't have sex. You can tell when a couple is not having sex. The way their bodies are with each other in a room. To live alone and have no sex, that's bad enough. But to be married and have no sex – that corrodes a person's insides, and eventually —'

Roza shut her mouth when Joe walked back out towards them.

'Was my mother saying appalling things?' he asked, with a stoic smile.

'Appalling beyond description,' Celia confirmed. 'Have you got time for a beer before you go?'

'Uh no, love to but can't.'

'Ah. Heather's mysterious surveillance system has alerted her that Josef might be having a pleasant time,' said Roza.

'Mum. At least do it so I can't hear.'

Roza made a show of pressing her lips together and put both hands in the air – an innocent party.

Joe offered Sheena and Kieran a generous smile. 'Good luck with the picking work.'

Kieran grinned. 'Thanks, Joe. Thanks, mate.'

'Uh – yeah – thanks and everything,' stammered the woman. She sounded so graceless, that Sheena, whenever she tried to be polite.

Roza watched her son slot himself back into the car and drive away, weighed down by the duties of the joyless household to which he was returning. What can any mother do about the person her child chooses to marry? Just hope for the best. And if the best hasn't happened – if, for example, a son has married Heather – there was nothing to be done but sigh and keep the mouth shut.

There was not much of the day left for picking, and Celia decided it would be best to use the remaining hours of light to sort out the cabin as living quarters. She hoisted one of the mattresses onto her head and started down the slope.

'Come on, Kieran, we're supposed to be helping,' said Sheena.

'No worries. Let's get scrubbing,' said Kieran, grabbing an armload of cleaning paraphernalia. But then he twisted his head to throw a cheeky smile to Zoe and as a result, he tripped and scattered bottles of cleaning products across the yard, whooping with laughter at his own clumsiness. He reminded Roza of a new foal not yet in control of its limbs. She'd seen many young men who didn't grow fully into their bodies for a long time.

The woman, Sheena, hurried to gather up the items on the gravel. 'Sorry about this,' she said. 'Kieran can be a bit of a —'

'A bit of a clueless fuckwit,' Kieran confirmed with a smile.

'Grab that other mattress. Stop mucking around,' said Sheena, shooing him down the slope.

Celia was already halfway to the cabin. She was focused on what needed to be done, throwing herself into the work, the way she always did.

Roza recalled the very first time she had laid eyes on Celia, striding across the yard of the peach farm, carrying baby Zoe in a backpack. Within a few weeks of their arrival, the story had whooshed around the district, the way such stories could. Celia's husband had been paying for petrol at a service station – this was somewhere in the city – when the place was robbed by a man armed with a shotgun. The husband, standing by the fridges, was killed.

At the time this terrible thing happened, Celia had been late in her pregnancy with Zoe.

When Celia moved onto the property with her ten-month-old daughter, people around the district thought she was crazy. *She can't run that place on her own.* But right from the start Roza had seen that Celia was a strong woman. A fretful woman, yes, but robust.

TWO

Celia wasn't sure she'd made the right decision, having these people here. Possibly, in the moment, she'd been too worried about the harvest to think clearly. Her judgement might have been skewed by gratitude towards Joe for trying to solve her problem. Or maybe she was operating from some misguided notion of politeness – the couple had come all the way out to the farm, willing to work, and Celia didn't want to seem churlish or suspicious. But was that the best way to make a decision? Did it make sense to have two strangers live on the property, when she had no way to cross-check their identities and reassure herself? She smiled at her own convoluted thinking – ridiculous.

Whether or not it was wise to have Kieran and Sheena stay on the place, Celia wanted to treat them decently. After a shower and a quick meal, she headed back down to the cabin from the house, carrying a baking tin with homemade lasagne the two of them could eat tonight, plus an esky with other food supplies.

It was dusk by the time Celia approached the cabin. She was pleased to see the place looked surprisingly homey – the gas lamp was going inside and the one window of the little hut was now a warm yellow square glowing in the dark orchard. She called out – a cheery *Yoohoo!* – and Sheena swung the door open.

In the limited interior space, the bunk beds were arranged in an L-shape, red paint flaking off the old metal frames. The two bottom bunks were now made up with foam mattresses and bedding. There was just enough room for a fold-out picnic table with a camping stove and the basic kitchen items Celia had put together. On one of the unused top bunks, she had hoisted a container of drinking water – a big plastic drum with a dispensing nozzle.

'How you going? Is it fit to live in?' Celia asked.

'It'll do us,' said Sheena. 'Thanks for the lasagne. You didn't need to do that.'

Celia smiled but felt a little sting. Sheena had a spiky manner and it was decidedly ungracious for anyone on the receiving end. But it was worse when Sheena was aware of her own rudeness and then scrambled to smooth things over.

'Anyway, it looks delicious. Kieran loves that kind of food,' she blurted. 'He's just gone up to have a shower.'

It had been agreed that the two of them would be able to use the shower and toilet in the lean-to on the back of the packing shed.

Celia unloaded the bag of food onto the little table. She was resisting the temptation to interrogate Sheena. Was her nosy impulse fuelled by simple curiosity or was it unreasonable anxiety? Whatever, she should ask nothing. Leave them be for now. But then she figured it counted as a legitimate desire to understand the situation and so she gave in to the urge to ask.

'So, have you and Kieran been on the road a fair while?'

Sheena stiffened up. 'Couple of months.'

Celia should have taken the hint from Sheena's defensive tone and left it there, but she couldn't stop herself. 'You headed somewhere in particular?'

'You need to know for some reason?'

'No reason. I just wondered . . .'

'Does it make a difference to the job here?'

'Not at all. Just curious, I guess.'

'So, why does it matter to you?'

'It doesn't. I'm sorry. Didn't mean to be nosy. It's none of my —'

'We're not gonna rob you or anything,' Sheena snapped back. But a second later, she retracted her fangs and attempted a more matter-of-fact tone. 'Kieran and me want to earn some money and then move on.'

'Of course.'

'I know my brother comes across a bit weird.'

'Brother?' queried Celia.

'Well, half-brother. I mean, if you got a problem with us being here . . .'

'Oh, no, it's not . . . Sorry, I thought you and Kieran were together.'

'*Together* together? A couple? Kieran's eighteen. I'm twenty-seven.'

'God, sorry, Sheena,' said Celia, laughing. 'I figured you must like younger men.'

'Uh, no.'

'Sorry. My mistake. He's your little brother. Good-o. Anyway, I'll leave you guys in peace now. Let me know if there's anything else you need.'

'Thanks. Yeah. Thanks,' mumbled Sheena. Then she bunged on a cheerful voice. 'We really appreciate you giving us this work and, y'know, the food and the place to stay and that. Oh – what time do you want us to start tomorrow?'

'Soon as there's enough light to see the fruit. Five okay?'

'Five's okay.'

'I can honk the horn on the ute as a wake-up call at quarter to,' offered Celia.

'Sounds good.'

By the time Celia walked back to the house, Zoe had finished cleaning up their dinner things. She was leaning against the kitchen bench, rolling a tumbler full of ice cubes back and forth across her forehead.

Celia laughed. 'First stinking-hot day knocks you round, doesn't it.'

'Definitely. I'm trying this new method to cool my brain down.'

'Give us a go.'

Zoe leaned over to hold the icy glass against her mother's temple.

'Yeah, that's good. That works.'

Zoe filled another tumbler with ice cubes and handed it to Celia.

'Thanks, sweetheart.'

The two of them flopped against the bench side by side, letting the ice cubes draw some of the heat out of their skin.

'Hey,' said Celia eventually. 'She's a prickly customer, Sheena.'

'Bit old for the guy, isn't she?'

'Ah, see, we were wrong about them. They're half-brother and -sister.'

'Oh,' said Zoe, nodding slowly. 'That fits.'

'Hope I haven't made a mistake having them here.'

'Why would you say that?'

Celia immediately heard the sharper edge in Zoe's voice and felt the conversational ground shift. This was how it could be between them these days – flipping, sometimes with dizzying speed, from a warm and companionable moment to a tense confrontation in which Celia was always, apparently, the unreasonable one.

'Well,' said Celia, 'I just think Kieran and Sheena seem sort of . . .'

'What, you're into judging them already?'

'No. No. Well, a bit, maybe.'

'More than a bit,' pronounced Zoe with the slightly self-righteous tone that always made Celia spring to defend her position.

'It's a matter of trying to read people. That's a perfectly reasonable thing to do.'

Zoe rolled her eyes, gearing up to debate this further. But Celia didn't have the energy right now to wrestle with her daughter's judgemental attitude about *her* supposedly judgemental attitude. They were both ragged after a day of hard work with the added stress about the picking team.

'Come and watch some rubbish on the telly with me,' Celia suggested. 'Just for the fifteen minutes before I sink into a coma.'

'Sure,' said Zoe, and her expression softened. Maybe she wasn't up for a tense exchange right now, either. 'But I get to choose what rubbish we watch.'

'Deal.'

They'd already missed the ABC TV news bulletin, which Celia watched from time to time to maintain some idea of what was happening in the world. As a young woman she'd prided herself on being informed about global events, but these days she found it daunting to fill her head with so many distressing stories – massacres in Lebanon, earthquakes in Guatemala, riots in Soweto, nuclear-weapon tests, hijacked planes, IRA bombs. Here, in their house, on this farm, it was easy to feel very far away from all of that, but Celia realised she should make some effort to stay aware of events beyond this place.

She brought two bowls of caramel ice cream through to the sitting room, where Zoe was flipping the channel knob on the TV set. There was a choice of *On the Buses*, a rerun episode of *Matlock Police* or the second half of an old movie involving women in crinolines, which they figured was the best option.

Celia didn't care what they watched – she was happy just to sit with her daughter. Zoe stretched out on the old floral sofa and put her feet on Celia's lap. They ate ice cream and let the prattle of the movie characters wash over them.

Celia noticed Zoe staring out the window for a moment and asked, 'What are you thinking about?'

Zoe smiled and shrugged. When she was little, she'd been such a chatty child, sharing all her thoughts, fantasies and opinions with Roza, Joe, her aunt Freya, and especially with her mother.

For years, here in this house, it had been just the two of them. As Zoe grew older, she had fallen into the role of Celia's companion, discussing plans and social arrangements and jobs that needed doing, developing their own private jokes and verbal shorthand and tacit understandings, always attuned to each other's moods.

Celia had been aware this was happening and she was wary of her child taking on an inappropriate emotional burden. As a corrective, she'd been conscientious about ensuring Zoe had plenty of time with little-kid activities. Celia had constantly taken readings, checking herself against the families they knew, regular families. But it was so hard to know what really went on in other households, what mechanisms hummed along in other people's lives. And Celia and Zoe's circumstance could never be regular. They could only do their best. Zoe had always seemed playful, never solemn or weighed down. And if she was also a very responsible kid who confided in her mother, that was a good thing, surely.

Of course it wasn't so much like that lately. Celia could tell there was plenty going on in Zoe's head that she didn't share anymore, which was probably fitting. A natural process. A sixteen-year-old should be allowed to have her own private thoughts, without being pestered.

Celia must have fallen asleep while trying to focus on the TV, because the next thing she recalled was Zoe shaking her gently, coaxing her to go to bed. 'Come on, Mum, you'll wreck your neck if you sleep here all night.'

Celia allowed Zoe to steer her out of the living room towards her bedroom.

*

It was giving Sheena the shits to be trapped in this festy shack with Kieran, especially if he was going to keep yapping and bouncing around the whole time.

'Sit down. This place is too small for you to go on like a hyper-fucking-active baboon.'

Sheena immediately regretted saying that – she should've real-ised it would inspire Kieran to have a crack at doing a baboon impersonation. He swooped down into a primate squat and made a few hooting calls.

'That doesn't even sound like a baboon – sounds more like a chimp,' she pointed out.

'Almost made you smile, but. Almost.'

He jumped to his feet again and made a grand sweeping gesture around the cabin, as if they were in a magnificent hotel suite. 'Look at this place! Our little cubby's nicer than any place I've ever lived,' he said. Then he flipped open the door and shone a torch out into the orchard.

'Check out those peach trees.' He picked out tree after tree with the torch beam. 'Look at them, all in rows – wap, wap, wap. Growing food. What a top thing. What do you reckon it'd cost to buy a place like this?'

'Oh right, and where would you get the money?' asked Sheena.

'I'm just saying, if you could, if you could, it'd be incredible.'

'Kieran. Don't get carried away. We only just got you a bit settled down.'

'Yeah, I'm too much of a spaz to run a farm.'

'I'm not saying that.'

Kieran suddenly flicked the torch off and spun round to face Sheena. 'Hey, what do you reckon about Zoe?'

Sheena shrugged. 'Bit up herself.'

'You reckon? I didn't think up herself. She's really – ah – what's the word . . .' Kieran whacked himself in the side of the head, trying to dislodge whatever was clogging his thought process.

'Kieran. Go to bed. You and me are gonna work our guts out tomorrow. The more peaches we pick, sooner we get the car back.'

'Roger that,' said Kieran, saluting. 'Thanks, Sheena. Have I said thanks?'

'About four thousand million times.'

'Ha! But I mean it,' he said and darted across to pepper her hand with grateful kisses.

'Get off me. Sleep. Now.'

Sheena turned the gas lamp off as they climbed into the two bottom bunks. Kieran's feet hung a few inches over the edge and the foam mattresses were thin enough to feel the wooden slats jabbing through, but thirty seconds after he bunched up the pillow under his head, Sheena could hear her brother's breathing fall into the slow, regular rhythm of sleep.

He was lucky – deep asleep within a minute of closing his eyes. He wasn't one to be awake half the night, head full of prickly thoughts. Kieran didn't hold anything in his head for long. Ten seconds tops. So he never had black thoughts poking him awake every few minutes. It was up to Sheena to do the thinking and worrying for him. Lucky Sheena.

Kieran had always been an impulsive kid. A disastrous idiot on many occasions. But never malicious. There wasn't a single nasty bone in that body sprawled over there on the bunk. Especially compared to Sheena's other maggot brothers. Compared to Sheena herself. Kieran was a way nicer human than all of them.

She wasn't sure how that had happened. They'd all grown up in the same hopeless-joke house with the same custard-brained mother, but some of them had different fathers. Kieran's dad was a good-natured, if useless, lump of a man. So, maybe that was it – genetics.

For whatever reason, Kieran turned out a good guy – not necessarily in terms of what he *did*, but in his heart. Sheena didn't see that in many people. So she didn't want to watch it get taken advantage of. Which could easily happen to a kid like Kieran. He could get sucked in by the wrong people – like his poisonous mate Mick – and end up in a mess, because he had no protective coating.

One handy thing about this godforsaken place they'd been marooned was the lack of telephones, not counting the owner's phone. It was a relief to think Kieran couldn't ring Mick or any of his deadhead cronies. The longer without contact with those losers, the better.

The sound of Kieran's sleep snuffles was beginning to shit Sheena to tears. She had a spiteful urge to reach across and thump him in the guts. But if she did that, he'd wake up and start yapping about something and that'd be even more annoying.

Sheena yearned for some form of amnesia, to wipe the mind clean, forget every person and every event that had ever happened in her life. She tried a breathing exercise she'd seen on a yoga TV show. She really needed to get to sleep, as rapidly as possible. They had to get up at fucking dawn to pick fucking peaches all fucking day.

*

Physical exhaustion usually allowed Celia to sink into deep sleep for four hours, but it wasn't enough to let her stay there. Most nights, like tonight, she would find herself awake at two a.m. Sometimes she would lie in bed and try to bully herself back to sleep. But often, like tonight, she made herself some herbal tea and prowled the house in bare feet, careful not to wake Zoe.

Celia had always been an anxious person. But on the normal scale. At the anxious end of normal. Then when her husband Marcus was killed, the fact of it blasted through her life like a meteor that scorched away all the calming fixtures people install in their minds to defuse anxiety. An unthinkable malignant thing had happened, so anything could happen. The world was a dangerous place. Most people had the luxury of ignoring that, but she could not.

Celia was generally okay in the daytime. In daylight, her mind was busy with the thousand jobs that needed doing, but the middle of the night was a different universe. In the middle of the night, she would wake up and the dangers would be *there*. They must have oozed up while she slept, until her brain was awash with panic. The panic was sometimes formless, but often about Zoe.

When Zoe was born, they had put her on Celia's chest and the baby had looked her mother straight in the eye. The challenge was there. *I must protect this human being.*

Celia had maintained a policy of never cottonwoolling Zoe and she followed the policy as an act of will. She didn't want to infect her daughter with the fears. So she had let Zoe run, climb trees, dive off high boards.

But now Zoe was older, it was becoming more difficult. Now there was so much, so many more terrifying possibilities that silted up in Celia's brain. The only way not to feel overwhelmed during the night panic was to repeat certain thoughts over and over. Acknowledging the potential dangers ensured they could not sneak up on her. She would keep her eyes fixed on them and be ready.

A quarter of all road fatalities were in the fifteen- to twenty-year-old age group. Youth suicide had increased thirty-five per cent over the past ten years. The leading cause of death for teenagers was now drug overdose, and reports of sexual assaults of girls were up more than forty per cent. And on and on. So many terrifying numbers.

Celia ran the numbers through her head, meditated on the risks so they wouldn't happen. She knew this was unreasonable. Superstitious thinking. She was compelled to do it anyway. Just in case. Just in case. Mother's voodoo.

This was the trade she had made: the night worrying meant that in the daytime, she could be normal and sturdy and get on with things.

THREE

Pickers needed to start early, so they could get as many peaches as possible into the coolroom before the heat of the day. Warm fruit didn't handle or travel so well.

Early was not a problem for Roza. Like other old crones she knew, she never slept much past four a.m. anyway. A cup of tea, some yoghurt with fruit, and she was ready for the day.

Roza's yellow-painted house was perched at the crossroads where the gravel lane that led to several properties, including Celia's farm, intersected with the bitumen road into town. For one year Roza had lived in this house with her husband Sandor, and for seventeen years, since Sandor died, on her own.

It was a twenty-minute walk from Roza's house to Celia's packing shed. Maybe thirty minutes at the judicious pace she tackled the pathway these days. The pre-dawn light was delicate, fragile, as if maybe, today, the sun might not manage to haul itself fully over the horizon. Lovely.

Celia was already moving briskly around the shed, setting up for the work. And just as Roza arrived, so did the boy, Kieran, bounding up to the yard from the cabin.

'G'morning, Celia!'

'Morning,' she said. 'Sorry about honking the horn so early. A bit brutal, I know.'

'No worries. Not brutal. No way,' he assured her. He spun round to grin at Sheena, who was dragging herself, still not fully awake, into the yard. 'Sheena! This is the absolute best time of the day, don't ya reckon? Magical.'

Sheena did not seem convinced anything magical was occurring.

Kieran carried on, undeterred and loud. 'It's completely fucking magical! I've stayed awake until dawn but I've never, like, *approached* it from this angle.'

'Kieran,' said Sheena with a scowl. 'Use your indoor voice.'

He reduced his volume, which was a relief to Roza. Even for her, it was a little early in the day for this level of boisterous enthusiasm.

In what Roza supposed was his 'indoor voice', the young man addressed Celia. 'I gotta tell you, I am totally psyched about this picking thing.'

'Well, that's great.' Celia smiled, encouraging. 'Today we'll be picking the Red Havens.'

She used some peaches already in the shed as examples to demonstrate to the newcomers. 'We start with what's called a "colour pick". We take any fruit coloured from this . . .' She held up a deeply red, almost overripe peach. 'To this.' She showed them another peach that was just blushing its way there. 'After that, we do the "strip pick" – we take off whatever fruit is left. Does that make sense?'

Sheena and Kieran both nodded.

'Let me set you up with bags.'

While Celia moved to the side bench to find two of the better picking bags, Kieran reached for the peaches she'd shown them. He held the peaches close to his face and turned them back and forth with his eyes scrunched up, as if absorbing the colours. Then he sniffed both of them like a curious animal. It was when he started to brush the furry skin of the fruit against his cheek, trying out the sensation, that Sheena flashed him a warning glare. *You look weird.*

The boy didn't see Sheena glaring at him, or perhaps he was deliberately ignoring her – Roza was not sure which. But a moment later, when Zoe appeared, he forgot about those peaches in a flash. His attention was entirely captured by her.

'Hi,' said Zoe, in a general greeting. 'Mum, I found some hats.'

'Terrific. Thanks, sweetheart,' Celia handed the comfortably battered straw hats to Kieran and Sheena. 'You'll need these. It gets very hot out there.'

'Hot. Got it,' said Kieran, tucking some of the longer loose strands of his hair up under the brim.

'A steady working pace is the go,' Celia advised.

Sheena eyeballed her brother. 'Hear that, Kieran? Steady working.'

Kieran grinned. 'You watch me. I'm gonna be so good, you'll be going, "Is that Kieran? Is that hardworking legend really my little brother?"'

And then he glanced at Zoe. He was showing off for her benefit. That was obvious to Roza and indeed, would be obvious to any person with eyes in their head.

'Let's get cracking,' said Celia.

Zoe drove the little tractor out of the yard, down between the orchard rows, taking the trailer and the stepladders to the section to be picked that morning. Celia followed on foot with Sheena and Kieran. She adjusted the picking bags to suit the two of them. It was always best to make sure the webbing strap hung comfortably on the neck and shoulders, and the bag sat at the correct level against the body.

She then showed them how the picking was done: how to select which peach to take, ease or gently snap it away, taking care not to tear the skin on surrounding sharp branches, then place the fruit in the canvas picking bag. Once a bag was full, they would release the straps in the bottom and let the peaches roll gently into the bins on the back of the trailer.

Kieran and Sheena started on the colour pick with Celia working alongside them, answering any questions. But once the bins began to fill up, she was busy ferrying the fruit back to the shed, helping Roza with the packing, and working the phone to liaise with the markets and hunt for more pickers. Whenever there was a gap, Celia would hop in and do some of the picking, but mostly it was Zoe who stayed out in the orchard with the newcomers. As for Kieran and Sheena, they were tentative at first, wary of making mistakes, nervous of damaging the peaches.

When the sun really got itself going and the heat intensified, Celia drove the tractor back into the orchard with a plastic cooler to refill the pickers' water bottles. Kieran, Sheena and Zoe all stopped work for a few moments to guzzle water.

'Thanks heaps for this,' said Kieran.

'You need to keep the water up,' Celia advised.

'Reckon. Feel like my guts, my liver, my entire insides have melted and sweated right out of me.'

Celia smiled. It was hard not to like this young man. 'You're going really well.'

'Yeah? Well, it's fun.'

Later, in the middle of the day, Celia insisted everyone take a two-hour break – for the sake of the fruit but also for the sake of the people. Kieran and Sheena retreated to the cabin, planning to lie 'like comatose vegetables' on the bunks.

It occurred to Roza that these two, having taken off the picking bags and tasted some blessed rest, might decide to give up. They might refuse to come back to the orchard for more hard labour in the heat. She had seen that happen more than once, over the years, often with the big-mouth types who had made the most noise about how hard they planned to work. But these two, Kieran and Sheena, fronted up in the yard at the agreed time, ready to put on the picking bags again.

By the end of the second day, the new pickers had grown in confidence and were bringing in the fruit at a decent rate. Any fair person would say they were good workers.

The young man – he was clowning around one minute, working fast like a crazy person the next minute, but added together, he picked the same amount as a good picker. And from what Roza had seen and heard, Kieran was not a stupid person, unruly perhaps, but not stupid by any means.

The sister would sometimes nag at him to stay focused on the task, snappy with him like a she-wolf nipping and growling at a boisterous cub.

*

After the first morning in the orchard, Sheena had removed her bracelets, neck chains, hoop earrings and ear studs. There was too much risk of catching them on a random branch and garrotting herself or tearing off an earlobe or something.

She got the hang of the job in the first couple of days and then it was just a matter of tolerating the physical shittiness of it – burning neck and shoulder muscles, shredded hands, aching spine, all to be endured in brain-frying temperatures, wearing clothes clammy with sweat. She did appreciate the fact that when she was absorbed in the task – selecting which peaches to go for, filling the bag, emptying peaches into the bin, moving the ladder, selecting more peaches – she could pretty much switch off all other thinking. It was preferable to fill her brain up with peaches rather than the other miserable stuff that could creep into her thoughts if left unattended. It was just a shame this welcome mind-numbing effect involved working in foul heat and making her entire body hurt.

Celia, the owner, never seemed to take a break, shuttling back and forth on the green midget tractor, helping the old Hungarian lady in the packing shed and then jumping in to help with the picking every now and then. Her vigorous, gung-ho routine irritated the shit out of Sheena but she had to grant that the woman seemed to be a decent operator. She was paying reasonable money and the fact was, she had given Kieran and Sheena a go.

Even so, Sheena knew Celia's judgement of them was buzzing whenever they were in contact. From the first moment they'd met, her skin had prickled under Celia's critical gaze – assessing, scrutinising, disapproving. Sheena was used to copping that most places she went.

Now, after four days working on the farm, she could still feel Celia's eyes on Kieran and her. She could practically hear the suspicious questions whirring in the woman's head. And occasionally, some of those questions would come out of her mouth, always with a fake chatty tone that didn't fool Sheena for one second.

'So, Kieran, you would've finished school – what, this year?' asked Celia as she refilled their water bottles from the cooler on the trailer.

'Oh, well . . . not exactly,' said Kieran.

'Did you leave early?'

'Kind of.'

Kieran threw Sheena a look – *What should I say?* He had enough sense to avoid blurting out too much to this woman, but he was never much chop at lying.

And Celia, she wasn't going to let it go, even if she was smiling as she said, 'Well, school's broken up for the year now anyway.'

'Yeah. Yep.'

'So, you guys are using the break to explore the country a bit, are you?'

Kieran shrugged. 'I guess. Is that what we're doing, Sheena?'

'Have you got a wish list of places to visit?' Celia asked.

'Oh, not really . . . I mean . . .'

'I suppose it depends how much time you have and if you need to be back by any particular date. Have you got plans for —'

'Oh, well . . . see, things got a bit messy and Sheena thought —'

'Oi, Kieran. Help me move this ladder,' said Sheena, shifting her body between the two of them, shielding her brother from any more of Celia's 'friendly' questions.

'Sure,' said Kieran and grabbed the ladder.

Celia went back to work, rearranging the bins on the back of the trailer.

Sheena assumed the woman thought Kieran was some kind of thicko – on account of him not finishing high school, plus how he came across generally. Actually, Kieran was of above-average intelligence. Officially. A counsellor at one of the primary schools had tested him. But without a steady family and all the proper stuff that should have been assembled around him, there was no firm ground for any brainpower to rest on. And once you chucked in the brain-frying drugs and the impulsive streak that ran through him, it was no wonder people thought he was retarded. Then again, the part of Kieran that *seemed* dumb was wound in tight with the part of him that was playful and kind. The way he acted gave Sheena the untold shits most of the time, for sure. But other people, strangers – they had no right to judge or ridicule her little brother.

Celia was lifting the cooler into a shady spot when Zoe, the daughter, appeared out of the trees.

'Hey, gorgeous,' said the mother.

'Hi, Mum. I'm nearly finished in that row. Ooh, is that cold?' Zoe pointed at the cooler.

'Yep. I just filled it with ice.'

'Brilliant.'

As the girl crouched down to replenish her water bottle, her mother smiled. It struck Sheena that it would be lovely to have someone smile at you like that – good if there could be one other human being on the earth whose face lit up just at the sight of you. A lot of things might be more bearable if you had that.

Sheena was sticking with her assessment that Zoe was up herself. Sure, yeah, the kid was out there in the heat, working as hard as anyone. She wasn't being a princess about the fact that she was grimy and sweaty, hair plastered to her skull with perspiration. But even if they were all engaged in the same earthy slog, Sheena still reckoned Zoe considered herself a much higher class of individual than them. Of course she would: she was the daughter of the owner, for one thing. She was unblemished, pretty – you would have to describe her as *glowing* with prettiness. An academic star at her school, according to the Hungarian lady. The only reason Zoe was out here working and sweating like a loser was because it was school holidays and she could earn some play money. This was a girl who was all set to go to university to land some high-end career and then marry some rich guy; a girl who'd never end up stuck with a job picking fruit because there was no other choice.

Most of the time, Zoe worked in the next row of trees, away from Kieran and Sheena. And that was fine by Sheena, because whenever the girl was anywhere nearby, Kieran would start showing off something chronic.

Once – this was the end of the fourth day – Zoe came over to empty her picking bag into the bin at the same time as Kieran.

'How you going this arvo, Zoe?' he asked.

She shrugged and smiled, a bit stand-offish.

'I am going gangbusters,' Kieran announced. 'Except for . . . actually, you know what I need to do?'

He darted across to the tractor and grabbed the secateurs from the little toolbox. He whipped off his hat, then took hold of one of the long hanks of hair that kept escaping from the brim of the hat and getting in his face. He used the secateurs to hack the hair off, half an inch from his scalp. 'Easy!' He proceeded to move round his head, cutting off every long section of hair.

When he'd finished, he looked at the hacked-off shreds of hair on the ground around his feet, ran his hands over his unevenly shorn head and whooped a laugh. 'The self-haircut! A fucking guerilla haircut!'

Zoe laughed. Sheena was pretty sure she was laughing *at* him, but Kieran thought she was laughing *with* him. Encouraged by that, he started to strike extravagant poses like a male model. 'So, Zoe, what do you reckon? Am I an unbelievable spunk now?'

Zoe looked unsettled then. The girl was definitely not comfortable. Kieran was coming on too strong – which he had a habit of doing, especially with girls.

'Uh . . . yeah . . . looks good,' Zoe mumbled, and quickly scooted away to the adjacent row of peach trees.

As he watched her disappear from view, Kieran still had a big dumb smile hanging on his face, not realising he'd just been given the brush-off.

The truth was, his ridiculous self-haircut looked fine. Better than fine. The new choppy hair kind of suited him. Sheena just wished he wouldn't make a fool of himself over some princess, a girl who would never take a guy like her brother seriously.

*

From what Zoe had seen so far, Sheena was pretty much permanently pissed off, like one of those tough cartoon characters stomping through the world, ready for something to jump out at her from any direction. But the thing that made Zoe nervous around her was the way Sheena's magpie eyes registered everything going on.

Kieran mostly did what his sister told him to do, but Zoe could see he had his own methods for handling her. It was one of the things she liked about him – the way he worked so hard to cheer up his grim-faced sister, goofing around, not caring if he looked like an idiot, not if there was any chance he could make Sheena laugh.

One afternoon, when Sheena was looking especially exhausted and testy, Zoe watched Kieran grab three of the overripe peaches off the ground and juggle them, making percussion and trumpet noises with his mouth as musical accompaniment to his performance.

'Sheena, look, look! I could be a busker,' he said.

'For fuck's sake, give it a rest,' Sheena snapped back.

Kieran didn't even flinch at the way his sister spoke to him. He just laughed, as the already squashy peaches turned to mush in his hands. Then he turned to Zoe. 'Hey Zoe, I reckon Sheena disapproves of my new career as a peach-juggling busker. Check out the face,' he said, pointing out his sister's scowling expression. 'Ouch! Who could ever make Mrs Crankypants smile?'

Sheena was primed to lash back at him, but then she relented and actually smiled.

'Ah-ha! Ha!' Kieran danced around triumphantly, attempting to juggle what was left of the pulpy peaches.

Zoe realised she was staring at him, so she quickly looked down to fuss with the picking bag. A moment later she darted back through the trees to the next row.

She'd hardly said a word to Kieran, even though they'd worked together in the orchard for five days now. Sure, he was staring at her a lot, and a few times he had maybe tried to flirt with her. There was a boy at the bus stop near her school who sometimes had a clumsy go at flirtation, but that felt entirely different, like a kid doing a lame impersonation of transactions he'd seen in movies. It wasn't like that with Kieran. When Kieran looked at her, it felt extraordinary. It made her *skin* feel electrically charged. That was why she had to dash away sometimes, so she could settle every nerve in her body. And there was no way she could attempt to flirt back because that would surely turn out an embarrassing mess. If a guy like Kieran actually got to know her, he'd be disappointed. That was why she had to avoid him – so he wouldn't realise what a tragically inexperienced kid she was.

This avoidance policy didn't stop her from holding Kieran in her head most of the time, flicking through images of him in her mind, resisting the urge to hear herself say his name out loud.

She contemplated ringing her friend Mandy, who was spending the summer with her grandmother in Melbourne. But what would she say? *Hi Mandy. Hey, guess what . . . There's this good-looking guy at our place doing some picking. He's tall, he has beautiful eyes and the most incredible smile, and he's unlike anyone I've ever met.*

Any wording she considered just sounded like silly, girly blathering. This feeling was too elemental, too special, to be diminished like that, so she didn't ring Mandy to talk about Kieran.

And of course she couldn't discuss him with Celia. She didn't even dare say 'Kieran' in her presence for fear Celia would somehow detect Zoe's feelings in the way she uttered his name.

Kieran was all Zoe thought about now, so she ended up saying almost nothing to her mother in the evenings. She didn't want to devote mental energy to any other subject, so she had grown uncharacteristically quiet.

'You okay?' Celia asked her over dinner.

'Just tired,' Zoe responded and, given how hard they were working, such an excuse could easily hold.

She stared at the TV for an hour after dinner and Celia had no clue Zoe was really projecting her own imagined footage of Kieran onto the screen the whole time. Then she professed to be exhausted and retired to bed early.

Already – for some time before Kieran landed in her world – Zoe had been growing skilful at controlling how many of her thoughts she transmitted to Celia. It seemed the best way to manage things.

Sixteen years ago, Zoe had been born into the narrative of her mother's suffering. Yes, yes, Celia had made an effort to ensure her daughter's childhood was not defined by grief. And Zoe considered she'd been given a happy childhood – at least as far as she could judge, in comparison with other kids she observed. Even so, it was always there: the awareness that her mother had faced a terrible loss and lived with the sorrow of it every day.

Ever since Zoe could remember, she had been able to identify the sadness in her mother's face and any signs she had been crying in the bathroom. When Zoe grew a little older, she used to try her hardest to imagine what it must have been like for Celia when her husband was killed. At the very least, she could always summon up huge sympathy for her mother, often weeping for her. Sometimes she felt she could achieve small traces of understanding. But mostly it was too overwhelming to comprehend. And Marcus, Zoe's father – he only existed for her as photographs and a few stories.

Roza had been a surrogate grandmother to Zoe, with Joe the equivalent of an adored uncle. There had been times when she had yearned for Joe to be her dad. When it was clear that wasn't going to happen – he was an honourable man who went home every night to Heather and their two sons – Zoe had decided to be glad he was around in whatever capacity, as long as he was around.

Last winter, Joe was the one who had noticed that Zoe was sulking, chafing against her mother's nervy scrutiny. There was a Sunday afternoon when he and Zoe were carrying groceries from Celia's house down to Roza's place.

'So?' was all Joe had to ask for Zoe to pour out her grievances.

He had listened patiently as she described the way Celia watched and worried. Zoe's complaints were twisted around, intersected with disclaimers and self-reproach, but constantly looping back to frustration.

'I think I can understand,' Joe said.

And Zoe knew he did understand a lot of it. Joe was also the child of parents who had suffered. Zoe had been told the stories. In 1938, the anti-Jewish laws were introduced in Hungary.

Roza and three-year-old Josef had fled Budapest at the urging of her husband, who planned to join them later. There were years with no word, and then Roza learned her husband had perished. After the war, she met Sandor, an older man, a fellow refugee. Both went searching for their families and found no one alive. 'We will be each other's family,' Roza had said, and eventually they migrated to Australia to make a life together. Joe was their only child.

'When I was your age, I had a list,' Joe explained to Zoe. 'Whenever my parents mentioned someone – a person who died, relatives who went missing – I wrote the name on a list I hid in my stationery drawer. I kept a tally of all the dead people, so I could get my head round it.'

'Did it help?' Zoe asked him.

Joe pulled a face. 'Not really. Anyway, the thing is, I always felt an obligation not to add to Mum and Dad's suffering in any way.'

Zoe nodded. She knew about that.

'Even just the obligation to stay alive,' Joe continued, 'so they wouldn't have to put one more dead person on the list.'

It wasn't exactly the same for Zoe. She didn't feel pressure to stay alive – dying wasn't an immediate possibility plonked in front of her. For Zoe, it was the pressure to be *happy*, so her mother wouldn't feel bad.

In recent months, there had been times Zoe felt herself sinking into black moods she found hard to decipher or regulate. Some days at school, she would suddenly, involuntarily, tune into the currents that flowed between the human beings around her, becoming hyper-alert to their meanness and lies, as if she had acquired an extra sense. An unwelcome extra sense. The volume was turned up on the nasty things the girls said or thought about each other. A fierce light was shone onto the faces of her schoolmates so she couldn't help but see how sad or angry they really were. And Zoe understood she wasn't a better person than any of them – she could be just as spiteful and scared and selfish and phony. She found herself worn out by knowing this, rendering her feeble, so she would have to push her limbs to move in what would appear to be a regular way.

That frame of mind would pass and she could barely remember seeing such things or feeling like that. And then some time later, another dark mood would sweep through her, inescapable and snaky as the sinuous lines of a weather map. Zoe suspected there was something wrong with her, something inside, right down into the cells of her body. She realised she wasn't physically ill. She wasn't afraid of that. She feared another kind of wrongness. And if any person were to come close, close enough to know her, they would surely detect the wrongness and find her repulsive.

People looking at Zoe, on the bus, at school, at home, wouldn't notice any difference. They would just see cheery, considerate, well-behaved Zoe. And often – most of the time – she really was that girl. But sometimes, she was secretly performing an acrobatic trick while keeping the smile steady on her face.

She could not let on to Celia, nor could she tell Joe or Roza or her aunt Freya in case they said something to her mother. She would just have to manage on her own and so far, she had managed it.

Now Kieran had arrived and shaken Zoe up in a way she could not manage.

She couldn't risk giving away any hint to Celia about her fixation on Kieran, because her mother would worry. (Even though there was no need for her to worry, because a guy like Kieran would never be interested in a kid like Zoe.) But more than that, more than any of that, Zoe didn't want to hear Celia discuss Kieran.

She didn't want any more of Celia's thinking patterns installed in her brain – patterns full of warnings and boundaries and logical reasons why this guy was a concern. Zoe wanted to be left alone to think about Kieran. He was like an electric charge, but in a good way, connected to some energy or – whatever – whatever this feeling was.

In bed, in the dark, Zoe imagined running her fingers up Kieran's arm, along the lines of the tattoo and then beyond the tattoo to the unmarked skin of his shoulder and chest. Would it feel different? No, that was silly. The surface of his bare skin would feel the same. But she imagined doing it anyway.

FOUR

Celia couldn't put off a supply run to Narralong much longer. And she had agreed to pay Sheena and Kieran in cash, which would require a visit to the bank.

'I'll head into town when we break for lunch,' she said to Zoe. 'Want to come with me?'

'One of us needs to drive the tractor in the afternoon,' Zoe pointed out. 'You don't want Kieran or Sheena driving it, do you?'

'No. But we could make it snappy and get back in time to —'

'But if I just stay here,' said Zoe, 'you won't need to rush.'

Celia could hear the delicate thread of excuse-making in her daughter's voice. The two of them had their favoured routine on trips into Narralong – playing pinball at the milk bar, flicking through stacks of second-hand records at the St Vincent de Paul, then trying on whatever new garments had appeared on the racks at Faye's Frock Shoppe, before attending to the list of supplies to take back home. Celia had no doubt Zoe enjoyed those days in town together but it also seemed fair enough that she might want some time on her own. And anyway, there was sense in what Zoe said about managing the day's picking tasks.

If Celia felt uneasy about leaving the place today, even just for a few hours, she couldn't be sure if this was an instinct she should heed or just noise from her constant low-level buzz of anxiety. She asked herself, as she often did, *What would a Reasonable Woman think about this situation?* And then she laughed out loud at the ridiculousness of her own imagination. She had developed a mental picture of this Reasonable Woman: an individual who looked a bit like Celia, but with more smoothly groomed hair and dressed in a diaphanous white garment for some reason that could probably be traced to an illustration from a childhood storybook. Sometimes the Reasonable Woman gave Celia the shits, with her smugly beatific smile, dripping with tranquillity. But the Reasonable Woman had her good points, always urging Celia to make judgements based on evidence.

And the evidence of Celia's eyes was that Sheena and Kieran were not a problem. They'd been doing well with the picking all week. The boy could be boisterous but not in a way that created trouble. They largely kept to themselves during the work day and retreated to the cabin during the break. At knock-off time, Sheena would hustle her brother straight to the shower, and that was the last Celia and Zoe would see of them until dawn the next day. They had proved to be surprisingly hassle-free workers. So, according to the Reasonable Woman, there was little risk in leaving the place for a few hours.

At midday, Celia handed Sheena scrap paper and a pen. 'Why don't you make a list of food and whatever else you guys need and I can pick it up for you in town.'

Sheena responded with her usual abrasive awkwardness. 'What? Oh. Right.'

She met every overture with a mistrustful frown – she seemingly had no way to process basic good manners from other people. Celia realised there must be reasons for this – a tough childhood, most likely. She felt sorry for Sheena. But that didn't make engaging with her any more pleasant.

As Celia drove the ute out towards the road, she called Zoe over to the passenger window. 'I won't be long. Couple of hours. If there's any problem, I'll be —'

'There won't be any problem.'

The journey into town always gave Celia pleasure. She loved winding through the mix of orchards, vineyards, acid-yellow fields of canola, green swatches of lucerne and hillsides thick with eucalypt forest. Some days, the days when she was feeling depleted, she would pull over to the side of the road, hop out of the driver's seat and take a long breath, stretching out her ribcage to suck in more air. If Celia filled her lungs and saturated her field of vision with all that physical beauty, it could reset the mechanism of her mind to something more serene, or at least something more manageable.

Celia never regretted her choice to make a life away from the city. Through the initial blur of grief when Marcus was killed, her friends had been supportive, solid, loving. But at every dinner table, she had been conscious of where Marcus used to sit and it was like tearing open a surgical wound over and over. She'd wondered if there might be some relief in moving to a new place where no one knew her as the remaining half of the Celia/Marcus couple.

But that wasn't the most powerful impetus. After Zoe was born, Celia had found the city too much. Too many people moving too fast, too much noise, too many volatile elements coming from all sides. She stumbled through several panic episodes out in the street and she started to concoct reasons to avoid leaving the house at all.

Celia seized on the idea of finding somewhere peaceful and safe. She knew this wasn't logical – bad things could happen anywhere – but it felt right. She held good memories of holidays on her uncle's stone-fruit farm, remembered the satisfaction she had felt helping in the orchard. She browsed rural property ads in the newspaper, calculating her funds – Marcus's life insurance plus a chunk she'd inherited from her parents. She came across a farm she could afford, one that seemed manageable. The owner, Les, was retiring to Queensland, but he agreed to stay on for a handover period to teach Celia the running of the place.

Her city friends had worried about the plan. How could she possibly cope with a farm and a baby on her own? Did she know anything about growing peaches and nectarines? Celia had been oddly confident about it – hard to believe, when she thought back on it. Probably it was self-delusion. Maybe it was the seductiveness of the vision – a simple, self-reliant life, work that was nourishing and productive.

It was a thirty-minute drive from Celia's property into Narralong. The town had just under five thousand people, four pubs, and three churches. There was an elegant old movie palace that had been closed down and a newly built monstrosity of a council chambers plonked in the wide main street, a liver-coloured brick fortress.

Celia was fond of Narralong but it had never felt like her place. Her place was the farm, and her connection to the town was a practical and fragmented business. For seven years she had driven Zoe in every day to the smaller of the two primary schools, Narralong North, and had ferried her around to piano lessons, swimming classes and to play with town kids. Celia had to push herself to fulfil the social requirements of being a mother – the chatting by the side of the pool and the swapping of anecdotes over cups of tea at pick-up time.

When the time came for Zoe to move on to secondary school, the choice wasn't so simple. There were stories about Narralong High – drugs, brawls, a spate of teenage pregnancies – although you had to be careful which scraps of parental gossip to believe. Some local kids were sent to boarding schools but Celia would never have sent Zoe away, even if she could have afforded it. In the end, she opted for the Catholic girls' school in Evatt's Bridge, despite her lack of religious belief.

On the town trip today, Celia was determined to move through her list of tasks quickly, so it was disappointing to discover that Neville from the water-pump place was out on a job until two-thirty. She figured she'd make the most of the waiting time by doing some paperwork in the one cafe in town that was air-conditioned.

In the cafe, Celia ordered a toasted sandwich and a pot of the milky coffee the place was known for (apart from its air-conditioning). Sitting at a table in the front window, she had a clear view of the main street. Almost immediately she spotted Joe across the road, juggling a sheaf of papers and checking his watch.

When Celia first moved to the district fifteen years ago, Joe had been living in Sydney for some years, studying and then working as a public prosecutor. His bond with Roza and with his stepfather Sandor was very strong. Even so, he must have needed to establish some separation from such intense parents. Roza herself understood that. 'It's good to have some air flowing between people,' she would say, sweeping her hands to demonstrate this healthy current of air. Roza knew Joe had girlfriends in the city but he was careful not to offer up too much information about them for his mother to pick over.

Back then, Celia was busy working out how to run a farm while also raising a baby, and there was no time for socialising. She and Joe met a few times when he came home to visit. He was aware how abruptly and violently she had been widowed, but he wasn't nervous around her. So many people were afraid of another person's grief and were awkward with her. Joe was never like that, and Celia appreciated it.

She was about to wave hello to him through the cafe window when she saw Heather walking along the street to join him. Celia let her arm drop.

Heather wasn't a totally unlikeable person. It was true she could be humourless and quick to blame other people, and she did talk about money an inordinate amount. But Heather was not the evil creature portrayed in Roza's mythology, even allowing for Roza's hyperbole and sly humour.

Soon after Sandor died, Joe had moved back to Narralong to support his mother. Within weeks of returning, he coupled up with Heather, an old schoolfriend. Roza painted Heather as 'a scavenger bird' who had swooped over the town and grabbed hold of him with her 'talons'. Joe was presumably a dying wildebeest in this scenario.

To Celia, Heather mostly seemed an unhappy person. She and Joe had trouble conceiving and the poor woman had endured many visits to city doctors, curettes, surgery and whatever treatments she could find. There had been signs that Joe regarded his marriage as an unfortunate mistake and maybe, if things had gone differently, he would have left her. (The demise of the marriage remained Roza's fervent hope.) But Joe was kind and stalwart when Heather was almost broken by the struggle to have a baby, and Celia respected him for that. Not long afterwards, their son Hamish was conceived, and two years later, Fergus.

Celia observed Joe and Heather talking on the footpath. Was Roza right that their body language was a clue to their sex life? Would that be something an observer could detect when two people were standing in the main street of Narralong? Celia's mind flashed on Joe and Heather in bed, naked, humping away, moaning, but that felt weird and unfair, so she banished the image. Anyway, you could never know what really went on inside other people's marriages.

There was certainly no evidence of sexual frisson between them right now. Heather was hectoring Joe about something. Celia could see – even from this distance – his resigned smile and his braced posture, allowing Heather's bad mood and torrent of opinions to wash over him. She'd seen Joe adopt this position with his wife, and with Roza too, on many occasions. Not that Celia regarded Joe as a weak man. The opposite, really – it was more a matter of him being sturdy enough to handle the circumstances of his life without sliding away from responsibility, without complaint or self-pity.

Even so, Celia wished, as a friend – well, they were virtually family – that Joe might one day claim a bit more joy for himself. The man had been so thoughtful and strong for her and Zoe over the years. When someone not related to you offered your child their devotion, the way Roza and Joe had done unreservedly with Zoe, it warranted a special kind of gratitude. Celia wanted very much for Joe to be happy. She wondered how she might broach the subject with him. *Are you wretched, my friend? Surely you and Heather can't be making each other happy.* But people never wanted to be subjected to that kind of questioning. Better to leave them be. Everyone had their own methods and accommodations to make life bearable.

A few moments later, Heather and Joe crossed the street together and Celia realised they were about to walk past the cafe. She didn't want to look as if she'd been spying on them, so, on a ridiculous impulse, she ducked down from her chair behind a display celebrating regional produce – a series of wicker baskets and cornucopias overflowing with real pumpkins and wheat sheaves mixed with plastic peaches, cherries and bunches of grapes.

Crouching, Celia was concealed by the display, but once down there, she realised she had no way of seeing if Joe and Heather had gone past. How long should she stay ducked down? A couple of other cafe patrons were staring at her, so she made a show of rummaging in her bag as if she'd dropped something.

'Celia. Hello.'

Celia spun round on the floor to see Joe and Heather standing beside her.

'Lost something?' asked Joe. 'Do you need a hand?'

'Ha. No. Well, my keys. But found them now,' said Celia, jumping up. 'How are you guys? How are you, Heather?'

Heather twisted her face, indicating she wasn't jubilant.

Celia nodded and then realised the nodding might look like an endorsement of Heather's unhappiness. But she was unsure what to say to remedy that, so she said nothing.

The three of them stood awkwardly for a moment, until Joe broke the silence.

'How are the new pickers working out?'

'Good, good. No, good. Good.' Celia heard herself sounding like an idiot. That was too many 'goods'.

'What?' asked Heather, irritated that she'd not been informed about something.

'Oh, Joe found me a couple of people to help get the picking done. He saved the day, actually.'

'Ah,' said Heather, still peeved.

When Celia had first moved to the farm, quite a few of the women in the district had been wary of her – a 27-year-old single mother who was presumably poised to seduce their husbands. Which was, in reality, a fucking joke. She was barely holding the shreds of herself together in those early years after Marcus died. The last thing she would have contemplated was a romantic relationship, let alone a spot of husband-stealing.

There had been a couple of attempts by well-meaning people to matchmake Celia with available local gentlemen. They had been pleasant-enough guys but it had never felt right to pursue things. Running the farm and raising Zoe had been enough for Celia to handle. And now, at forty-two, she couldn't imagine connecting her life to a man again. So, she was certainly not a threat to anyone else's marriage.

Heather, though, had always seemed suspicious of her. There'd been times Celia had fought an urge to grasp the woman by the shoulders and pronounce, 'I'm not going to run off with your husband, Heather. I don't want another husband.' But there was no point saying anything.

'Anyway, I must get a move on,' said Celia, slightly too loudly. She gulped down the remains of her coffee and took a last bite of the sandwich. 'See you.'

Standing at the counter, waiting to pay, Celia suddenly felt the burn of tears. This was one of the risks of coming into town or visiting her old life in the city. Being in close proximity to other people as they trundled along with their lives, seeing husbands and wives walking down the street, however wretched they may be together, she might abruptly feel the pain of losing her man as freshly as when it first happened. If she had ever let herself experience the deficits and the loneliness full pelt, there was a risk she would crumble, which would be of no use to Zoe.

The cafe girl was distracted, flustered by the complexities of a new cash register, so Celia pushed a five-dollar note across the counter. It was way too much money, but it was better to get out of there quickly before she started to cry and became the subject of Narralong gossip.

On the way to the water-pump place, she stopped in at the bakery and bought a couple of vanilla slices, with their lurid yellow filling and neon-pink icing, a favourite of Zoe's since she was a little kid.

*

With Celia away for the afternoon, Zoe was the one conveying the bins of fruit to the packing shed. The next time she drove the tractor back into the orchard with empty bins, Kieran was tackling a new row, while Sheena finished the low-down stuff on the previous section.

'Hey there, Zoe,' he said.

She watched him pause to take a drink, head stretched back, the muscles of his throat rolling with each gulp of water.

Without making a big deal of it, Zoe grabbed a picking bag and started work on the peach tree next to Kieran's. When he realised she was helping, he flashed a smile at her through the branches and mouthed, *Thank you*. Kieran hadn't shaved for a few days now and she noticed his stubble was growing out a shade darker than his toffee-coloured hair.

Zoe had been observing Kieran during the day and thinking about him at night. She decided he wasn't a person who would ever ridicule someone, not in a mean-spirited way, so she now felt brave enough to risk talking to him.

Working side by side, picking fruit, was the perfect opportunity to test-drive talking to him – they were close enough to have a conversation, but because they were focused on the task, Zoe could avoid eye contact with him. That way, she wasn't so exposed.

They chatted about random stuff to begin with, and laughed at each other's lame jokes. After a while, Zoe felt a small surge of boldness, enough to say, 'The thing you have to know about me is that I'm socially retarded.'

Kieran laughed. 'What?'

'Let me explain how it works. I go to a single-sex school in Evatt's Bridge, right?'

'Where is that?'

'So bloody far away from here,' Zoe replied. 'Which means I spend a total of two-and-a-half hours a day on a bus, usually with a few old people going to the chiropodist in Evatt's Bridge to get their toenails scraped out. So, my day consists of bus, all-girls' school, bus, home. On weekends and holidays I'm helping out round here. That's it. Goody-goody daughter whether I like it or not. I live in protective custody.'

'Yeah? It doesn't look to me like . . . Your mum doesn't chain you up at night, does she? I mean, she seems pretty cool.'

'Oh, Mum's cool in some ways,' Zoe agreed. 'She never *forbids* me to do anything. She doesn't have to.'

'I don't get it.'

'She does it by emotional blackmail,' Zoe explained. 'I can hear the worry clunking round in her brain, even though she tries to hide it.'

Kieran stopped working and looked directly at her. 'Roza told me what happened to your dad. I'm so sorry. That was . . . far out. He was just standing there, buying petrol and – bang – some psycho shoots him. Your poor mum. Poor you.'

He was looking at her so intently, Zoe had to turn away for a moment. 'Yeah, well – yes.'

'Sorry,' said Kieran, 'I didn't mean to sound —'

'No, don't say sorry. And yes, you're right – that's the thing. There's a worm in Mum's mind: *People go off in the morning and then never come home.* So, if some . . . Like, I missed the bus once and I couldn't find a phone. When I got home, Mum tried to sound reasonable but I saw the panic on her face. She was packing shit. I never want to see that face, so I don't do anything. That's how she keeps me locked up in protective custody. That's how you end up a sixteen-year-old who's done fucking nothing. That is, you end up socially retarded.'

Zoe took a breath after that mouthful of words and realised Kieran was staring at her in that intense way again.

'What?' she asked.

Kieran shook his head.

'I'm talking too much. Sorry.'

'No, no. I like it,' he said. 'I like it a lot.'

A moment later, they heard the sound of Celia driving the ute up from the gate. Zoe dumped her picking bag into the bin and hurried over to help her mother haul the shopping and gas cylinders inside.

After dinner, Celia and Zoe shared one of the vanilla slices so they could save the other one for the next night.

Possibly Zoe went on about the vanilla slice a bit too much. 'Mm, so disgusting but so perfect,' she said. 'The icing's sugary enough to make your teeth hurt, but then you sink into gooey custard in the middle and it's just – ah . . . Thanks for getting these, Mum.'

'You're welcome,' said Celia. 'Oh, hey, how did you all get on this arvo?'

'All good,' said Zoe, as lightly as she could utter the words.

FIVE

Sheena could hardly believe that Kieran had held it together for a full week, putting up with the heat, the slog, the crushingly early starts, then being crammed into the airless little cabin at night, with only his testy sister for company, offered nothing by way of entertainment and without chemicals of any kind to distract him or embellish the experience. Really, her little brother was surprising the hell out of her with this new diligence. A few times, Sheena had glanced across from the ladder she was standing on to observe Kieran working away, focused – quiet for fucking once! – and it struck her that he appeared to have sprouted several mature brain cells right there in front of her. Maybe it was the fresh air.

At the midday break, Celia was hovering in the yard, waiting to speak to Sheena but trying not to make it obvious. The band of muscle across Sheena's lower belly contracted, like tightening a belt. She was always primed for hassle, suspicious questions, dismissal.

'Something up?' Sheena asked. If Celia wanted to sack them, let her get the hell on with it.

'We should talk about Christmas.'

'Sorry? Christmas?'

'It's the twenty-third today.'

'Is it?' Sheena puffed out a laugh. 'I lost track.'

Celia smiled. 'Yeah, easy to do. I guess you and Kieran will want to take Christmas Day off?'

Christmas had never been a jolly procedure in Sheena's experience. On 25 December her family was either scattered, or if there had been any attempt at a gathering, it would fragment into alcohol-soaked disputes and, in especially merry years, would involve visits from the police. In recent times, wherever Sheena found herself during the festive season, she would sign on for any available work shifts in order to snag the penalty rates.

'I hadn't thought . . .' said Sheena. 'I guess if you guys aren't working, we can't work.'

'Well, when we're pressed for time, as we are this year, Zoe and I usually pick for part of Christmas Day, then knock off early.'

'Right. We'll do the same, if that's okay with you.'

'Great,' said Celia.

Roza was eavesdropping, as the old lady often did. She gave Sheena the heebie-jeebs – the way she watched everything, keeping up surveillance from under her wrinkly eyelids, sending out that *I'm a white witch* aura. Not that Sheena was fooled. She knew people could spin a vibe like that to unnerve you, but it didn't signify anything real. Still, Sheena didn't enjoy being stared at by that peculiar Hungarian duck in her mirrored Indian skirt as tizzy as a Christmas decoration.

'They should come to my house for the Christmas evening meal,' Roza announced to the world, then turned to Sheena directly to explain. 'Celia and Zoe always come. You and your brother can come too.'

Sheena looked to Celia, not sure what to make of this. Celia was smiling but she was noticeably uncomfortable. She was the type of person who wouldn't want to appear mean-spirited, but even so, she surely wouldn't fancy having Sheena and Kieran invade her Christmas festivities. Sheena was just about to decline the invitation, when Celia dialled her smile up from polite to hospitable.

'Yes, that's what you should do, Sheena,' she said. 'Come to Roza's. Joe and Heather will be there, and their boys.'

'Oh . . . no. Thanks, though.'

'Please come. You're doing us a big favour – working through this period to get our peaches off the trees – so the least we can do is make sure you have a good dinner on Christmas Day.'

'But we wouldn't have anything to contribute,' Sheena mumbled.

Roza flapped her hand. 'Don't worry. Plenty of food. Of course, I should warn you: you'll have to put up with the wife.' And as she uttered the word 'wife', there was the vinegar face whenever she mentioned Heather. 'There's nothing I can do about the wife, I'm sorry to say. But a table full of good food – that's no problem.'

Sheena was formulating an excuse to wriggle out of the event, but then she glanced over to see Kieran hauling two heavy bags of peaches towards the yard, working hard, not complaining. The image of her and Kieran eating tinned food in that fusty cabin on Christmas night was so bleak it was almost comical. Being a stray at someone else's Christmas had to be an improvement on that. Or a distraction at least. And Kieran loved a party – even if this party was sure to be a tense affair with Celia being awkward, the old lady being white-witchy, her daughter-in-law being vile. Sheena could handle that. She'd endured a lot worse.

'Okay,' said Sheena. 'Thanks. That'd be really good.'

Roza clapped her hands together – it was all settled – then took off her work apron. She was taking the afternoon off for Christmas food preparations, but she must surely be in need of some rest as well, given how seriously ancient she was. Sheena had been shocked and secretly impressed to see an old lady work so hard in the heat, day after day.

Sheena watched Roza trudge down to her house, at a slow but tenacious pace, with her dusty red sneakers crunching on the gravel and that ridiculously long skirt flicking back and forth as she swayed her hips, making the tiny mirrors glint in the sun.

For the rest of the afternoon, Celia took over Roza's role in the packing shed, in addition to driving the tractor. The woman was flat-out busy, marching around the shed and the orchard in work boots, khaki shorts and blue singlet.

Sheena reckoned Celia was a good-looking woman – even sweaty and grubby, with no make-up, her mass of dark hair pulled back in an elastic band. She had the kind of olive skin that looked good with a shine of sweat on it, unlike Sheena's pale, freckly hide. Celia wasn't pretty – not in a pretty-girl way – but her face was strong, with beautiful eyes. She was tall, with the womanly figure you would see on a 1950s movie star (big breasts, rounded hips, solid thighs). That sort of body could easily plump up, if the woman with the body didn't work as hard as Celia did every day. The point was, the whole package was quite sexy, in Sheena's opinion. Not bad for a forty-something woman. So, what a waste that she'd been living out here on her own – well, with a daughter, but no man.

At first Sheena had assumed there was something going on between Celia and Joe, but now she figured it was more of a brother–sister thing. Which was a shame, really. According to the old lady, Joe wasn't getting any at home, and there was Celia right in front of him not getting any either. But maybe if you'd always had a brother–sister vibe, it would feel creepy to crack on to each other.

Possibly Celia drove into town for a sneaky fuck every now and then. She could have an arrangement with some local guy for her sexual needs, but Roza said she didn't and Sheena reckoned the old duck was right about that. So, Celia had spent sixteen years living like a nun, a peach-growing nun, a peach-growing nun with a child. Weird. Of course Sheena wouldn't have a clue what it was like to have a husband, let alone a husband who had got killed out of the blue when you had a baby in your belly. Still, it seemed a shame Celia's sexiness was being wasted, especially since she was getting older and there wouldn't be many sexy years left.

Through that hot, windless afternoon, Sheena, Kieran and Zoe picked fruit, then finished up at five, an hour earlier than usual.

While Sheena loaded the ladders and bags onto the trailer, Kieran was pulling at his shoulders, doing exaggerated groans of agony, making Zoe laugh.

Sheena chucked a water bottle at him. 'I told you to take it easy with that high-up stuff, deadhead. You always overdo it and end up shredding yourself.'

'But I kind of like the feeling,' he said. 'I can locate all these muscles exactly. Makes me think about my insides like one of those charts at the hospital – you know, with the man's skin taken off so you can see the red stripy muscles wrapping and crossing over his body. How wild is that!'

He grinned at Zoe, who proceeded to encourage the annoying idiot by laughing more.

'Kieran,' Sheena snapped. 'You better have a good scrub. I'm not sleeping in that sauna of a cabin with you all stinky and cheesy.'

'I love you too, Sheena.'

They were about to head off to the shower when the girl said, 'Hey, um, I was thinking – since we finished early and it's still light – which means, y'know . . .' She trailed off, but Kieran was smiling at her, expectant, so Zoe dredged up the courage to say what she planned to say. 'The thing is, there's a good swimming spot at the creek. I could show you. Well, you can't *swim* but you can cool off there, if you guys feel like it.'

'Fuck yeah, we feel like it! Don't we, Sheena?' Kieran swivelled his body to face her with a grin of appeal. 'Come on, Sheena. Yeah? Come on.'

Her brother had worked hard for seven days straight without whingeing, so Sheena figured he deserved some kind of treat. And for that matter, Sheena deserved whatever treats might be available in this place they'd found themselves.

'Sure,' she said. 'Whatever.'

The three of them refilled their water bottles, then Zoe led the way around behind Celia's house, down towards the creek. Kieran galloped ahead, as if they were on their way to an amusement park or some amazing attraction. When the rough track became steeper, zigzagging around rocks, all three of them had to pick their way more slowly.

The creek was like a photo out of a tourism brochure. It sat snugly at the bottom of a gully lined with trees that arched over the stream to create a shaded canopy. Clear water, almost knee-deep, flowed over smooth stones. Along the banks, between the big rocks, were stretches of soft grass as if someone had mowed the stuff to look even more perfect.

Zoe pointed out a section where she had piled up rocks when she was nine years old, in an attempt to construct a swimming pool. She showed them spots where her little-kid self had hidden treasures and built cubbies and found an injured wallaby. It was like the childhood in a fucking book.

Sheena yanked her shoes off and sat on a smooth rock. From that position, she could swish her feet around in the creek and scoop up handfuls of water to splosh over her face and arms.

Kieran clambered straight into the water in the grubby board shorts and singlet he'd been wearing all day. He stretched out and rolled around on the creek bed until he was wet all over, like a labrador in a puddle. Then he started to whoosh himself from side to side more vigorously.

'Sheena, check it out! You can make it like a washing machine! Saves time on washing my clothes. You hopping in the washing machine, Zoe?'

Zoe laughed, shaking her head. Like Sheena, she was sitting on the side, swirling her bare legs in the water. 'See that rock there?' she said to Kieran. 'Sit with your back against that.'

Kieran shuffled his bum along and wedged himself against a rock that protruded from the middle of the creek like a low chair back. Instantly, the water was forced up, spraying high around him. He whooped, turning his head to catch the spray, flapping his arms like a little kid frolicking under a sprinkler. 'This is like a jacuzzi! Better!'

Not that Kieran himself had ever been in or anywhere near a jacuzzi. He must've seen one on TV and was comparing that to a bit of water splashing against a rock in a creek.

Sheena sometimes envied the way her brother could find delight in things, even if it involved being blind to the ugliness of whatever reality he was stumbling through. She wondered if it was a better way to be. But no, it really wasn't – that kind of childlike, unguarded state meant Kieran was too vulnerable, susceptible to individuals who took advantage of him.

Sheena closed her eyes, relishing the shade, the sound of the water and the peacefulness of this place. A few moments later, there was a splash and she opened her eyes to see Zoe in the middle of the creek, her shorts and T-shirt now soaking wet. The girl propped her back against the rock next to Kieran and the two of them were laughing.

When they'd first turned up at the farm, Zoe had kept her distance from Kieran, but in the past couple of days, from what Sheena could see, the girl must've changed her policy. Now, during the long shifts working in the orchard, Zoe and Kieran were yabbering to each other at every opportunity.

Zoe was careful not to let Celia notice her talking to the low-life guy. Sheena admired the way the girl handled the mother, the subtle way she sidled in and out of one-on-one chats with Kieran without Celia sussing it out. When Sheena was sixteen, she hadn't needed to use any such furtive manoeuvres. She could get away with anything. Her mother wouldn't have given a flying fuck if – well, it was more that she never *noticed* when any of her offspring were engaged in unwise activities. Their mum was always off her face or preoccupied chasing after Scumbag Boyfriend of the Month or sprawled in bed, weeping, blowing her nose on scrunched-up toilet paper because Scumbag of the Month had left her.

Sheena had made a strategic decision not to worry about her brother engaging in a bit of low-octane flirting. Sure, Zoe came across as more mature than Kieran, but she really was just a kid, especially compared to the scheming sixteen-year-old bitches Sheena knew in the city. For all Zoe's delicate manoeuvres around her mother, she remained thoroughly under Celia's thumb and she'd never do anything to risk her good-girl status. And if a flirtation with the blonde princess helped keep Kieran settled for long enough to earn some money, that was an advantage. It meant they could fix the car and move on as soon as possible. Back on the road, with a wad of cash, they could then cobble together a longer- term plan.

Kieran and the girl climbed out of the water and lay on a slab of flat rock, warming themselves like beautiful animals in the syrupy light of the late afternoon. Kieran kept glancing at Zoe's wet T-shirt clinging to her bra, outlining the shape of her breasts. Oh Jesus, it was like a classy, soft-focus wet T-shirt competition with only one entrant. Zoe's eyes were closed, her blonde eyelashes against her pale skin, her chin tilted up, but even with her eyes closed, that girl knew exactly what effect the whole shirt-clinging-to-breasts thing must be having on Kieran – on Sheena's poor gullible brother.

Then out of nowhere, the girl sat up and said, 'I want to know how you guys ended up here.'

Sheena shrugged. 'This is the place my car broke down.'

'Yeah, but I mean, where were you driving to before the car trouble?'

'We weren't driving *to* anywhere,' said Kieran. 'It was —'

Sheena flashed him a warning look that would usually have shut him up, for a moment at least. But this time Kieran held her gaze with a kind of firm composure she wasn't used to from her brother.

'Come on, Sheena, I want to explain. To Zoe. Let me explain about when you found me.'

If Kieran described that scene, the girl would realise he was a bona fide fuck-up and not some innocuously scruffy guy. And maybe it would be just as well if she understood that.

'Okay,' said Sheena. 'You can tell Zoe about that day.'

Kieran grinned, excited, like a puppy let off the leash. 'Okay. So. A few weeks ago, Sheena came back to Sydney. She'd been living up the Gold Coast. She was living up there with this dude who —'

Sheena slammed her hand against the air to shut him up. The princess didn't need to hear details about Sheena's fucked-up love life. 'Let's just say I was with a guy who turned out to be a bit of dickless wonder.'

Kieran nodded emphatically. 'Sheena always picks the biggest dropkicks. Our aunty reckons Sheena could walk into a room packed with fifty nice guys and she'd manage to find the one slack dickhead in the place and fall for him in five minutes flat.'

'That's probably a fair call,' Sheena conceded. 'But where are these rooms with fifty nice guys in them? There are no such rooms. If someone showed me where I could find a room with fifty nice men inside, I'd go there right now.'

Zoe laughed and made eye contact with Sheena – which was unexpected, given the way the girl generally avoided Sheena's gaze.

'Anyway, anyway,' said Kieran, eager to get to the story, 'Sheena comes back to Sydney and she asks our mum, "Where's Kieran?" And Mum goes, "I think he's been staying at his mate Mick's place." So then Sheena asks, "Which Mick? Brain-dead Mick Fraser or Mick the Toxic Snake?"'

Sheena frowned, not sure it was the best idea to go into such detail with the girl. 'Well, yeah, I had to ask because —'

Kieran leaned across to explain to Zoe, 'Because I've got two different mates called Mick. Well, three if you count Dean's brother Mick – who's in jail now.'

'The point is,' Sheena continued, 'Mum had no clue. She just —'

'Oh, oh, oh, let me do it.' Kieran was stabbing his hand in the air like a kid eager to answer a question in class. 'When our mum has no clue, she does this —'

Kieran did an impersonation of their mother – sighing, jaw slack, fluttering her eyelids down – an impersonation so accurate it gave Sheena the shivers.

'The poor woman's *very* tired,' Sheena explained to Zoe.

Kieran added, mock-earnestly, 'It's all too much for her to handle.'

'She still hasn't worked out that the pills and the Bacardi don't contribute a huge amount to her mental alertness and problem-solving skills.'

Sheena took a swig of water and glanced over to see that Zoe was getting off on the thrill of hearing about this low-life family. A bit more of the sordid detail might properly freak her out, and that wouldn't be such a bad thing if it scared the kid into keeping her distance from Kieran.

'So, anyway,' Sheena continued, with more relish and purpose now, 'I took a guess on where Kieran was and gunned it round to Mick the Toxic Snake's place. I could smell the putrid house from two doors down. There was so much blood in the living room, I thought someone had their throat cut with a chainsaw in there.'

'What was the blood from?' asked Zoe.

'Those geniuses got hold of industrial quantities of a vet drug called ketamine.'

'Some guy told Mick how people can take it even though the vets use it on animals,' Kieran explained.

Zoe nodded, trying to play it cool. 'Yeah, it's for horses. It's a horse anaesthetic. My friend's dad is a vet.'

Ah, the princess was showing off, trying to impress them with her rural credentials.

'Well, Zoe,' said Sheena, 'I don't happen to know what effect ketamine has on horses, but I do know that if human beings pig out on the stuff, their feet and hands go numb. There was heaps of broken glass on the floor – from accidents with bottles none of those morons had enough functional brain matter to clean up.'

'Oh,' said Zoe. 'They couldn't feel they were cutting their feet on the glass because they were numb from the ketamine.'

'Yeah, so they tracked blood all over.' Sheena sighed. 'But actually that stuff wasn't what worried me.'

Again, Kieran leaned over to Zoe to explain. 'Sheena thinks Mick is a dangerous guy.'

'He is a scaly toad and a psycho,' said Sheena firmly. 'The kind of psycho who holds a shotgun to a mate's head as a joke.'

'That was only one time,' Kieran protested. 'Oh . . . well, twice . . .'

'Mick had gone into business for himself since I'd left Sydney,' Sheena went on. 'Dealing speed. He'd got Kieran frying his brains, plus using him as a runner. Mick's in business with bikers.'

'Those guys are pretty big in the speed business,' Kieran added as a helpful note.

'And now Mick was boasting to me how he's got a shotgun in the house. I didn't have to be Mystic Sheena to see someone's gonna go to jail or end up dead. And chances are it's going to be my little brother.'

Kieran struck a pose for Zoe and she spluttered into laughter. If the girl was laughing out of embarrassment or shock or admiration, it was hard to tell.

'So, anyway,' Sheena continued, 'I found Kieran in one of the back rooms.'

Kieran wiggled his fingers around his head in a scrambling gesture. 'I was far away down a pixie hole.'

'I dragged him out the door, his feet all cut up and bleeding. Shoved him in the back seat of my car and drove off. As far away from Mick and Sydney as I could get him.'

Zoe turned to Kieran. 'And what did you think about that?'

'Oh well, I slept the first ten hours.'

'But when you woke up, what did you do?'

'I started whining, didn't I, Sheena?'

'Yes, you certainly fucking did.'

Kieran laughed and flopped onto his back, so he could do an exaggerated demonstration of how he'd behaved in the back of the car. 'My feet hurt – ow, ow, ow! What are you doing to me, Sheena? How come I've got bandages on my feet? Where are you taking me? You're not the boss of me, Sheena!'

'Why didn't you just run off?' Zoe asked.

'I tried.'

'His feet were so cut up to begin with, he couldn't walk properly,' said Sheena.

'I couldn't. I was her prisoner in the back seat of the car. I go, "You're kidnapping me. This is an actual crime, you know, Sheena."'

Sheena rolled her eyes. 'Driving me mental.'

'So, you know what she did?' he said, sitting up. 'Pulled up outside a police station, and you know what she says to me?'

Sheena jumped in to play herself in the scene. 'Okay then, pop inside and tell the cops I'm kidnapping you.'

Kieran grinned at Zoe and shrugged – *What could I do?*

'But once your feet healed up, why didn't you take off then?' Zoe asked him.

Sheena answered for her brother. 'Because we'd been away from those deadheads long enough for Kieran to think straight. And now he needs to stay away from guys like Mick long enough to grow a brain in his thick skull.'

Sheena got to her feet, to make it clear the storytelling session was over. It was good to give the princess a bit of a scare, but no need to tell her more than necessary. 'We need to get dinner organised while there's still some light. Let's go.'

*

Zoe was expecting Kieran to jump up and follow his sister straight away. Instead, he lay on his back again and adopted the joke whiny voice, as if he were still in the back of her car with cut-up feet. 'Gimme one more sec off my sore tootsies. Please, please.'

Sheena groaned, but then she headed up the bank. 'One sec. Then come.'

Once Zoe was sure Sheena was far enough up the slope to be out of earshot, she asked Kieran, 'Do you mind your sister bossing you around?'

'Oh, well, she doesn't always boss me around.'

At exactly that moment, Sheena turned back to bellow down at them. 'Kieran! You said one sec. Get back up here! Now!'

Kieran gave a thumbs-up to indicate he was coming, but then he turned to Zoe. 'The thing you gotta understand, Zoe, is Sheena's always looked after me. Even when I was in kindy. Like, if she was picking me up from school and she found out kids were monstering me, Sheena would belt across the playground like Super Sister and yank their arms behind their backs. I had my own bouncer.'

Zoe laughed, easily picturing that scene. She was scared of Sheena but admired her ferocity. When Sheena was telling the blood-on-the-floor ketamine-kidnapping story, Zoe had never seen her so animated. It was a glimpse of the other ways Sheena could be, a sign she could be fun if you caught her in the right mood. But the main thing Zoe had felt, listening to the two of them, was envy. Envy that Sheena and Kieran had each other and could tell a story together as a double act, as brother and sister. And envy that they had a story to tell that was real and intense, like something out of a TV show.

Sheena was near the top of the slope by now but the screeching pitch of her voice was loud enough to make Zoe's ears hurt. 'Kieran! I can see you still sitting there on your fucking arse!'

Kieran didn't flinch. He just looked at Zoe and said fervently, 'Sheena's a good person. She deserves better than she gets.'

Again, the shrill voice from above them. 'Kieran!'

He bellowed up towards his sister. 'Yeah! I'll be up there in a minute! You have first shower!' He spun back to Zoe. 'Better get up there soon, I s'pose. Before Sheena rips my balls off.' But even so, Kieran made no move to leave.

Sheena scowled down at them before she walked out of view.

'Sheena's cranky with you,' said Zoe. 'Because of me.'

'Well, my sister is worried you're after my money.'

'Perhaps so. But she's also worried that you're just too immature and silly.'

They both nodded slowly, with mock gravity, until Kieran suddenly lunged sideways and scooped a handful of water from the creek to flick onto Zoe's legs. She squealed with the cold shock of it and then splashed him back, scoring a direct hit in the face. Kieran threw his upper body into the stream to swing his arms through the water and drench them both.

The splashing assaults escalated into a full-on water fight, the two of them scrambling over the rocks, laughing wildly, clothes and hair sodden again, until they eventually collapsed onto their backs on a grassy stretch.

For a few moments, all Zoe could hear was the sound of Kieran breathing and her own breaths loud in her throat. She was aware of his body, stretched out at a slight diagonal to hers.

'What are you thinking this second?' Kieran asked.

'Oh . . . you don't want to know.'

'I do.'

'Oh, no.'

'Um, *yes*.'

'Well, if you must know, I was thinking about how I think about things too much. Like, in my imagination I watch myself doing something before I do it and then I think about all the reasons it might be a bad idea and don't end up doing anything. I wish I could just . . .'

Zoe squeezed her eyes shut, flung her arms out wildly and made a yowling noise that bounced off the sides of the gully. 'I wish I could throw myself into things before I get a chance to . . .'

She opened her eyes to see Kieran staring at her. She dropped her arms, twisted up her face with self-mockery. 'You think I'm a fruit loop.'

'No! No, no, you're – uh – uh – uh . . .' Kieran thumped his fist against the side of his head, as if he could shake loose the word he was looking for.

Zoe laughed. 'Are you having a seizure?'

'No. I've gotta find exactly the right word. Ah! Yeah! You're spectacular.'

'Shut up. Don't take the piss out of me.'

'Don't you take the piss out of my word. I had to dig around in my scrambled brain to find that word. *Spectacular.*'

Zoe held her breath. She wanted so much for that to be true, for him to mean it, but the wanting it so much was almost more than she could bear. 'A spectacularly sad case, you mean.'

'Fuck me dead, you're beautiful.'

And that was enough to suck the breath out of Zoe's lungs so she was unable to bat him away with some comment. Kieran slid closer, close enough to kiss her. But then he stopped, waiting for permission. Zoe was going to have to make it clear she wanted him to kiss her. She was glad the sun had shrunk back out of the gully – it was getting close to sunset. The dim light meant it was possible Kieran wouldn't be able to see how nervous she was. She wrenched up the courage to lean towards him, and they kissed.

Zoe and her friend Mandy had practised pashing oranges when they were in Second Form. But she had never pashed a person – unless you counted kiss-chasey games in primary school that only ever resulted in giggly or disgusted pecks on lips. Zoe had imagined pashing Kieran many times over the last seven days – often during the daytime and even more at night.

It was good, a bit tentative, but good. Way better than kissing an orange. But Zoe was anxious, with no way to tell if she was doing it right from her side of the process. How much tongue? How much pressure? How much moving of the head? Was she doing it all wrong, revealing herself as an inexperienced kid?

Then Kieran made a small noise in his throat and Zoe felt the vibration on her mouth. Surprised, she drew back a bit, and Kieran smiled at her — *what?* She didn't want him to think she didn't want him to keep kissing her, so she dived for his mouth again, determined not to let anxiety twist and strangle this opportunity. After that, it was better. Much better. And then it became something else — more intense and dizzying. All they were doing was kissing but her whole body was humming with a glorious energy, as if she had finally been activated for the purpose she was ever in this body.

When they came up for air a few minutes later, Zoe didn't want to look at her watch, but she had to. It was dinnertime and she didn't want to give her mother grounds to worry — at least not until there was a chance to think this through.

She tugged her shoes on, threw Kieran a quick affirming smile, then scrambled up the side of the gully and ran back to the house.

SIX

In Roza's estimation, there was a choice about how to look at it – 'it' being the sight of Kieran and Zoe on that Christmas Eve, kissing, laughing, whispering, scampering between the orchard rows to kiss some more, so intoxicated with this kissing that they didn't care who saw them.

A person could have viewed it through a patronising and jaded filter. *Oh, those young lovers are too immature and foolish.* Or someone might have looked with bitter eyes. *How dare those young people have such rapture.* But Roza made what she considered a selfish choice. She saw herself as feeding off the energy that radiated from their passion. She was a geriatric vampire. When there were so many painful things in a life, why not let your eyes linger on a beautiful thing and soak in a little of its vitality?

Roza was aware that neither Sheena nor Celia was happy about the kissing going on in front of them through the day. Celia's reaction was to be expected – to see this boy, this wired-up, aimless, tattooed, stray young man with his arms around Zoe would ignite her anxieties like a spray of kerosene on a fire. Why Sheena looked unhappy was less certain. Perhaps it was simple envy – there was no one here for her to canoodle with, no man gazing at her the way Kieran was gazing at Zoe. Or perhaps Sheena noticed Celia's disapproval and she was worried this threatened the stability of their employment. Or it could be some deeper concern about her brother's emotional state. But neither woman said anything about it – not in Roza's hearing, anyway – they merely frowned at the young pair whenever they caught sight of them.

Kieran seemed unaware of the spiked glances fired in his direction by his sister and his employer. Zoe also appeared oblivious, but Roza knew that would not be so. That girl understood what her mother's reaction would be to this development. Which didn't mean Zoe's infatuation with Kieran was not authentic. From what Roza could tell, she was truly swept away by this young man.

In the late afternoon, Josef drove out to Celia's farm, bringing papers to be signed or whatever errand was the excuse for this visit. He always brought fresh milk and any other items from town he thought Celia might need. Roza was satisfied that she and Sandor had brought up their son to be a considerate man who would think about someone's need for milk.

When Joe pulled his car into the yard, Roza could see he was tired, tired into his bones. When he stooped to kiss her cheek, she grabbed his face in both hands so he couldn't escape close scrutiny.

'Show me your eyeballs,' she said. 'You have a deficiency.'

'What is it this week, Mum?' he asked. 'Vitamin B? Iron?'

It was, in Roza's opinion, a deficiency of the spirit, but she controlled the urge to point this out. Roza well knew that it was not easy being the son of a mother like her. Josef stood before her with that resigned smile of his and she decided now was not the time to destabilise the fragile truce he had made to get through his life. Instead, she planted robust, smacking kisses on both his cheeks. Some days that was the best you could do for your child.

'Sheena. Hi,' said Joe.

Sheena had ventured close to the packing shed to collect an empty bin. 'Hi.'

'How's it going?' he asked.

'Okay.' She shrugged and shifted uncomfortably. Even so, she lingered, in a spot where a wedge of shade fell across the yard by this time of day.

'Listen, I spoke to the mechanic,' said Joe. 'The parts came for your car. It's ready to pick up whenever you're ready.'

'Whenever I get the money together,' Sheena snapped back. 'We don't all have eight hundred bucks lying around.'

'Sure. Right. I know it's a sizeable chunk of money.'

Sheena winced, acknowledging how rude she sounded. 'Sorry. Sorry . . . I'm just . . .'

Joe shook off her apology with a smile. 'You've got a lot on your plate. Oh, hey, I grabbed you and Kieran some stuff in town.' He walked back to his car to fetch a supermarket box from the boot. 'Just some cold bits and pieces I thought you might be running out of. Especially with the shops shut for the next couple of days. Give me a yell if there's anything in particular you guys need next time I come out.'

Sheena jerked a smile and took the box of food from his hand – clumsily, as if she had never been handed an object by another human being. 'Ta. How much do I owe you for all this? I haven't got cash on me here but I could run down to the cabin and get some.'

'No rush. Whenever. Or never. It's just a few bucks' worth,' he assured her.

Roza wasn't surprised to see Joe being so kind to this spiky woman. Living with a dissatisfied creature like Heather for more than ten years had honed a special capacity in him to manage difficult people graciously. It was like a superpower he used at home that he felt obliged to exercise in other personal interactions.

Sheena was clearly puzzled by his kindness. 'How come you're being so nice to us? That's your job in town, is it? Being the nice, helpful guy.'

Yes, thought Roza, that was exactly the role Joe had established for himself. Sheena was more astute than a person might think just from looking at her.

'Eh?' responded Joe, thrown off balance.

'Oh – no, I don't mean . . . sorry,' stammered Sheena. 'I mean, shit. Look, y'know, thanks. I'll shove this stuff in our esky.'

Sheena seemed glad of the excuse to flee, heading down to the cabin with the box of food. Josef also looked relieved that his awkward encounter with the woman was now over.

As Celia walked across from the house, she saw Joe and called out to him. 'Hello!'

Joe swung his arm to indicate the row of fruit trees where Kieran and Zoe were working. 'You guys seem to be moving through the pick okay.'

'We're getting there,' said Celia.

She and Joe stood side by side in the doorway of the shed, looking out into the orchard, just as there was a fresh outbreak of passionate kissing between Kieran and Zoe.

'Oh,' murmured Joe.

Celia nodded. 'Mm.'

Before Joe could summon any more of a response than that initial 'oh' of surprise, the phone extension rang, reverberating through the shed. Celia answered the call, then mouthed 'Heather' to Joe. He whispered a quick 'Sorry about this' as he took the receiver.

'Hi. How are you? I'm just —' he began, before Heather cut him off.

This was how it so often went whenever Roza heard her son's side of a phone call to his wife, a woman apparently incapable of allowing another person to finish a sentence.

'No, I haven't rung them yet because —'

There was more yapping by Heather, then Joe managed to get a few words out: 'Sorry. But I thought we decided it was better to leave it a few —'

Heather then launched into a longer stint of talking, during which Joe nodded, capitulating to whatever position she was pushing. 'Okay. I will.'

Finally, his voice fell into a defeated cadence, the way these phone calls often ended. 'I'm sorry. I said I'm sorry.'

Roza should not have been eavesdropping on her son's call – out of respect for Joe's privacy and to spare herself the frustration of hearing him like this – so she moved away, out of the shed and into the yard, to avoid catching anymore.

Josef drove back into town the minute the phone call was over. According to Heather, there was a big list of Christmas Eve jobs not yet done.

*

Celia had noticed the flirting earlier in the week, given she wasn't sight-impaired or dimwitted. What she hadn't expected was that the flirtation would turn into anything physical. Zoe was by nature a cautious kid, so this brazen display of kissing had come as a surprise.

Surprise kept Celia's mouth shut when she first saw Zoe and Kieran together. It was so early in the morning, there was barely enough dawn light for the two kids to find each other's faces. As the kissing interludes continued through the day, what could Celia have said? *What are you doing?* It was obvious what they were doing.

Zoe had dodged any possibility of speaking privately with her mother, and then at the end of the working day, she ran ahead to the house. By the time Celia caught up, Zoe had showered and was in her bedroom, the door closed.

With anxiety fermenting in her belly, Celia dropped her sweaty clothes on the bathroom floor and stepped into the shower. She needed to hold her neck under the clear, cool stream of rainwater so she could think clearly and coolly.

The first time Celia had properly kissed a boy she'd been almost eighteen, wedged beside the cleaning-supplies alcove at the back of an ice-skating rink. She remembered that the moment felt good, a heady sensation despite, or maybe because of, the bleach fumes from the nearby buckets. But her overriding response was relief that this boy she had been pining for was willing to kiss her.

Celia used to worry she was too much for people. Through her teens and into her twenties she feared she was too intense, too ardent, and this would frighten men away. She assumed she would always, inevitably, be the one who wanted a man more than he wanted her. So, her strategy was to conceal how strongly she felt, withhold the full force of her emotions rather than let them loose onto some guy who would likely flee in horror. In her romantic life, such as it was, she always felt precarious, on the edge of being exposed, and always slightly ashamed.

Then Marcus came along, and it wasn't like that. Not on the evening they were introduced and not for one moment afterwards. Within days of meeting, he declared himself with such unqualified fervour that Celia knew she could reveal the full strength of her emotions. (Afterwards they used to joke about the two of them 'unleashing' themselves on each other.) And right from the start, she felt astonishingly relaxed and safe to show herself, because it was this man, Marcus.

Maybe it was a matter of timing – by then Celia was twenty-four, more confident, making her way at work. In the previous few years she had buried both her parents, a process that had left her tougher, more sure she could wrangle the world on her own. Maybe that was part of it. But meeting Marcus was more fateful and surprising than any logical explanation – she'd found someone who could match her feelings in a way that was thrilling and at the same time deeply calm. Lucky. She had always appreciated they were lucky.

At Zoe's age, Celia would never have dared kiss and grope a boy in front of her parents in glaring daylight. And she would never have gone for a guy as wild as Kieran. Probably Zoe was throwing this silly infatuation into the air as a show of independence, expecting her mother to forbid it, provoking Celia to challenge her. Zoe knew how her mother would react. She most surely knew.

Celia stayed under the shower, letting the water run longer than she normally would, and consulted the Reasonable Woman about how to regard today's events. It would all be fine, surely. She could even welcome the romance, the festival of kissing, as a sort of practice run for Zoe – a chance to rehearse with a boy who would only briefly flit through her life, without the risk of making a fool of herself in front of her friends. Celia could see the appeal of that. And Kieran would be moving on soon enough, so there was little danger this would escalate into something more troubling. If anything, she should be more concerned about the boy having his heart broken, being toyed with by a curious teenage girl. In fact, probably the best thing would be to let things run their course.

Even so, she should say something this evening, something brief and direct and calm, avoiding inflammatory wording.

Celia turned off the shower – she'd used up enough precious water – and wrapped herself in a towel. She didn't often wear dresses, but since it was Christmas Eve she flipped through to the far end of her wardrobe and chose a bright paisley-print dress. She tossed her sweaty work clothes into the laundry and then waited for her daughter to emerge from her room.

When Zoe finally wandered into the kitchen, her hair was still damp from the shower and she was pulling her fingers through the tangles like a rough comb.

'Do you want me to start on the meringue?' she asked.

'Uh, yes. That'd be good,' Celia said. 'You do that and I'll poach the chicken.'

On Christmas Eve, Celia and Zoe always prepared a chicken salad and a pavlova as their contribution to the Christmas Day spread at Roza's house.

She was surprised by the matter-of-factly domestic tone Zoe adopted, as if nothing unusual was going on. It threw Celia off balance, and for the moment, she figured it was best to say nothing, to let things go until the air around them settled.

For the next hour, the pair of them worked side by side in the kitchen, preparing food, poaching chicken, whisking egg whites with sugar, sharing the limited space between the benchtop, the fridge and the stove, moving around each other with the wordless efficiency of two people who had shared that kitchen for a long time.

Celia should mention Kieran soon, broach the subject somehow. She wondered if Zoe would say something, but she said nothing, other than remarks or questions about the cooking tasks. The longer this went on, the harder it felt to choose the words or find the moment. It was astonishing the way two people could be in close proximity and not talk about the thing that was thudding inside both their brains.

So Celia let the minutes unspool, until eventually it seemed impossible to blurt out a comment or ask a question. And by then she had let herself relish the simple pleasure of this Christmas Eve routine with her daughter. She didn't want to spoil it. So she said nothing.

In every year, there were obstacles scattered through the calendar – Marcus's birthday, the anniversary of his death, their wedding anniversary – dates Celia could get snagged on. She had developed rituals to mark such occasions and avoid being obliterated by them. She kept those observances to herself. No need to burden Zoe.

Early on, Celia had expected 25 December would be one of those jagged dates, but as a little kid Zoe had loved Christmas-time with such simple delight, it had proved easy to enjoy it with her. It helped that the workload on the farm in midsummer kept Celia too busy to dwell on visions of what should have been.

Over the years, Celia and Zoe had assembled their own Christmas traditions. On 18 December they would work together to drag a potted conifer in from the back porch and decorate it with ornaments Celia had inherited from her grandmother. On Christmas Eve, Zoe would mix up the seasonal 'cocktail' she had created as a nine-year-old – juice, crushed ice, mint leaves and small chunks of fruit, served in an etched-glass punchbowl the two of them had spotted together in the Narralong op shop.

Christmas Day usually involved a few hours of work, then during the midday break there would be a phone call to Freya, Zoe's Sydney aunt. Freya's kids had been just old enough last year to have a turn on the phone, chattering to Zoe. Late in the afternoon, Celia and Zoe would share an early dinner with Roza and Joe's family.

Jesus played no role in the celebration, not even in a perfunctory way. Religion had never been part of their life. Every Sunday when Zoe was little, her school friends would be dressed in their for-best powder-blue Courtelle dresses, lace-trimmed white socks, black patent shoes and flowery hairclips, then sent to church and Sunday school. Zoe never asked why she didn't go, in the way kids don't question the givens of their childhood. At the primary school, there had been scripture classes that mostly involved the gluing of cotton balls onto sheep and colouring-in of shepherds on roneoed sheets still reeking of inky chemicals. Those activities didn't spark any theological discussion at home.

When Zoe started at the Catholic high school, Celia kept her mouth shut and didn't directly challenge the religious instruction from the nuns, wary of forcing her child into an outsider position. Zoe had played along with the school scripture stuff – she was a dutiful, willing kid – and when she experimented with a bit of earnest prayer at bedtime, Celia decided not to comment.

Then, one day in her second year of high school, Zoe came home and announced, 'I don't think any of it is true.'

'Neither do I,' said Celia. And from then on, the two of them would talk in a relaxed, curious way about the various things people believed, including the version of religion the school was pitching.

Zoe checked the pavlova base in the oven, then lifted it out onto the bench.

'It's done, I think,' she said. Then, in a mock-mystical voice, she quoted the instructions from the recipe in their old cookbook: 'The meringue should be cooked at the temperature of a mountain hillside towards the end of summer when a light breeze is blowing.'

Every year, the two of them would send up that ridiculous other-worldly line in the cookbook. This year, Celia laughed a bit too enthusiastically, grateful her daughter would joke with her about the pavlova recipe, counting it as a sign that nothing significant had changed.

All evening, Zoe was sweet with Celia, but holding her at bay – as if she were clasping her mother's arms affectionately but in such a way that it maintained a gap between them. Any connection felt fragile, and Celia was careful not to spoil things.

Since Zoe had turned eight and grown too old for the Santa Claus pantomime, mother and daughter had exchanged presents on Christmas Eve, a tradition they liked to call 'being European'. Really, it was a practical matter, given that mornings during harvest times were always pressured and busy.

After cooking and eating, they followed their usual Christmas Eve routine and switched on the telly for the Carols by Candlelight tele-cast. They lit a dozen red and white candles around the living room and then both sat cross-legged on the floor to unwrap their presents.

Zoe gave her mother two gifts – an Iris Murdoch novel she'd asked Freya to post from Sydney; and earrings, red jasper set in sil-ver, that she'd bought from the slightly hippy shop in Evatt's Bridge.

'What a fantastic choice. I love them,' Celia said and put the earrings on straight away.

Celia always gave her daughter a stack of books. This year there were novels by Ursula Le Guin, E.L. Doctorow, Jane Austen, Chaim Potok – an odd mix but she was confident Zoe would devour them all happily. Another parcel contained an embroidered straw beach bag stuffed with a striped purple towel and other beachy items. This gift was meant to demonstrate Celia's enthusiasm about the plan for Zoe to spend the next Easter holidays with her friend Mandy's family at their caravan on the coast.

Celia's main present for her daughter was the riskiest. She'd seen the dress in a shop window on a trip to Young, and the urge to see Zoe wearing it was strong enough to make her spend more money than she normally would.

When Zoe peeled the sticky tape from the wrapping paper, the dress slithered into her hands – pale-blue silk printed with loose skeins of flowers tumbling down.

'Mum. It's so lovely,' she whispered. 'But it looks expensive.'

Zoe had always worried about their finances, even as a little kid, and as always, Celia fibbed to put her at ease. 'It was on sale. I hope it fits.'

Zoe ducked into her bedroom to try on the dress. She had never been especially modest about her body, even in her teens, but in the last year she had stopped wandering through the house naked, or even in underwear.

'It fits, I think,' said Zoe when she reappeared in the doorway.

The dress gathered softly at the shoulders, with a scooped neckline, then the silk skimmed over her waist and hips to fall like liquid into the loose folds of the skirt. She was breathtaking in the dress, just as Celia had imagined.

Celia couldn't speak for a moment, looking at her, and then, before she could say a word, Zoe darted forward to kiss her mother on the cheek.

'I love it. Thank you,' she said.

Celia felt Zoe's warm body against hers, and then the sleek fabric of the dress slid under her hands as Zoe darted away, back towards the hall.

'I'd better take this gorgeous thing off and hang it up,' she said. 'I feel so tired suddenly. Might go to bed.'

'Yes, do that. We need plenty of energy for tomorrow.'

Celia stayed on the floor for several minutes after Zoe left. But sitting there was only delaying the start of the hours she would spend lying in bed wondering if she should have said something.

SEVEN

Christmas Day.

As a child in Hungary, Roza had always enjoyed Christmas-time – even growing up in a Jewish family, she could enjoy the street decorations and the music and the food. She was proudly an atheist (and indeed she found it difficult to respect a person who could still believe in any kind of god, given the world they lived in), but she could ignore the religious nonsense in order to throw herself into a festival about food and generosity and gathering of family.

Of course there was the peculiar seasonal dislocation in Australia – celebrating Christmas in the hot middle of summer, surrounded by plastic holly and toy reindeer, with people exchanging cards depicting Cotswold villages draped in snow. But Roza was surprised to find she liked this oddness and reversal. It meant she could reinvent the occasion as a fresh thing, shedding its connections to the old world, crusted over with bad memories, and inject her own meaning into it.

She loved the idea of bounty, sharing a table of special food, taking pleasure in planning the dishes, negotiating with locals, buying fresh cherries from one neighbour, ducks from another, cream from the dairy farm on the way into town.

This Christmas, as well as roast duck with cherries and a variety of salads, she had prepared stuffed peppers, even if only Celia and Josef enjoyed them. She made *túrós tészta* because the children loved the cheesy noodles. There was always a potato dish so rich that her son declared it to be 'a heart attack in a baking tray', though that didn't stop him eating flattering amounts of it. And even if Josef needed to deal with his pudgy-belly issue, these were special festive dishes, not eaten every day, and not a thing to fuss about. Every year, Roza most enjoyed making *hamantaschen* – triangular biscuits filled with raspberries or chocolate or apricots – which her grandmother had taught her to cook.

By the time Joe, Heather and their two sons arrived at Roza's house on Christmas Day, it was half-past four. In Roza's opinion, it was an uncivilised time to have dinner but Heather insisted on this arrangement. She wouldn't contemplate missing out on Christmas lunch with her parents. One year, in an attempt to make things easier for Josef, Roza had accepted an invitation to Christmas lunch at Heather's parents' home, and was served a meal involving desiccated, overcooked pork, waterlogged vegetables and a brick of a pudding served with a whipped 'topping' from an aerosol can. She only attended the event that one time.

Roza would've been happy to celebrate with her son's family on Christmas Eve, in European style, but Heather declared this not to be 'proper Christmas'. Roza would not want any person to say she was obstructive, so she went along with Heather's timetable, which involved driving out in the afternoon in order to tick off the seasonal duty to her mother-in-law, then get her boys home to bed nice and early.

Roza was always intrigued, as well as disturbed, to see what dishes her daughter-in-law brought to the Christmas table. Heather chose to cook from packets of processed components – she regarded this culinary practice as 'modern' and 'sophisticated' compared to Roza's antiquated, peasant habit of cooking identifiable fresh ingredients.

For Christmas, Heather went in for torturing the food into shapes. This year there was a bright-green jelly mould with chunks of vegetables trapped inside, surrounded by a wreath of lurid yellow Cheezels. Some kind of tinned fish had been mixed with artificial substances and what appeared to be a can of pineapple chunks, then formed into a fish shape. Heather was clearly most proud of an object shaped like an igloo made from 'Deb' dehydrated potato, with a sausage-meat interior. The reconstituted mashed potato formed a dry grey crust like an unfortunate skin condition, and the stuffing gave off a greasy smell like dishwater left in a sink too long, the smell of resigned misery.

In theory, there could be something playful about a mother preparing food in fanciful shapes (such as an igloo) for her children on Christmas Day. But Heather wasn't that mother. She didn't cook to delight or nourish. She cooked for the admiring comments when she boasted of her culinary achievements later to her social-climbing friends.

Heather placed this year's monstrosities on the sideboard.

'Remarkable,' said Roza, which Heather took to be a compliment.

Josef, however, threw his mother a warning look – *Watch your tongue.*

'Boys, show Grandma what Santa put in your Christmas pillow-cases,' suggested Heather.

'Yes, please. Show me,' said Roza, and the two boys dragged in a laundry basket filled with their gifts – a board game called Mouse Trap, a Spirograph set, books and beach toys. Roza made a fuss of each item, asking questions and letting the boys chatter about them. Very quickly their chatter turned to the much more exciting presents they had also received that morning – scooters, remote-controlled car sets, walkie-talkies, an arsenal of plastic weapons and a fleet of Matchbox cars.

Roza exchanged a look with Josef as his two sons reeled off the long list of extra Christmas booty they'd left at home. Knowing that Roza disapproved of such material indulgence, Heather only allowed Hamish and Fergus to bring a selection of their more educational gifts to their grandmother's house. Joe had argued against Heather spoiling the children, but he never won that battle.

These days, Roza consulted Josef about what she should buy her grandsons. This year, with his advice, she gave Hamish a couple of Airfix kits to make World War I planes. She suspected it was a tactic by Josef to spend time with his TV-fixated elder son, just the two of them engaged in a task together. For Fergus, Roza bought a set of watercolours, brushes and quality art paper, because the seven-year-old reportedly loved painting and drawing. Roza figured this was also wishful – Josef would like to imagine his son was an artistic child.

Heather always gave Roza clothes, invariably matronly and hideous. These garments were made of synthetic textiles created by chemical companies out of their petroleum dregs – fabrics that would make a human being sweat like a sow swaddled in plastic wrap. Why any person with a choice would wear such fabric next to their skin was a mystery. Possibly Heather offered these garments as an unsubtle hint about how she would prefer Roza to dress. Or perhaps the woman was unobservant enough to think her mother-in-law would actually like them. Roza wasn't sure which explanation was more dispiriting.

Every Christmas, there was always another parcel tagged 'For Grandma, Merry Christmas from Hamish and Fergus', even though the two boys played no part in selection, purchase or wrapping the gift. This parcel would always contain candles and lovely bath oils chosen by Josef because he knew his mother enjoyed such things.

After the exchange of gifts, there was an awkward silence, which Josef valiantly tried to fill by pointing out things around the house. Heather looked panicky, trying to think of a way to make conversation.

'Oh, Roza, is that a new painting?' she asked.

'No, no, very old. But I have moved it from that far wall to this one,' Roza replied. Her habit was to move artworks and ornaments to different spots around the house several times each year so the eye could fall upon them freshly.

'Ah. I didn't notice that one when I was here the other day,' said Heather.

Heather talked as if she visited Roza's house often, but in truth, she only visited twice a year – Christmas and Joe's birthday. But they all went along with the fiction that they spent lots of time together. Such fictions lubricated the social occasions in many families, those events where each individual would rather not be there, everyone trapped and pretending.

Roza did make occasional visits to town. She would go to watch the boys play sport or perform in school concerts, and then she would treat them to iced chocolate in a cafe afterwards. This was a way to spend time with her grandsons without having to enter Heather's home, and all that entailed.

Leaving Heather to pretend interest in some artwork or other, Roza made an excuse to go into the kitchen to check on the food. From the stove, she could look back into the lounge room to see Hamish and Fergus setting up the Mouse Trap board on the carpet.

She searched the boys' faces for signs of Josef inside them somewhere, willing the genetic material to push its way through their skin. Joe made some efforts to influence his sons in positive ways but really, for the sake of peace, he gave in to Heather and her choices again and again.

Roza was heartened to see the kids giggling together over the game. She regretted that Josef had been an only child. Siblings could share the burden of their parents' fears and expectations. She wished Joe had had the benefit of that. She wished he had that now.

Then, a moment later, Roza observed Hamish snatch a red plastic piece from Fergus, and soon they were squabbling, whining for fizzy drink, dobbing on each other, both telling shameless lies to their mother, Hamish glowering at Fergus with hateful focus, as if his survival depended on destroying his younger brother.

As the afternoon wore on, the bickering would worsen. Heather aggravated the problem, playing the two boys off against each other, shaming one child while praising the other for some goody-goody posturing. It must be said that, regrettably, Josef did little to improve things, adopting a neutral, diplomatic role, only stepping in to negotiate the ceasefire terms. And through all this, there was nothing a grandmother could do or say.

Roza loved Hamish and Fergus fiercely, no matter how obnoxious they might one day become. It wasn't their fault this situation was allowed to go on. And however Roza might twist her thoughts and opinions, however much she might wish to cut dead her feelings for these difficult children, nothing would ever dissolve the visceral love for her grandsons.

*

Christmas Fucking Day. Sheena regretted she'd ever accepted the invitation to the old lady's house – an arrangement made before the kissing display had started.

The night before, she had contemplated giving Kieran a lecture about keeping his paws off the girl, but her brother's brain was too flooded with infatuated chemicals to process sensible thoughts. And anyway, the pashing in the orchard hadn't escalated into anything more. Kieran wasn't famous for self-restraint, so it had to be the girl who was maintaining those boundaries. Most likely, the whole business would stay at this teen-princess level: just kissing and besotted staring. Nothing to panic about, however nauseating it might be to witness.

This morning, Sheena had let Kieran have a sleep-in until eight, which he declared to be the best Christmas present he'd ever received. They picked fruit until midday, when Celia brought down ham-and-salad rolls for everyone. Then at three they all knocked off work to get ready for dinner at Roza's.

Sheena did have one more crack at wriggling out of the invitation – surely Celia would prefer they didn't go – but Zoe pushed for the day to run as planned.

So now here they were, Sheena and her brother – having washed off the sweat from the day's picking and put on the least-crappy clothing they had – walking down the slope to Roza's front door.

Kieran carried a box of wine and soft drink that Celia had brought to the yard earlier. Celia's arms were full, encircling a huge ceramic bowl of chicken salad. Zoe carried a platter with a dessert under a protective mesh cover to keep off insects. That girl always looked pretty, even when she was sweaty and filthy, so now, strolling along in a silky, flowered dress – a Christmas present, apparently – she looked like a film star in a movie about a fairy princess from the fucking forest.

'Merry Christmas,' Sheena murmured, adding to the chorus of season's greetings burbling through Roza's living room.

Sheena did not want to be here. Socialising wasn't exactly her strong suit. And today, with all the unsettling shit going on, it felt like the floor could fracture and collapse underneath her any second. She was sneaking looks at Celia, to suss how angry she was about the kissing business and what that would mean. She kept an eye on Zoe too, wondering how the princess was going to play it this afternoon. She flashed warning looks to Kieran – *Behave yourself.* And all the while, she fought the urge to bolt out the door and drag her brother with her.

Sheena heard her own voice come out with thin, breathy politeness as she was introduced to Joe's wife, Heather. 'Lovely to meet you.'

Heather had a pointy face like a fox, a face that would've been considered pretty in high school. Now she looked too sour to make anyone say 'pretty'. She was wearing so much make-up, with foundation and powder caked on her foxy little features, Sheena could smell it when she walked past. Heather's dyed-blonde hair had been given a determined going-over with a curling wand and then lacquered into submission with hairspray. Her beige skirt came with matching waistcoat, worn over a pink blouse that tied at the neck with a bow.

Not that Sheena had any right to be snide about this woman's grooming choices, given she herself was standing there with mousy roots coming through her cheap black dye job, zero make-up to cover her sun-damaged skin, and wearing a tatty shirt over black jeans.

'Shauna, is it?' said Heather. 'Hello, Shauna. Merry Christmas.' She retracted her apricot-frosted lips to show her teeth in an unconvincing forgery of a smile.

Sheena figured Joe hadn't told his wife very much about the two pickers from Celia's place who would be joining them for Christmas dinner, because Heather was eyeballing them with a mixture of disbelief and alarm. And when Kieran galloped over to join the two boys on the floor – 'Mouse Trap? Mad! I've seen the ads for this on TV!' – the woman looked downright scared. She thought Kieran's trashiness was contagious, infecting her precious high-class kids with low-life germs.

'You boys should pack that game away,' she said. 'We'll be eating soon.'

Hamish whined in protest, but when his mother glared at him, he shut up.

Fergus was busy sulking about the game being shut down, so Zoe coaxed him to show her how the Spirograph worked. The princess was sweet with both those boys. Sheena figured they were like cousins to her.

Celia swept through the living room, making an effort to smile, as if it was her duty to keep this event sailing breezily along despite the discomfort squirming close under the surface.

'Can I pour anyone a glass of wine? Sheena, have you tried one of Roza's yummy cheese pastries? Ooh, Heather, did you make that dip? I love the way it's shaped like a Christmas tree!'

After some polite eating of hors d'oeuvres, Celia gave Hamish and Fergus presents, which they unwrapped with mumbled thanks then quickly tossed into a laundry basket with the rest of their haul.

'Thank you,' said Joe with a wincing smile, embarrassed by his sons' lack of manners. Sheena saw Celia smile back at him – *Don't worry about it.*

The adults apparently had a long-standing agreement only to give presents to the children. Because Zoe still counted as a child, Roza gave her a diary, with '1977' in embossed numerals nestled in silver curlicues on the midnight-blue hard cover, the edges of the pages marbled with red and blue.

'It's such a beautiful thing, Roza,' said the girl, then she laughed. 'All my secret thoughts can go in here.'

Joe gave Zoe a globe of the earth with a light bulb in it, so the oceans and continents were illuminated from the inside.

'I wanted to give you the whole world,' he joked.

'Oh, wow . . . thank you, Joe,' said Zoe. 'I love it.' She spun the globe on its metal stand so the world flew round, patches of colour bouncing across her eyes as the different countries flicked past. Chances were a girl like Zoe would end up going to a fair number of those places.

When they sat down to eat, the nine of them just fitted around the fully extended dining table, with extra chairs brought in from other rooms. Kieran and Zoe chose seats on opposite corners, as if they'd agreed this beforehand. Presumably they knew they couldn't keep their paws off each other if they sat side by side.

There was a lot of strange food on the table Sheena had never seen before in her life. But some of it – like Roza's stuffed red peppers – was better than you would think just by looking at it.

Kieran was making an effort to display proper manners at the table, his eyes darting around the huge amount of food laid out, his hands twitching to stop himself grabbing for stuff. As he tasted each dish, he blurted out compliments – 'Roza! You're the best cook in the world!', 'Did you say this is a duck? I've never eaten a duck before!', 'Celia, your chicken salad is – far out, that is good.'

He struggled to keep smiling as he chewed a mouthful of the food Heather had contributed. Everything she cooked was oddly gritty and left a chemical coating on the inside of your mouth. Even so, Kieran managed to find a way to praise her – 'Food built to look like an igloo – that is mad! That is the coolest thing I've ever heard of.'

'Thank you,' said Heather and did a weird tight thing with her mouth. She didn't want to receive compliments from a yobbo like Kieran. The way she acted, you'd think he'd just spat in her face.

Sheena wasn't the most diplomatic person on the planet – she knew that. But even she was shocked by how openly mean Heather was about Roza's food, poking at it as if insects were about to crawl out. She winced when she tasted some of the dishes and turned to Joe to pull disgusted faces, trying to recruit her husband to make fun of Roza's cooking. As if that was ever going to happen.

Over dinner, Heather launched into a boastful monologue about her kids, bragging about school results and sporting achievements, with sniggering comments about the inadequacies of their classmates thrown in.

Sheena watched Celia, who was making the appropriate impressed noises in response to Heather's unabashed skiting. Celia could easily have boasted about Zoe too, but she had too much class to do that.

At one point, Roza asked everyone to raise their glasses for a toast. 'I just wish to say that I'm very happy to have you all around my table to share this Christmas meal.' There was a chorus of 'Cheers' and everyone took a sip of wine or beer or lemonade.

Once the desserts and sweet things were on the table, Heather pulled Joe aside for a hissed private conversation. She was spraying dirty looks at Kieran, whispering about him to Joe without even trying to pretend she wasn't. The woman was cranky as shit that her husband had allowed a pair of scumbags to come to their family event.

Sheena tried to catch Kieran's eye to remind him not to be a dickhead, but he was preoccupied, raving to Celia about the pavlova being 'incredible – I wish I had better words – just – ahhh – incredible'.

At least he wasn't pashing that girl in front of tight-arsed Heather and her precious kids. Thank Christ.

*

Celia was only there for Roza's sake, to help soak up Heather. And for Joe's sake, to help control Roza's tongue around Heather. And also for Heather's sake, to offer some neutral ground within the difficult territory of her mother-in-law's house.

Every year, the occasion would start out on a gust of good-will, then drift into a strained evening that everyone wanted to escape. And today there was the added strain of Zoe and Kieran. Even though that seemed on pause right now, the worry was still humming under everything.

After they'd eaten, Roza put one of her Elvis Presley Christmas albums on the record player – she was a big Elvis fan – which blessedly covered over any uncomfortable silences.

Joe was in the corner being berated by Heather. He was still and calm with her, as he always was, as if he could absorb his wife's irritable mood into his body to save innocent bystanders copping a spray from her.

Celia felt bad for her. Roza would be a difficult mother-in-law to please and Heather did make some efforts, however clumsily. And she was in an especially tetchy state this year because she hadn't been forewarned that two itinerant fruit pickers would be additional guests at dinner. Joe would have wanted to avoid an argument by not telling Heather beforehand, but that struck Celia as unfair, leaving his poor wife feeling ambushed and off kilter.

When Fergus turned up the volume on the Elvis record, Heather spun round to snap at him, 'Turn down the wailing from that disgusting man!'

But before the kid had a chance to do as he was told, Kieran turned it up even louder.

'This is the most excellent Christmas I've ever had in my life!' Kieran proclaimed.

It was cramped with so many people in Roza's living room, but Kieran found space on the available patch of carpet to start dancing, gyrating his hips Elvis-style. Heather fired Joe a look, as if the tattooed hoodlum cavorting in front of her children was his fault.

Kieran caught Zoe's hand to draw her over to join him. He spun her round until she was laughing dizzily, then the two of them twisted back and forth, playful and silly.

The next track was Elvis doing a bluesy number, 'Merry Christmas Baby'. Zoe and Kieran stayed on the dance floor, swaying to the slower beat, gazing at each other. They weren't blatantly kissing in Roza's living room as they had been in the orchard all morning, but anyone could see how they were with each other, the infatuated intensity, the way Zoe leaned her face close in to the scoop of Kieran's neck to whisper something to him and giggle.

Heather turned to Celia and raised her eyebrows. Celia didn't want to stand there and cop Heather's questions or disapproval, so she grabbed an empty food platter to carry out to the kitchen.

Once she was out of Heather's eye line, Celia took a breath to steady herself. She didn't give a toss what Joe's wife thought. In fact, she'd never cared much what other people thought about how she should raise her own child. Let people like Heather clutch their fistfuls of opinions. But right now, Celia had to work out how to handle this and having Heather sneering at her didn't help.

She deposited the platter on the sink and headed for the back door to reach the open air so she could think. She stepped onto the porch to discover Sheena was standing out there, alone.

Celia attempted a smile, a smile of solidarity. She was hoping she and Sheena could handle this together, as the two responsible adults in the story.

She flicked her head in the direction of Kieran and Zoe dancing in the living room. 'So.'

'Yeah,' said Sheena, not giving much away.

'Has Kieran had a serious girlfriend before now or . . .'

Sheena bristled. 'If you're trying to pump me for information, forget it. He's not telling me anything you can't see with your own eyes.'

'I'm just trying to get a sense of —'

'They're not fucking on Kieran's bunk bed, if that's what you want to know.'

'Fair enough, Sheena. I don't think it's weird for me to be concerned about my daughter.'

'Hey, no offence to your daughter, but I'm not too stoked about this either, okay?'

'Why do you say that?' asked Celia.

'Look, Kieran got himself in some trouble in Sydney so I'm —'

'Trouble?'

'I'm just trying to keep him settled, and this doesn't help.'

'Maybe it'd be best if you tell me —'

'Best thing is if I wrench him off your daughter quick smart and haul him to the cabin,' said Sheena, then dodged back into the house before Celia had a chance to ask another question.

'We better go, Kieran,' Sheena announced. 'We've gotta wake up dead-set early tomorrow.'

She thanked Roza for having them, muttered a general good-bye, and steered her brother out the front door at remarkable speed.

As the last of the daylight faded, Celia was washing up in Roza's tiny kitchen while Joe dried the dishes. Roza, exhausted by the effort of having everyone here, had been persuaded to go to bed. Zoe stayed in the living room, playing Mouse Trap with Hamish and Fergus, while Heather reclined in an armchair, nursing a bilious headache.

Celia turned to Joe but she kept her voice soft, knowing Zoe could emerge from the other room at any moment. 'Kieran's been in some kind of trouble,' she said.

'Like what?'

'The sister just said "trouble". That's why they're on the road. Kieran calls himself a "fuck-up". You'll think I'm neurotic —'

'I don't think that,' said Joe. 'But I doubt there's any reason to panic.'

'If he's in trouble with the police, would you be able to ask around your Sydney cop mates and find out?'

'Well, possibly . . .' Joe winced.

'Please, Joe. I've got nothing against this kid, but I've got them staying on my place.'

'I'm sorry if bringing them here was a mistake.'

'No, don't apologise. You rescued me, bringing them,' Celia assured him. 'I just need to know whether I should worry. Can you find out? Please.'

'Even if Kieran's been a bit wild, a lot of kids go through that. And if Zoe learns to deal with – I mean, you can't world-proof her.'

'Why shouldn't I pick out a path for my child through the minefield – to whatever extent I can?'

'But you can't limit the natural kind of – the natural sort of —'

'You wouldn't let nature take its course if a wild dog leapt into a baby's cot.'

'No, but a small baby isn't the same as a sixteen-year-old.'

'I know.'

The next moment, they both heard footsteps on the hall rug and the conversation was over.

'What were you guys talking about?' Zoe asked, leaning in the kitchen doorway. But she didn't wait for either of them to answer. 'Mum's doing the worried face. She thinks I can't see it, but I've been copping that face all day.'

Joe took a breath to respond but Celia threw him a look – *Leave it.*

Before Zoe or Celia could say anything more, there was an infuriated shriek from Heather in the living room.

'Enough! I'll throw that wretched game in the bin if you can't learn how to behave!'

A squabble had flared between Hamish and Fergus to the point that they were jabbing each other with the sharp corners of the Mouse Trap pieces.

'Joe? Joe!' Heather barked through to the kitchen. 'I told you we should have taken these two home half an hour ago! Can we please go now? Finally? Hamish, pick it up. Now. Now. Now. Pack the whole thing away quick sticks or I mean it, I will throw it in the bin.'

Joe jumped to, to wrangle his sons. Celia and Zoe helped Heather carry platters, parcels of leftovers and presents out to their car. Hamish and Fergus were hustled into the back seat, faces pinched from being roused on by their mother, but fingers poking each other on the sly, ready to resume their dispute on the trip home.

Celia and Zoe stood on Roza's front verandah to wave the family goodbye.

As Joe said his farewells, he tucked his head close to Celia to murmur, 'Try not to worry so much. See how things go.'

He kissed the top of Zoe's head, the way he used to do when she was little. 'Take care. See you guys soon.'

Once Joe and his family had driven away, Zoe didn't go straight back inside. She stepped off the verandah onto the grass. She did a few wandering dance steps around the front yard, barefoot, with the sheen of the blue silk dress catching the little bit of light that spilled from the house.

Celia, leaning against one of the verandah posts, couldn't tear her eyes away from her daughter. So lovely, it was almost painful to look at her. Celia usually kept her body taut with readiness to tackle whatever needed doing in the present or whatever problem might materialise in the future. Now, gazing at Zoe, all Celia's limbs, her shoulders, her throat, her belly, melted with overwhelming love for this girl, and rendered her defenceless.

'I can feel you staring,' said Zoe.

'I was thinking how beautiful you are.'

'You want to reach into my head and check out every thought that's in here.'

Celia smiled. 'You used to tell me every thought. But I know that time's over.'

'Really?'

'I just want you to be careful.'

'We haven't had sex or anything,' said Zoe.

'Okay,' said Celia cautiously.

'That's what you're worried about, I assume.'

'If I'm worried, it's because you know so little about Kieran.'

'You don't understand,' said Zoe flatly.

'I understand this is the first time you've – I get that you're giddy with this.'

Zoe twisted to face her mother, fierce. 'No. You don't want to understand. I can see from the way you're setting your jaw, that warnings will come out of your mouth. The "what if"s and "always remembers".'

Celia flinched at Zoe's excoriating tone. 'But sweetheart, can't I —'

'No. Shut your mouth. I won't listen to you pour poison on this. Shut your mouth.'

Zoe strode around the side of Roza's house and out of sight.

Celia couldn't move, as if pinned to the verandah post by a knife that had sliced right through her soft belly.

*

Zoe walked away from the house quickly, then even more quickly, until she was running up the slope. The impulse wasn't to escape or hurry anywhere in particular – the running was to burn up the excess energy fizzing through her blood. Zoe had never defied her mother like that, never unleashed her full power at Celia before. She was afraid that something inside her would explode or the earth would lurch out of orbit or something – some terrible and potent aftershock. But nothing had happened. She was okay. Exhilarated. That was why her heart was pounding – this was exhilaration, not fear.

The next thought in her head was overwhelming: she needed to see Kieran right now. She kept running until she saw a light shining at the end of the packing shed. Kieran was emerging from the lean-to bathroom, straight from the shower, wearing board shorts and sneakers, with a towel hanging over his bare chest.

'What's up? You okay?' he asked, reaching for her.

Zoe must've looked crazy to him – breathless, wild-eyed, gaping at Kieran but not letting him touch her. She gulped a breath, in order to summon up a coherent and mature voice. 'I was thinking we should have sex now.'

'Oh. Right. If you want to . . . uh . . .'

If Kieran sounded freaked out, it was because this morning she'd told him her sexual experience was zero. Zoe knew she could be honest with him. And Kieran could be completely honest with her too. They'd already talked about the fact that he'd been fucking since he was fourteen. The first time, he'd been stoned, seduced by the 32-year-old woman who was shacked up with one of his stepfathers.

So now, as Zoe blurted out her suggestion, Kieran hesitated. It felt like a long silence to her. Really, he only paused for two seconds. Less than two seconds. Then he said, 'I mean, yes, yes . . . y'know, *great*. That'd be great.'

He flicked the towel off his shoulder onto the ground with a jokey flourish and reached for Zoe. Again, she ducked out of his arms – if he touched her right now, it would mess with her head when she was determined to think clearly.

'But what are my reasons for wanting to have sex with you? Would I just be using you?'

Kieran laughed and lunged forward to slide his hands onto her hips. 'You can use me. That's cool. Use me.'

Slipping sideways out of his grasp, Zoe went on. 'But would I just be fucking you to rile up my mother? Or for the sake of getting rid of it? I've never understood why people say "losing virginity". What are you losing? The absence of something. Which is nothing. Really you're gaining non-virginity. You're gaining sexual experience. Which in a way is – sorry, I'm yabbering at you.'

'Which is cool. I just don't know —'

'Nervous. Sorry,' she said. 'But it's complicated. I want to be sure what my reasons are. Sorry.'

'It's okay, Zoe. But I'm not sure what you want me to do. We can keep talking if —'

'No,' she said, 'no.' And she took his hand.

The daylight was completely gone now, but even in the dark Zoe knew this place so well she could pick her way around the farm, finding a soft pathway for her bare feet. When they were close to the house, Kieran stopped.

'Zoe, where are we going? We can't – not in your mum's house.'

'I know. Stay here a sec.'

Zoe left Kieran to wait by the camellia hedge that formed a kind of dark wall between the packing shed and the garden of the house. She slipped inside to her room, without turning on the light, and fished around in her bedside drawer. Last term, a girl in

her class, Donna, had brought a pack of condoms to school and
paraded around, flashing the packet, skiting about how many guys
she'd rooted. Donna had then flung the condoms onto the asphalt
in front of other girls, like a queen throwing bread to starving peas-
ants. Zoe had picked one up and taken it home. Now she retrieved
it from its hiding place in the drawer. On her way back outside, she
grabbed shoes, a torch and a rug from the laundry.

By torchlight, the two of them hurried down the slope to the
creek. Zoe flung the rug out over a patch of soft grass. She switched
off the torch, then turned back to Kieran and puffed out a nervous
laugh. After that burst of purposeful activity, she was suddenly
frozen with embarrassment – until Kieran pulled her close, kissed
her, and it felt right again.

As Kieran slipped her dress off, Zoe realised he was also nervous.
'Your hands are shaking,' she said.

Kieran looked down at his own hands. 'Oh. Yeah.'

'Why would you be nervous? You've done this before.'

'Never when I wasn't off my face on something.'

'Which is different, I guess.'

Kieran nodded and then dropped his head onto her bare
shoulder. 'And I've never done this with you.'

'And what, that makes you nervous because —'

'Doesn't make me nervous,' he said. 'It amazes me.'

She pulled him down onto the rug. Kieran was worried his
palms would feel too rough on her skin, but she pointed out that
her hands were just as shredded and callused from the picking work
as his.

Before now, Zoe had tried to form a useful working model of
sex from *Cleo* magazine, bits she'd seen in *Penthouse* and scenes in
movies. She'd then cross-checked that information with stuff girls

at school had said. She was prepared for the fact that the first time was usually pretty lousy, something you just had to get through, that guys could be rushed and clumsy. But it wasn't like that with Kieran. He kept stopping and checking she was okay, to such an extent that she started to get paranoid.

'Don't you really want to?' she asked.

Kieran laughed – well, it was a sort of breathless, strangled laughter, as if he were in pain. 'Zoe. Fuck. Zoe . . . I'm an eighteen-year-old guy. I want to have sex every second I'm awake, and a major amount of the time I'm asleep. But I mean, this is different. I don't want you to – if you're not sure, I don't want to, even though, fucking hell, I want to . . .'

Zoe wanted to demonstrate she was sure, so she yanked down his board shorts and grabbed his cock. She wasn't certain how much force she should use but it was important she not appear tentative.

Kieran yelped with pain. So, she had, in fact, grabbed too hard.

'Sorry, sorry, sorry, sorry!'

Kieran was groaning, his body scrunched up, but a few moments later he managed to joke, 'Right. So, you *are* keen, then.'

The two of them laughed, lying there while he recovered. Some of the nerves had been laughed away, breaking down the self-consciousness between them. This wasn't a girl losing her virginity. This was *them* – Kieran and Zoe – and that was special and different and right.

'Fucking hell, look at you. You're beautiful,' said Kieran.

Zoe shook her head, but in fact, she believed he meant what he said. There was such intoxicating pleasure in having her body looked at – not her own critical gaze in the mirror, examining her-self as a sexual entity in the abstract, for some hypothetical point in the future – but appreciated by the eyes and hands and mouth of someone who kept murmuring how gorgeous she was. There was pleasure too in getting her hands on the body she'd been staring at and imagining for days now. She was torn between the urge to focus on every second and record every sensation in her mind, and the desire to suspend normal consciousness.

Afterwards, they lay on the rug, staring up into the dark mesh of the trees, happy to have the cool night air on their skin.

'You okay?' Kieran asked. 'Was that okay?'

She laughed and nodded, mock-earnest. It was better than she'd imagined. In fact, it wasn't even right to think in those terms. There was no point applying some teenage-girl grading system she'd been carrying around in her head. This was more profound and incredible than anything her silly sixteen-year-old self could have imagined.

EIGHT

Sheena sat on the front step of the cabin, swinging the door back and forth, trying to get a few slugs of fresher air mixed into the cube of stale gases inside.

Kieran wasn't offering much in the way of detail (thank Christ) but as Sheena understood it, he and Zoe had their first, apparently transcendent, fuck on the Picnic Rug of Love by the creek, and there was more of the same the following two nights.

Sheena was angry in that way she could get sometimes, her gut manufacturing a corrosive substance that burned its way through her circulatory system. This time her anger was mostly directed at herself, for miscalculating the situation so stupidly. She'd banked on the Kieran and Zoe flirtation, even the displays of pashing in the orchard, being a diversion that would keep her brother safely in one spot, occupied and under her watchful eye. She hadn't expected that Zoe – such a shielded kid – would take things all the way so quickly. They could at least have chosen to go at it in secret, but no, there was no secrecy about the consummation of their week-long acquaintance. Who knew the girl would shove this in her mother's face so blatantly?

The past two nights, after a session down at the creek with Zoe, Kieran had slipped back inside the cabin at one or two a.m. to grab a few hours' kip. He'd try to be quiet but really, that was redundant. There was no risk he'd wake Sheena, because there was no risk she'd be asleep when he came in. Splayed out on the bunk bed, she was scrounging even less sleep than she usually did, and even then it wasn't restorative. It was more like the crumbly dozing she did on long-distance bus journeys, frequently waking with unpleasant jolts and always unrefreshed.

Sheena had let Kieran take the packet of condoms out of her toiletry bag – a packet left over from her last attempt at a relationship with the Dickless Wonder. Sheena herself had no need of condoms right now. The romantic offers weren't exactly flying in. There was not a parade of available guys sauntering through the stone-fruit district of central New South Wales. And if one were to stumble across Sheena's path, she would hardly be an arousing sight. She'd been avoiding looking at herself in the mirror – pretty easy here given the absence of reflective surfaces, other than the tiny mirror Kieran had propped against the corrugated-iron wall of the shower so he could shave. But Sheena had no doubt she was looking like a piece of shit. Her hands were roughened up from the picking work, so they were now leathery old dog chews. She'd stopped bothering to shave her legs and given up wearing eyeliner because it wasn't a good mix with sun-cream and sweat. Her hair must be looking rank, with a stripe of brown regrowth because she hadn't touched up the colour on the roots. Plus she was so exhausted – working from five every morning and worrying herself into a lather over Kieran – her face must surely be haggard.

Sheena could make herself look attractive enough when she made an effort. She'd never been up herself, but the truth was, she was the kind of woman that certain kinds of men hit on, and she'd always had a decent strike rate with the guys she went after. But the way she was looking now – no chance. The point was, Kieran might as well take the condoms. It occurred to her that Celia could have the shits with Sheena for providing contraception to her daughter. She shouldn't have the shits. At least this way there wouldn't be a pregnancy to add to the mess.

Zoe and Kieran were only managing three or four hours of sleep, max, but they were still working hard picking peaches, presumably powered by whatever magic fuel was being produced in their bodies by all the sex at night.

During the daytime, in the orchard, Sheena could feel the air crunching and hissing between Celia and Zoe. Whenever mother and daughter were in close proximity, the two of them held their bodies tight, avoiding eye contact and only addressing each other with the few necessary words the job required.

Sheena was surprised Celia hadn't gone ballistic. Possibly she was giving Zoe hell inside the privacy of their house, but Sheena didn't get the sense that was happening. For Celia to see Kieran and Zoe together, knowing what was going on at the creek at night, it was astonishing the woman wasn't shrieking and prising the two apart with a shovel, then slamming the tractor into Kieran before driving back and forth with its knobbly tyres over his pulpy body. Then again, Sheena realised why Celia wouldn't do that. She couldn't stop her sixteen-year-old daughter engaging in a legal activity, short of locking her in a cupboard. And arguably, a mother could choose to be relieved her daughter was conducting her sexual initiation with an eighteen-year-old and not a forty-something PE teacher with lips crusted with dried spit.

Whatever was going on in Celia's head, she kept slogging through the harvest tasks, looking more strung-out each day. As for Roza, the weird Hungarian lady, she watched the goings-on with a benign, knowing vibe as if she'd predicted it all. Sheena would happily slap that unnerving smile right off Roza's face.

Sheena was still sitting on the front step as Kieran walked back to the cabin from the shower – well, not so much walked as *skipped* through the orchard. Skipping, for God's sake. Men who were getting plenty of sex were so predictable, even her drug-stewed little brother. Every guy she'd been with was the same: if they were in a grumpy mood for whatever reason, she could always cheer them up with a root. One minute, they'd be cranky or worried or sad, but then post-root, they'd grin like gormless dopes, prancing to the bathroom making lame jokes. Transforming a man's mood really could be that simple. Once she'd cottoned on to how easy it was to manipulate their primitive psyches, it was even harder to respect them. Which was not to say Sheena wasn't into sex herself. She missed it when she went too long without. But she wasn't sure a bout of good sex was worth all the other bullshit that surrounded the procedure.

Of course, Sheena knew this was not a simple case of Kieran having a mood-lifting sexcapade. This wasn't simple at all. Her little brother had catapulted himself into a dangerous situation that he needed to be extricated from as soon as possible.

As Kieran approached the cabin door he smiled at Sheena – one of those *I'm happy, so I want everyone else to be happy* smiles.

'Hey, big sister. Y'know, from over there you can get a massive lungful of warm peaches and it's – ahhh . . .' He sucked in a big breath and staggered as if stoned. Then he righted himself and adopted a deliberate, sober tone. 'I've been thinking, Sheena . . .'

'Thinking? Steady on. Remember what happened last time you did that.'

'No, listen – I was thinking I could get a permanent job on a farm. That's something I could do, I reckon.'

Sheena was thrown off guard. That wasn't the conversation topic she'd been expecting. And she was thrown because it wasn't an entirely stupid idea. A physical job, away from the city, would be a good move for a guy like him. If he could stick with it. Once she recovered from the shock of Kieran having a half-decent idea, she capitalised on this thought of his, in order to steer him clear of trouble.

'Well, you know what,' she said, 'we could follow the picking circuit if you like – soon as we earn enough here to get the car back. We could do the grapes in Mildura, then head along the Murray in time for the tomatoes.' She'd been asking Roza a few questions about the harvest timetable, figuring it might be a good plan for Kieran, given how well he'd taken to the picking work. Deciding on the next step had become more urgent now that he and the girl had got their pink bits tangled up.

Kieran was smiling at Sheena, but he wasn't going with her plan. 'Why leave here? There's still plenty of work on this place,' he said. 'We could finish the peaches for Celia, then do the nectarines.'

'Oh right. And do you really think you're Celia's favourite person right now?'

'She's a bit freaked out, sure. But you know what happened to Zoe's dad. I mean, that poor lady. That's how come she gets nervous when unexpected stuff happens.'

'Right from the start, Celia was sniffing around, asking questions.'

'Yeah, she's worried, but that's —'

'*I'm* worried. This little girl's using you. I sussed Zoe from the first day we got here. She's out to get her thrills and give Mummy the shits and have something to boast about to her little princess friends at school. *What I did in my summer holidays: I fucked a wild trashy boy from Sydney.*'

'That is not true.'

'And when she's had enough of her little adventure, that girl won't give a toss what happens to you.'

'Sheena, don't talk like that, okay?'

'You've gotta trust me on this. The sooner we get away from here, the better.'

There was a swishing sound from the orchard, and Sheena looked over to see the pale shape of Zoe standing out there, her creamy hair luminous amid the dark rows of fruit trees.

The girl held a rug up in the air as a signal for Kieran to follow her. His face lit up the instant he saw her. There was no denying that look.

Kieran pointed to the plate of sandwiches Sheena had prepared while he was in the shower. 'Can I have some?'

'Yeah, der. That's why I made them.' Sheena leaned sideways so he could reach past her to the little fold-out table and grab a hand-ful of the food.

'Thanks. I'm starving,' he said. 'Hey – I don't want to fight with you, Sheena, and I know you're looking out for me and everything but . . . y'know . . .'

Sheena shrugged. She wasn't going to argue with him right this second. What could she say? *Why don't you stay here in this festy cabin with your grouchy sister instead of romping away to have sex with that luscious girl?*

Once Kieran had disappeared with Zoe into the orchard, Sheena stayed on the front step. She was stuck for a moment, stunned by how different Kieran had sounded, how calm – no, not calm exactly, because his manner was intense and obviously the blood was rushing to his groin and not his head. Maybe resolute was a better word.

*

Zoe loved the way their bodies looked together as they lay on the rug. During the couple of hours they'd been down by the creek tonight, a mass of cloud had filled the sky and the moonlight bounced off it to create a diffused glow, even down in the gully – enough light to appreciate the sight of her white limbs against the caramel colour of his skin.

They were both exhausted, happily. But lovely as this sweet sleepiness felt, they shouldn't risk falling properly asleep. So, Zoe rolled around to reach into the creek, scoop out a handful of water and splash her face, to wake herself up. When she wriggled back around, she saw Kieran looking at her.

'What?' she asked him.

'What are you thinking about right now?'

'Why do you keep asking me that?'

'Because I reckon there's always something interesting going on in your brain. More interesting than the gloop in my skull.'

She reached across to run her hands through his hair and cradle the back of his head. 'Don't say that. It's a beautiful skull with a beautiful brain inside it.'

He pecked kisses on her wrists like a crazed chicken and she giggled, pulling her hands back.

'Promise you won't laugh at me,' she said, 'but I have this list in my head – a list of things I want to try.'

'You mean sex things?'

She jiggled her head, embarrassed, worried the idea of a list sounded goony and childish.

Kieran sat up straighter and announced, mock-earnest, 'Well, Zoe, I want you to know I will help you work through your list, no matter how long it takes us.'

She adopted the same jokey solemn tone, as if they were research scientists. 'We need to be methodical.'

'Fuck, yeah. You can never be too methodical.'

'And we should revise as we go,' she added.

'We certainly should,' he agreed, and pulled her in close.

Later, as they walked back up from the creek, hand in hand, a shiver went through Zoe.

'You cold?' asked Kieran, offering to wrap the rug around her shoulders.

She shook her head. They were dressed again and it was a warm night. She shivered because the connection to him was gripping her so forcefully that she wasn't sure she could withstand it, or absorb it or whatever she needed to do to avoid exploding into a thousand pieces.

Kieran could *see* her, the way she'd never realised someone could truly see another person. She could be her whole self with him, without the need to edit bits out, without worrying that bits of her might cause him pain.

She loved hearing Kieran say her name, not just during sex, but all the time. The sound of 'Zoe' from his mouth transmitted to every cell of her body as if it were a signal she had been waiting for, without realising she'd been waiting for it.

When the two of them reached the top of the gully, they knew they would have to separate soon – Zoe to pad barefoot into her bedroom and Kieran to continue on to the cabin. Still, they couldn't bear the idea of saying goodbye. So Kieran swung Zoe off the path, coaxing her to veer away from the house garden and into the orchard.

'A few minutes, yeah?' he said. 'So we can say goodnight properly.'

They laughed and ran, so they were breathless as they kissed. When they came up for air, Zoe flopped down on the ground. Kieran spun himself round between the rows of fruit trees, tipping his fingers gently against the leaves.

'You're so lucky to live here,' he said. 'I like the way, if you feel like a feed, you can just reach up and grab something.'

'It's not always like this. Only for three months. Half the year it's just grey sticks.'

'But you know that inside the grey stick trees there's little tiny peaches waiting to come out,' he said, and shot her a radiant smile.

Kieran suddenly crouched down in front of Zoe and his tone shifted, tentative, intense. 'One of the things I've been thinking about . . . Okay, the thing is, I have been off my face a fair whack of the time since I was thirteen. But since I've been on the road with Sheena, it's like I'm waking up and seeing things for the first time. It's like – I want to explain this to you . . . I've been replaying stuff in my head.'

'Like what?'

'Dumb stuff I did, like going to a meeting with bikers, off my face, knowing Mick had a shotgun in the boot. It didn't rattle me then, but now I'm scared shitless. It's like *now* I'm feeling the fear I should have had then. My brain's catching up with what my body's been doing. Mental, eh. All out of sync.'

'Maybe you were out of sync before. But not now.'

Kieran jumped to his feet again, suddenly hyper. 'The thing is, the thing is . . .'

Zoe reached her arms out to him. 'Come back.'

But Kieran stayed out of her reach, hopping from foot to foot. 'Just let me say this, okay. You know I got in trouble with the cops when I was younger?'

'Yes,' she said. She was thrilled that he trusted her enough to tell her everything.

'Well, there's been some other stuff in the last few months. Then I didn't show up in court and that means I'm in deeper trouble. And it's – oh fuck . . .'

He was prowling around, his hands drumming against his thighs as if an electric charge was running down his arms. It looked uncomfortable, distressing. Zoe didn't want him to suffer for one second ever. She grabbed for his hand, trying to make him be still.

'Kieran, I don't care. I trust you, whatever happens.'

'But I don't trust myself,' he said. 'Because sometimes I only see what's in front of me. A mate'll say, "Let's do this or that, Kieran" and I think *why not* and I forget the important things and I fuck up and . . .'

This time Zoe succeeded in grabbing his hand. She held it firmly, wanting to absorb some of his distress into her own body. 'I'm right here.'

'You are,' he said, staring at her in disbelief. 'Why would you want me?'

She pulled him back down to the ground. 'You're the most alive person I ever met.'

The rain started a few minutes later and eventually became so heavy they had to clamber to their feet and run, Zoe to the house, Kieran to the cabin, to avoid getting drenched.

When Zoe climbed into the single bed in the room she'd slept in since she was nine months old, her wet hair made the pillow damp.

NINE

Celia lay in bed, listening to the rain – light at first, then drumming more firmly on the roof tin. She heard the rasp of the flywire door being closed carefully as Zoe came back into the house, then the scuff of feet along the hall and finally the yielding sound of her daughter's body settling onto the mattress.

Celia forced herself to conjure up the Reasonable Woman and hear what that serene, unneurotic dame in her diaphanous gown had to say about this situation. Maybe there was no need to consider the sex a big deal. She should be relieved Zoe wasn't being furtive or secretive. And at least this boy seemed to adore Zoe and would treat her with tenderness, however clumsily. But no – bugger that. The Reasonable Woman could get stuffed. Zoe was too young, too young, too young. She'd only just turned sixteen and this guy was much older in real terms. And she didn't really know Kieran, who had shown up here barely ten days ago from Christ-knew-where.

It was a mistake Celia should have predicted and stopped. And underneath all the arguments pinging back and forth in her mind – contentions formed into sentences, words threaded together with grammar and logic – there was an ongoing rumble of fear that could not be processed with language. Impermeable to logical thought.

She and Zoe had barely spoken in the past three days. Celia kept rehearsing brief speeches but she didn't want to misjudge it, afraid she would inspire contempt and be forced to endure the serrated edge in her daughter's voice. But it turned out the silence was worse, making Zoe seem inaccessible, out of range, even if she was sleeping only a few feet away from her mother. Celia would have to say something. She would have to risk saying the wrong thing.

The heavy downpour through the night settled into steady rain before dawn. Celia hauled herself out of bed and was pulling on work clothes, when Zoe yelled down the hallway. 'Is it too wet to pick this morning?'

'Yep. I think so,' Celia called back.

'I'll tell them.'

Celia heard the flywire door thwack shut as Zoe hurried out to let Sheena and Kieran know there would be no work done this morning. This suspension of work wasn't to spare the pickers. It was to protect the fruit. After heavy rainfall, there was a risk the peaches would take on too much water, and with any handling the skins would split.

Later in the morning, Celia was working in the shed, alone. She should be using a wet day during harvest to catch up on paperwork, but there was no chance she could concentrate on invoices and columns of numbers. Too agitated to keep still, she zigzagged around the place, sweeping, fiddling with the gear, scrabbling for ways to keep her body and mind occupied.

Close to midday, she heard the squelch of car tyres on the wet driveway and emerged from the shed to see Joe pull up.

'Hi,' he said as he stepped out of the driver's side, his shirt immediately speckled with rain.

'Come in out of the weather,' said Celia.

'I quite like being out in this.' He smiled, spreading his arms out and turning slowly to get his shirt evenly wet. Then he tipped his head back to offer his face to the rain. 'I spend most of my waking hours in offices. So, this is – y'know . . .'

Celia smiled her understanding. She had always avoided jobs stuck in offices – all her life, long before Marcus was killed – and now she couldn't imagine herself living an indoor existence.

'Your mum's not up here,' she explained. 'We won't be packing any fruit on a day like this.'

'I came to see you,' said Joe. 'Is Zoe around?'

Celia shook her head. She suspected Zoe had taken Kieran down to the old woolshed so they could avoid the rain. And avoid her.

Joe walked over to join Celia under the awning of the packing shed. 'So, I talked to a bloke I know in Sydney. A cop. Kieran was in some trouble as a juvenile.'

'He's legally an adult now so . . .'

'And as an adult, there are a couple of warrants out on him.'

Celia forced herself to match Joe's measured tone. 'Warrants for what?'

'Minor stuff, mostly. A break and enter. Story is he got caught up with some nasty characters and police want to talk to him about a couple of more serious matters. There's one robbery where a security guard was assaulted, I gather.'

'Oh my God, Joe.'

'Probably the wisest thing is for them to move on. You could suggest they leave now rather than stay for the rest of the pick.'

'Zoe talks about travelling with them when they move on.'

'Well, tell her she can't.'

Celia shrugged, helpless. 'She'd hate me for it.'

Joe nodded and let a silence go. One of the things she liked about Joe was that he understood so much without Celia having to unpack the whole crate of tangled shit in her head. His other, more unsettling tendency was that he sometimes answered her unspoken thoughts.

'Kieran seems like a good-hearted kid,' he said eventually. 'And obviously Sheena's trying to straighten him out.'

'Listen, Joe, I don't want to destroy this boy. All I'm thinking about is Zoe.'

'I know you are.'

Joe flicked his head and Celia followed his eye line to see Zoe striding between rows of fruit trees, towards the yard. She was wearing gumboots, with a light-green cotton dress soaked dark green from the rain, her wet hair swept back from her face.

'Oh, Joe, I don't know what I should do,' Celia whispered, as Zoe approached them.

'Talk to her. That's the best thing.'

'Mm.'

'Do you want me to stay?' he asked.

'No. Thanks, but no. In fact, might be better if you head off now.'

'So Zoe won't feel we're colluding?'

'Yes.'

Joe made the dash through the rain to his car door. 'I'll call you later.'

He curled the vehicle round on the gravel, just as Zoe reached the yard. Joe waved extravagantly to her and drove away towards the road.

Zoe swung to face her mother. 'What were you talking to Joe about?'

'Listen, sweetheart, I'm going to have to ask Kieran to leave.'

'I knew it. I knew you'd end up doing this.'

'He's wanted by the police.'

'I know. He told me.'

'Wanted for robbery. Serious stuff. Someone was assaulted. Did he tell you that?'

Celia could see Zoe was thrown for a second, but then she recovered, with a more defiant edge in her voice. 'Yes. He told me. Because he trusts me and I trust him. Which you wouldn't know any fucking thing about. Since you don't trust me one tiny bit.'

'I do trust you.'

'Bullshit. That's bullshit. Did you sic Joe onto Kieran? To spy on him? That's disgusting. No, actually, it's sad. Your life is so dried up, you have to snuffle around in the dirt until you —'

'You can say as many cruel things to me as you like, Zoe. I have to do what I think is right.'

'If you make Kieran leave, I'll go with him.'

'Please, if you need to have a battle of wills with me, don't do it about this.'

'You don't get it,' snapped Zoe. 'It's not about *you*. I love Kieran.' She flashed a smile – invincible, as if this were unanswerable proof of her love for the boy. 'Me and Kieran'll be back up here to work once the rain stops, okay?'

Zoe strode away again, through the orchard.

Celia counted out a few slow breaths. What she needed to do now was gather up her strength, think her way through this, absorbing whatever pain might be necessary in order to do the right thing for her child.

*

In the late afternoon, Sheena woke up groggy, her face sweat-glued to the pillow. She remembered lying down on the bunk, just for a minute, to rest her eyes and maybe plan the next move. But it was hard to think clearly in the muggy air inside the cabin. The rain hadn't let up all day, and as the moisture mixed with the unrelenting heat, Sheena felt as if she were breathing soup. After falling asleep for three clammy hours, what she needed now was a shower.

She flicked open the cabin door to find the rain had stopped. The whole place was sodden but the air was cooler, cleaner. Stepping outside, Sheena wondered for a moment if her eyeballs had grown a coating of mildew in that humid cabin – everything her eyes fell on was draped in a layer of mist. She then realised it was steam, rising from every surface, as the warm, soggy land met the now-cooler air. Vapour wafted up from the shed roof, from the fruit trees, from the ground itself. Still dazed from her nap, Sheena was caught off guard by the beauty of it, this layer of white mist – potent, as if the earth were in transition from one mysterious phase to another.

The shower was so good – sluicing off the sweat and the layer of gritty stuff that had stuck to the sweat. Sheena relished the tingly chill of the cooler air against her wet back. She could feel the ropes of muscle in her arms and shoulders, distinct under the skin after these days of picking work. She would've loved to stand there swaying under that shower spray for hours but she couldn't do that. She needed to work out where the fuck Kieran was.

On her way back to the cabin, Sheena noticed Celia's ute winding up from the road. She must've spent the afternoon doing errands in the town or whatever. When Celia spotted Sheena through the trees, she stopped the ute and signalled – *Wait.*

Walking across the orchard, Celia looked different. Maybe it was the white shirt she was wearing, unexpectedly brilliant in the diminishing light. Maybe it was her hair – normally she kept it tied back for work, but the dark curls were untied now, spilling over the shirt.

'Do you need help with unloading stuff or anything?' Sheena asked. 'I'm not sure where Kieran is right now but I can find him.'

'I want you and Kieran to move on.'

Blunt. Rude, even. Okay. Celia usually had a pretty straightforward way of speaking but this was different. Sheena could see some new mechanism had ignited inside this woman.

'Well, that's what I want,' said Sheena. 'Soon as I get enough money together for the car and we've built up some travel money.'

'I just paid your bill at the mechanic,' Celia replied. 'I've asked Joe to drive your car out here for you tonight. I withdrew the cash I had in the bank. One thousand six hundred.'

She pulled a yellow envelope out of her bag. The car money plus that much cash – it was more than she owed them for the work so far. So this was a bribe, not payment for the job. 'It's yours,' Celia said. 'Travel money.'

Sheena could see Celia was shaking a little but her gaze was steady. If she was shaking, it was from the intensity of her purpose. 'I want you and Kieran to leave tonight, without Zoe knowing about it.'

'He won't go for that idea,' Sheena pointed out.

'You should know that I know about Kieran's police trouble.'

'Oh. Right. So, you'll go to the cops if we don't leave.'

'I'm not threatening you.'

'Yeah, you are,' Sheena shot back.

'Well, I don't want to make threats. I'm just trying to . . . Look, you want to stop this before it gets out of hand.'

'Yes.'

'So, this is a solution that suits both of us.'

Sheena looked down at the envelope Celia was holding out in her hand. 'Fair enough.' She took the envelope, tight around the fat wad of banknotes inside.

Celia exhaled then, as if she had been holding herself too tightly to breathe. 'Thank you,' she said. 'Make sure Zoe doesn't know about this. Please.'

'She's going to wonder what the hell's happened.'

'I'll work that out. Once he's gone.'

Sheena winced. 'Yeah, well, good luck with managing that.'

For a second it looked like Celia might respond, but she just gave a brisk nod. She walked back to her ute and Sheena continued down to the cabin, with the yellow envelope folded up in the bundle of sweaty clothes she'd peeled off for the shower.

Sheena couldn't believe she was agreeing to this. Except that Celia had given her no fucking choice. Sheena was caving in to a threat rather than agreeing to a deal. Offensive was what it was. The woman thought Sheena and her brother were scum, such repulsive, dangerous scum that she was willing to clean out her bank account to pay them to rack off. Evidently, it was worth several thousand dollars to Celia to make them vanish from this lovely little fruit world she'd created for herself and her precious daughter – the precious daughter who had set her sights on Sheena's gullible brother and his stupid eighteen-year-old-guy cock.

By the time Sheena was back in the cabin, her gullet was burning, resenting not just Celia and Zoe but every person on the planet with money and university degrees and peach farms and lovely peachy families and the power to make things go the way they wanted, the power to disrespect losers like her and Kieran, the power to eradicate her brother from their smug universe. And now those privileged fuckers were giving Sheena a gut ache from resenting them, which was one more crime to add to the list of shit that had been done to her.

And the most annoying thing was that the deal Celia was offering, this act of blackmail, was the best idea going in the current almighty mess. She hated Celia for it but in another compartment of Sheena's brain, she was forced to respect what she was doing. Celia had balls of steel, or whatever the right expression was for what she had. Ovaries of steel. A uterus of steel. Whichever. The woman was doing what she needed to do. Fair enough.

Sheena flinched when she heard Kieran bound up to the cabin in one of his bouncy moods. It would make what she was required to say that much harder.

'Sheena! How you going? Zoe and me've been hanging out at this old shearing shed, left over from when the farm had sheep way back.'

'Kieran, listen.'

But he was too juiced-up to listen. 'All the wood inside has a sheepy smell. Zoe reckons it's the lanolin that's still soaked into everything, even though there hasn't been a single sheep there for a lot of years. It's mad.'

'Kieran, shoosh up and listen.'

'You've gotta come and check it out. Now the rain's stopped —'

'Kieran, shut up!'

'Okay.' Once he'd shut his mouth, he engaged his brain suffi-ciently to notice there was a backpack sitting on Sheena's bunk bed. 'What are you doing?'

'We're leaving tonight. You need to pack your stuff.'

'What? Why?'

'Celia knows about the Sydney mess. She'll dob you in to the police if we don't clear off. We leave as soon as our car gets here.'

'I don't – huh? What are you talking about?'

'She's paid the bill on the car and given us a wad of money on top of that. The deal I made with Celia is we go tonight.'

Kieran started to move in the small space of the cabin, scuffing his feet from the edge of one bunk to the other, twisting his body back and forth as if he could wriggle his shoulders into some new space that would open up to him.

'No. Hang on,' he said. 'I gotta talk to Zoe about this.'

'That's the other part of the deal. You can't tell Zoe.'

'What? No way, no way, no way.'

Sheena aimed to sound implacable without being cruel. 'There's no choice.'

'Wait, wait. Let me think a second. Let me think,' muttered Kieran.

'Plenty of time to think once we're in the car,' said Sheena. 'I reckon this is the best thing.'

'It's not the best thing for me! Fuck.'

Kieran was circling now, waggling his hands in front of his chest, muttering to himself. He was generating too much frantic energy in the tight space, creating a density in the air that was pressing in on Sheena's skull. She had to do something. She had to settle him down quickly. She resorted to the familiar slap-down.

'What makes you think a fuckwit like you is a good thing for this girl?' she said, loud and sharp enough to cut through to his brain. The words tasted bitter in her mouth, but she was doing what was needed to extract him from trouble. 'Come on, mate. The way you are – you're no good for a girl like Zoe. Wake up. No wonder her mother wants you gone.'

Kieran turned to her, with the bewildered face of a slapped child. 'Why would you say that to me?'

'I'm sorry,' said Sheena. And she was sorry, but she couldn't risk losing momentum. 'I've gotta look out for you. What if Celia went to the cops? Do you want to get done for the vet-lab thing?'

'No.'

'Do you want to go to jail?'

'No, no.'

'So, we have to go.'

Kieran was cursing in staccato bursts, revving himself the way he could do sometimes, like a toddler trapped in a self-lacerating tantrum.

'I get it, Sheena. I get it. But I need to see Zoe before we go.'

'Not a good idea.'

'Listen to me, okay, I'm just asking if —'

'I'm the one who has to look at things realistically.'

'No, you're not listening to me! I love her.'

'I know you think that.'

'You don't know. You don't,' said Kieran firmly. 'You've gotta understand – when I'm with Zoe, it's not a screeching mess in here.' He jabbed his fingers across his skull. 'When I'm with her, things are so clear in my head and I think, *Right, Kieran, this is what it should feel like.* It's fucking incredible. Are you listening to me?'

Sheena was listening, still trying to get used to this version of her brother.

Kieran stood still and resolute in front of her. 'Let me just see Zoe one more time before I have to go. Please, Sheena. Please.'

Sheena knew she should say no to him. But she was so sick of saying no all the time. Why did the job of looking after Kieran – keeping her stupid, beautiful fuckwit of a brother alive and safe and out of jail – why did it require her to be a negative bitch so much of the time? And now look at him, enraptured, as if getting himself love-struck over this girl was his conversion to a religion that promised all the solutions to life's shitful smorgasbord. The burning smile on Kieran's face – Sheena had seen that smile on a girl she knew who'd been sucked in by Pentecostal Christians, to the point where she'd started swooning onto the shiny tiled floor and yabbering nonsense. The full three courses of crazy. Kieran was as misguided and as likely to crack his head open as that girl. Still, it felt vicious to be the one saying no to him in the middle of his rapturous state. Maybe Sheena could allow him a couple more hours to paw at Zoe or gaze into her eyes or whatever the hell they did.

'What if I said you've got until ten o'clock?' she offered. 'A bit of time before we have to head off.'

'Yes. Yes. That's all I'm asking. That'd be brilliant, Sheena.'

He grinned at her. Now he was too buoyant. She needed to hammer down a few tent pegs around that giddy happiness to keep Kieran on the ground.

'But then you stick with the deal and leave without making a fuss. Okay?' she said sharply.

'Okay.'

'You don't want to go to jail, do you?'

'No.'

'And you don't want to get Zoe in big trouble, do you?'

'No. No.'

'You want to protect this girl, don't you?'

'Yes.'

'Which means you can't tell her we're going. Tell me you understand that. Say it aloud.'

'I understand that.'

There was definitely fear on Kieran's face when she pointed out the risk of jail. Then the suggestion that he could bring trouble to Zoe – that was the clincher. He would want to protect the princess. Sheena had managed to scare him sufficiently. He would go along with the plan.

'Okay,' she said. 'Take my watch so you can keep track of the time. Ten o'clock, be back here and we go.'

'Thank you. Yes, yes. Thank you, Sheena.'

And he disappeared through the orchard, on his way to find Zoe.

It didn't take long for Sheena to finish packing – their piss-weak pile of possessions only half-filled her backpack and Kieran's sports bag. She stripped the sheets off the two mattresses and rolled them into an efficient bundle for Celia to wash. Maybe there would be two new pickers staying in this cabin after they'd gone and those people deserved clean sheets if they were going to work their arses off picking peaches. She swept bits of grass and leaves off the tiny floor area of the cabin and out the door, using the edge of one of Kieran's thongs.

Very quickly, Sheena exhausted the jobs that needed doing. She lay down on the bare mattress, figuring it might be good to get an hour or two of sleep, to bank up energy to drive, once she had the car back.

The smartest plan was to drive all night, to transport Kieran rapidly away from this place and from Zoe. Judging from the parade of destructive behaviour Sheena had observed so far in her life, people were more likely to make moronic decisions during the night, in the dark. Kieran was a shocker for such misguided night-time choices. She could envisage her brother hurling himself out the car window onto the pitch-black embankment of a country road in order to run back to Zoe, howling like a mongrel dog. But if Sheena could just keep him sitting in the car long enough, hopefully sleeping, hurtling along that highway through the night, then when the dawn came he would be more likely to see the sense of the thing.

It turned out there was no way Sheena could sleep now – because of that sweaty nap earlier and because her bones were gritty, scraping inside her flesh with self-loathing. She was lonely, cranky and worn out from making decisions on her own for so long. Mostly lonely. She thought about Kieran and Zoe holding each other right at this minute, skin to skin. It would be good to have that for a moment, however self-deluded you'd have to be to think it solved anything. But it would be good to have that for a little while.

After ten minutes of that soft-headed, self-pitying rubbish, Sheena shook herself back to the thumping reality of how things worked on the surface of the planet. It struck her she might be sweating on the bare mattress, so she jumped up, untied the bundle of bedding and put one of the fitted sheets back on. But then, instead of lying back down on the bed, she decided some fresh air might help her toxic mood.

She dragged the esky across to wedge open the cabin door and then sat on the front step, gazing out into the dark orchard. She might as well make the most of her last hours here. She'd never spent time in the country as a kid, and as an adult she'd always felt out of place in a rural setting, as if her presence there was a distasteful or laughable mistake. The old Hungarian lady said that when you worked hard on a piece of land and the sweat from your labour had soaked into its soil, you grew a connection to that land. Sheena was not taken in by such mystic bullshit but she had to concede she felt some affection for this farm now, a sense that she had some right to be here after the hours of shredding work she'd put into it. Part of her was sorry to be leaving – admittedly a very small part that was crusted around with resentment.

Some minutes later, Sheena heard footsteps swishing across the wet, mulchy stuff on the orchard ground. It wouldn't be Kieran – she didn't expect him back until the agreed time – so it must be Celia, wanting to check things were going to plan. Then Sheena realised Joe was the one walking towards the cabin.

'Hi,' he said. 'I left your car down by the gate.'

'Right. I guess I should say thanks.'

Joe dropped his head down a little. Was that a smile on his face? What the fuck did that look mean? What had Celia been saying to him? Joe had always appeared less judgey about her than she expected a guy like him to be. He had even, amazingly, seemed respectful towards her. Had that soured now he had more information? Did Joe reckon she and Kieran were low-life scum? Well, whatever. Sheena didn't have the emotional stamina to take that on right now.

As he stood at the cabin door, she asked him, 'How will you get back into town?'

'I'll stay the night at my mother's. Wouldn't mind escaping my place for a bit.'

Sheena wasn't sure if that was an invitation to ask further questions about his home life. It was better to keep her snout out of his business, so she responded with a noncommittal tip of the head.

'Where's Kieran?' asked Joe.

'He'll be back soon, then we'll head off. Don't worry. Kieran knows he doesn't have any choice, unless he wants to get arrested. What time is it?'

'A bit after eight.'

Joe came close enough to drop the car key into her hand. Then, to Sheena's surprise, he gestured at the empty section of the step – *Can I sit there?* She shuffled sideways to make room for him beside her.

'You know, Sheena, you made things harder for Kieran by helping him skip town.'

'By the time I found him, he'd already missed those court dates.'

Joe nodded. 'Well, the cops want to talk to him about some other matters now.'

'Oh. Right. Doesn't surprise me.'

'The vet-science lab.'

'Yeah, those morons stole a shitload of drugs the vets use. The security guy wasn't supposed to be there at the time.'

Joe nodded, letting Sheena run off at the mouth.

'But the guard was there,' she said. 'And then – I don't know, exactly. Mick laid into him. Beat the poor guy up pretty badly, from what Kieran told me.'

'And Kieran was part of it?'

'Not the bashing, I don't reckon. But he was there. Trailing after Mick like a brain-damaged puppy. With Kieran's record, he'd end up in jail for a serious deal like that, wouldn't he.'

'Most likely, yes. Look, the best move is for Kieran to hand himself in to the police.'

'Maybe so. But I'm worried he'd get blamed for all the stuff Mick did. Kieran'd blab out more than he should, make things worse for himself and end up in jail for a long time.'

'I get what you're saying, but —'

'And you know, jail for a soft kid like Kieran . . .'

'Sure. I know.'

'He needed rescuing. I rescued him,' Sheena said flatly.

She waited for Joe to rip into her short-sighted strategy. But instead of doing that, he flopped his head back with a weary smile. 'What will you do now?' he asked.

'What we were doing before the car broke down – drive round, doing big figure eights on the map.'

'But in the long run – what?'

'I'm hoping the cops get their paws on Mick sometime soon and he soaks up some of the blame. Make things easier for Kieran. Meanwhile, my job is: keep my brother alive and out of major trouble.'

Sheena knew that sounded pretty feeble, she knew it wasn't much of a plan, but Joe didn't try to argue her out of it. He just said, 'Well, good luck.'

Sheena was waiting for Joe to get up and go. But he stayed there, sitting beside her on the step. It was nice to have another human being – other than Kieran – to talk to. With the police trouble out in the open and the decision to leave the farm already in place, she could afford to let her guard drop. And anyway, she was sick to death of the effort it took to keep that guard up.

'The last couple of weeks, Kieran's been so grounded, really got into the work,' said Sheena. 'But I dunno . . . I've always been scared my little brother is doomed.'

'I don't think he's doomed.'

She wanted to believe Joe was right about that. It was incredible to hear another person, a sensible person, say it. Listening to this man offer a smidgen of hope for Kieran made the wretchedness come rushing up from her belly to tighten around her throat.

'He'll hate my guts for making him leave. Ooh yeah,' said Sheena, attempting a laugh. 'The next few weeks are going to be seriously shitful. Kieran miserable, blaming me, me feeling like a bitch.' And now there was no way she could stop her voice trembling.

Joe fumbled in the inside pocket of his suit jacket to retrieve one of those small packets of tissues. He was the kind of guy who carried little packs of tissues in his pocket. He probably never even used them himself. He probably just kept them on hand in case some sneezing child or injured elderly gent or weeping woman needed a tissue. Right now, Sheena was the weeping woman. She pulled a tissue from the packet, bunched it up and pressed it against her eyes to blot up the tears.

'Thanks,' she said. 'You're a kind man.'

'You reckon? Not so sure about that.'

'At least you think about what's going on for other people.'

Joe puffed out a defeated breath. 'For all the good that does.'

'Well, it's more than the self-obsessed dicks out there in the world ever do.'

'Maybe. You know, one of the things I really like about your brother – he thinks the best of everyone.'

'Ha – he does do that. But it means they take advantage of him. He doesn't know what people are really after.'

'But you do?'

'Yes, I do,' replied Sheena emphatically. 'They still end up taking advantage of me, but.'

Sheena pulled a stupid face and Joe laughed.

'I've been a tiny bit jealous,' she said, 'watching Kieran and Zoe with their pashing and staring into each other's eyes and all that shit. Kidding themselves – obviously.'

Sheena instantly regretted speaking that way to him. She was an idiot. Joe shook his head, staring out into the orchard, not looking at her, and she worried she'd offended him somehow.

'What?' she asked him.

'The way you look at me – like you can see every dark secret in here.' He tapped his own forehead.

'I can't really. It's a trick I do with my face. I know bugger-all about what's going on in people's heads, but pretty much everyone's got dark shit inside them, so if you do this look —' she demonstrated a suspicious, slit-eyed stare, 'the other person's mind does the rest and they imagine I'm on to them. That's the trick.'

'It works.'

'Yeah, freaks people out. Sometimes they blurt stuff out without me doing anything.'

Joe frowned, as if doing a quick audit of his own mind. 'I've never gone in for blurting stuff out. Too careful. Too much in the habit of filtering every single thing that comes out of my mouth, making sure there's no risk anyone could get hurt.'

'Well, that's a good way to be,' said Sheena. 'Better than being a tactless fucking big mouth.'

'Is it, though? Or is it just fucking repressed?' He grinned at her with a boldness she hadn't seen from him before. Then he dropped his face away. 'But the thing is, I've got responsibilities, I've got people I have to worry about, I've got history I have to remember. You get used to censoring yourself.'

He looked back at her – *Do you understand?* Sheena was aware of the history he was talking about. She knew stuff about his parents, she knew Celia's story, she'd heard the tales from Roza. And even if she couldn't entirely understand, she wanted him to feel understood, so she nodded.

He went on. 'After a while, after always talking yourself into the responsible choice, you end up talking yourself out of impulses. You lose connection with your own – I can't explain it – sorry . . .'

'No, I think I get you.'

Joe looked at her intently for a moment, as if working out another way to explain himself. Then he suddenly slid along the bench and kissed her.

Sheena remembered thinking Joe was a good-looking man when they had first met on the outskirts of Narralong. She had been marooned with her piece-of-shit car rolled onto the roadside dirt, farting grey smoke, her little brother wandered off into the neighbouring paddock, trying to lure the sheep to him by offering them Twisties. Joe had pulled his car over and gave them a lift to the mechanic in town. On the drive, he had chatted to Kieran with a simple courtesy that made her ache with gratitude.

Later, once the car had been towed into town, Joe had stopped by the garage to check they were okay and mentioned the chance of fruit-picking work. That first day, Sheena had definitely found the guy attractive, even if he wasn't really her type, in his suit and his staid job. And she had sensed he was attracted to her too. But since then, in all the times Joe had been out to Celia's farm, he had never shown any sign of lusting after her, so she figured she had misread those initial cues. There was no mistaking the cues now.

They kissed each other for a moment, but then Joe pulled back and dropped his face away again.

'Oh,' Sheena said, 'now you're thinking, "This is a mistake, this'll cause problems." I mean, you're right, we shouldn't do this.'

'You really are no good at reading thoughts. I'm thinking how incredibly soft your mouth is.'

They kissed again, and this time it wasn't *I wonder what it would be like to kiss you*, it was *We might be about to have sex with each other*.

Sheena scrambled to reason with herself, but it was difficult to think rationally when she was kissing this man. Maybe it wasn't a terrible idea. She was leaving in a couple of hours and they would never lay eyes on each other again. She wasn't wrecking his marriage – no one need ever know if they fucked each other tonight. If Roza was correct – and she most likely was – Joe was starved for sex, so Sheena could tell herself there was a charity element. He was a lot older than her but he was a gorgeous man and she wanted to fuck him. Maybe it could be as simple as that.

Sheena stood up, and Joe seemed uncertain if she was about to slam the door against him or invite him inside. She flicked her head to indicate he should step into the cabin, then she shoved the esky between the end of the bunk bed and the doorway. She was almost certain Kieran would cling to every minute with Zoe until ten, the agreed time, but just in case, the esky would be an effective barricade if Kieran came back early and tried to push the door open. The moving of the esky felt like a bold move, the certain signal that she wanted this to happen. Joe shrugged off his jacket, chucked it on the top bunk, then pulled Sheena to him.

There was a degree of awkwardness – having sex on the single bunk bed, crowded under the top bunk. It required a fair bit of 'Sorry, let me just move sideways' and 'Watch your head on the rail'. But Joe was decisive as he gently manoeuvred their two bodies in the limited space. And that didn't seem to diminish the intensity of the encounter, with its weird mix of politeness and lust. Joe was simultaneously the considerate man and a guy who desperately needed a fuck.

Sheena knew this wasn't sex between two people because they cared about each other. Well, they probably did care about each other, but that was beside the point. He wasn't having sex with her in particular – he just needed to fuck someone. But there was tenderness and no darkness or anger in it.

TEN

Roza had cooled off by lying in a tepid bath, happily allowing the house to grow dark as it filled with the milder night air. Afterwards, she did switch on a few lamps, then pulled on cotton harem pants and a matching top made from a fabric shot through with gold thread. There was rarely anyone in her house to see this sparkly and exotic ensemble, but she liked to wear it most evenings anyway.

She filled her belly with a chicken, wine and vegetable concoction she had cooked because the dish was one of Josef's favourites. She ate without him – she was hungry, and anyway, he hadn't mentioned a definite arrival time on the phone. She put the leftovers in the fridge on an elegant platter in case her son needed food when he eventually drove up.

When the nine o'clock news came on the radio, Roza turned up the volume to hear the weather forecast. Tomorrow it would be forty-two degrees, well over a hundred on the old scale. After the bout of heavy rain, tomorrow's high temperature meant there was a risk an extraordinary thing could happen in the orchard: the fruit might cook on the trees. True. Roza herself would never have believed it if she hadn't seen it with her own eyeballs one year.

She put fresh sheets on the bed in the spare room for Josef. He hadn't said why he was coming to stay the night at her house and Roza didn't ask, even though the question was rattling in her throat, desperate to jump out of her mouth. She hoped it was a sign that he might be reconsidering the future of his marriage, but she didn't dare set her heart on it. Better not to set up expectations that could fall short. Better to allow events to roll towards you in their own time, then choose your moment to duck out of the way or let them slide over you.

The knock on the door just after nine was too insistent to be Joe. He would never knock in such a demanding way.

'Who is that?' Roza called from the hallway.

'It's me,' Celia called back. 'Sorry if I gave you a fright, Roza. Sorry.'

When Roza opened the door, she saw that the woman looked as anxious as she sounded. Celia had been running across the property, the ground still soggy from the rain, so her bare shins and sandalled feet were spattered with mud, as if she had been pulled out of wet soil like a deracinated plant.

'Joe's not here yet?' Celia asked, staying outside, keeping her muddy shoes off the verandah mat. 'Thing is, he should be here by now and I need to – I'm just wanting to know where Zoe is. You haven't seen her? I checked down at the shearing shed and – anyway, don't worry, I'll . . .'

She turned, flicking on the torch in her hand, and hurried away from the house.

'Wait!' Roza called after her. She hauled on the gumboots that lived on the verandah and picked up the torch hanging from a hook just inside the front door. It was a large black metal object, heavy enough for Roza to cosh a robber over the head – that is, if her old-woman arms had enough strength to cosh any robber.

She headed outside after Celia. Roza wasn't sure what was happening but it was clear Celia needed help. She followed the beam of Celia's torch up the path to the farm and then into the orchard.

Roza was much slower on her feet than the younger woman, especially so when galumphing in gumboots. But there were chances for Roza to close the gap when Celia stopped to look along the other pathways, the torch-beam startlingly bright in the dark orchard. By the time Roza caught up with Celia, they were almost at the cabin where the young man and his sister had been living. The gas lamp glowed golden through the front window.

'Hello!' Celia yelled out. 'Sheena? Kieran? Have you seen Zoe?'

From inside the cabin, Roza heard the scraping sound of something heavy sliding across the floor before the door opened a little way.

Sheena poked only her head out. 'Hi. No, I haven't seen . . . sorry, no.'

The young woman must have looked furtive to Celia. Guilty even. Suspecting Sheena was hiding Zoe behind her in the cabin, Celia lunged forward and with one decisive thump, pushed the door wide open.

'Zoe? Are you in there?'

Sheena was revealed to be bare-legged, wearing only a T-shirt, stretching the fabric down at the front to cover herself. Behind her,

Josef was pulling his suit pants on, the rest of his clothes in a pile on the floor. He looked embarrassed, flustered, as you would well expect him to be when discovered in such a tableau.

It was the kind of ludicrous scene that might ordinarily make Roza sigh indulgently or even laugh at the way most of us fumble around in the world, trying to grab what we hope will be chunks of happiness or pleasure. There was a bounce of surprise for Roza that her overly considered and straitlaced son had ever found his way into another woman's bed, let alone the bunk bed of this prickly young woman. But right now was not the moment for amusement or speculation about Josef or moral interrogation of this bunk-bed farce. Celia's panic about her daughter drowned out all other concerns.

'Where's Kieran?' Celia asked Sheena. 'Do you know where Zoe is?'

'No, sorry, no, I don't.'

Sheena made a *please wait* gesture and ducked into the corner of the cabin to pull some shorts on under her T-shirt. At the same time, Josef, shirtless and barefoot, moved forward into the doorway.

If Celia felt distressed or betrayed by what Joe had just done, she did not waste energy on that now. 'Did you drive their car here?' she asked him.

'I did. I did. Just let me check something.'

Celia avoided direct eye contact with him and Joe seemed relieved not to meet her gaze. And when he jumped over the front step to the ground, she lurched backwards to stay well clear of him, not wanting him to touch her as he brushed past.

Joe ran off to check this 'something' and at the same time Sheena started blathering at Celia, urging her not to worry. Kieran would be back soon and then they were definitely leaving. All his belongings were here, packed, ready to leave as agreed. Sheena held out her palm with the car key Joe had brought, displaying it to Celia as proof they were really going. But Roza could see Sheena recognising, in this one crumbling moment, that she had mis-judged this and that things had spun out of any control she ever imagined she had.

Joe hurried back towards them, his suit trousers spattered with mud. 'Sheena's car – I parked it by the gate and now it's gone.'

'Does Kieran have spare keys to that car?' Roza asked.

Sheena groaned. 'He doesn't need any. My brother could hot-wire an old car like that one in thirty seconds.' She looked at the key in her palm as if that key was the problem and the reason she had been fooled.

Joe handed Sheena her watch, which he'd found sitting on the gatepost. Then he turned to Celia. 'Did Zoe say anything at all? Did she take any clothes or money from the house?'

Celia was silent, holding a lungful of air without exhaling. She was immobile, suspended in the last fraction of time before this slammed into her.

'Celia,' said Joe. 'Listen to me – it's fine. I'm sure it'll be fine.'

But Celia didn't seem to hear him speaking to her.

'I'll find her,' she said to herself, but aloud.

Then she hurried away, into the orchard, with the torch aimed ahead of her like a weapon, its yellow beam slicing through the air.

PART TWO

ELEVEN

One thing Roza had never liked about Australia was the feeble excuse for seasons. In summer, grey–green leaves; and in winter, the grey–green leaves would still be stuck there on the trees. No one could call that a proper season. The year had no rhythm to swing a person through. For this reason she had been glad to settle in a fruit-growing area. Living around stone-fruit orchards, the leaves changed colour, and later, when the trees were bare, at least it *looked* like a winter.

This winter was proving surprisingly cold, even in the first days of June. So when Roza contemplated leaving her warm house to walk up to Celia's packing shed, she put on the alpaca sweater her son had brought back years ago from a trip to the United States. It was the lightest, softest sweater she had ever owned, yet almost inconceivably warming, as if spun from some magical substance. Joe had chosen a blood-red colour for his mother, knowing her tastes well, so this was a garment she was very happy to wear once the weather was cold enough.

Fourteen-and-a-bit years ago, Roza and Sandor had been living in the yellow-painted house surrounded by orchards for little more than thirteen months when his body failed, the electrical circuits in his heart fried and frizzled. That was the problem with marrying a man so much older.

Sandor had been a wonderful husband, if you overlooked his labile moods and the teeth-sucking noises. But Roza would never complain, because those were the kind of faults you should over-look when a man was as thoughtful, amusing and honourable as Sandor, and as generous and skilled a lover. They had been a blessed pair, no question. For many years she had adored him and he had adored her, each conscious they had rescued the other from the miserable lives into which they could easily have stumbled.

After Sandor died, Roza had one consoling idea in her head: now, apart from Josef of course, she just had herself to worry about. She could suit herself. She could eat sardines followed by chocolate mousse every night if she fancied. But the truth was she did not eat a lot of mousse. She drank vodka. Because the consoling idea was not so consoling. The vodka was much more effective.

It was a couple of years after Sandor died when Celia said, 'Roza, I need help with packing the fruit.' Roza knew this was a plan that Celia and Josef had cooked up to get her out of the house and busy. But it turned out she was bloody good at the job.

After that, for the next ten years, it went like this: summer and autumn, Roza would be up at five to work for Celia. Sober. Winter, she could retreat to her little underworld, with vodka and silly tele-vision shows to keep her company. Celia would stroll down to check on her sometimes but she eventually gave up inviting Roza for meals in the winter. She let her be, accepting that a sozzled hibernation was the choice her neighbour had made.

This winter was different. Any person observing Roza walk into the yard of the packing shed in her red alpaca sweater would see she was completely sober. She had to keep herself clear-headed because there were people who might need her help.

In the first days after Zoe had disappeared, Celia had stayed mostly in the house – making phone calls, contacting the girl's friends, waiting for messages that might come, hoping her daughter would simply return home.

During this time, the remaining peaches and nectarines were left to rot on the trees, or fall to the ground and rot there. In the heat, thousands of dollars' worth of fruit cooked down into a worthless, nasty jam, spread across the mulch. The smell was potent, a sticky–sweet substance clinging to the nostrils and the lining of the lungs.

Apart from money being lost in the pulpy mess, Roza worried that the putrefying fruit might cause problems with fungus and crawling beasts. But Celia would not listen to anyone who suggested she bring in some help. She couldn't give her mind to such matters. The only thing she cared about was her daughter. Of course.

Celia stayed close to home for two weeks after Zoe left, until one morning she abruptly left the property without telling anyone. That was over four months ago now.

Roza had tried to keep the vegetable plot going, tramping up the slope every day to water and weed and flick off any bugs eating the foliage. But it proved too much to manage. Eventually, Joe dug the remnants of the vegetable plants back into the soil, so they could at least be of use as compost in the garden beds.

Since then, Roza had persisted with a daily walk up to the farm, taking the longer route, via the front gate, to check Celia's mailbox. She would then make a slow circuit around the packing shed and the house. This way she could check if there had been any damage done by wind or robbers or creatures overnight, and it was also a way to keep her ancient limbs awake and mobile.

Roza had always had a key to Celia's place, but these days she used it for a special task. With Celia gone away on her search, there was no one to hear a phone ring in the empty house or the idle packing shed, and so Josef had connected a telephone answering machine to Celia's home line. He had originally bought this machine for his office in town, but his secretary would not touch the thing for fear she might break it or the device would leap up off the desk to tear out her throat.

Roza was not afraid of the machine, installed on Celia's kitchen counter in its fake-wood laminate casing. In appearance and operation it was much like a cassette player, so not an object any sensible person would regard as monstrous. In fact, Roza respected and admired the contraption – it had the power to capture messages that could otherwise be lost. Of course there was a risk it was storing distressing messages in its metal and plastic innards, but that was not the machine's fault. And it was always better to know.

Every morning, Roza let herself in through Celia's kitchen door and checked the tiny red bulb on the front of the device. If the light was flashing, she set out notepaper and pencil before hitting the playback tab, ready to write down messages from the police or anyone with information she must relay to Celia. Before hitting the button, Roza also readied her own body, taking a big breath and bracing her rib cage, in case a voice coming out of the machine were to deliver bad news about Zoe.

The first weeks, the tape was filled with confused voices stammering their way out of the little holes in the speaker. 'Sorry – uh – have I got the right number? Is this – oh . . .' People were flummoxed, unused to speaking to an answering machine. 'Celia? You there? Is this thing recording me or am I supposed to – oh, I'll ring back later.'

Sometimes there would just be the fragile sound of a person breathing, barely audible through the swish of the tape between the tiny rollers. Roza fancied she could hear the person's brain clunking around as they tried to work out what to say.

There was also the hope that the flashing bulb heralded good news or even the voice of the girl herself, saying she was okay, saying she was coming home. Maybe some of the breathing noises on the tape had been Zoe, but Roza doubted that. She believed she would somehow divine if it had been Zoe breathing, hesitating, letting the tape hiss on.

There had been almost no useful dispatches on the machine – a few possible sightings of the girl, but all proved to be dead ends. Some friends and neighbours had recorded their concern for Celia, words tight in their throats, tight with worry or the inadequacy of the words. In some cases, there was a tinge of unspoken smugness ('*My* child has not run off'). Roza was happy to filter these messages for Celia. People's best wishes were so often bound up with their own fears or vanities or self-absorbed notions about the way things went in the world. It was better if Roza was simply able to say to Celia 'Mrs So-and-So is thinking of you', 'Santino sends his love', and 'The lady from the P and C offers any help she can give'.

This particular day, the red light was not flashing. No messages. In fact, there had been no messages for over a week now.

Roza had finished her checklist – letterbox, garden, house, answering machine – and was coming back towards the packing shed when Joe drove into the yard. He climbed out of the vehicle and gave his mother a kiss.

'Thought you might be prowling around up here, Mum. I just dropped off some bags on your front verandah.'

'What bags? Bags of what?' Roza asked.

'We're sorting through stuff at our place. There were some things Heather thought you might be able to use.'

Roza snorted. 'Are these "things" items of overpriced foolish junk Heather bought and now throws out so she can buy new?'

'Basically, yes.'

'Will they be useful to me?'

'No. Except as a physical reminder of your contempt for Heather,' said Joe with a small smile. Even though he was always patient with his mother, there were times Roza could hear the scrape of irritation in his voice. But other times – right now being an example – he appeared to enjoy the game, at least a little.

'Well, so, please drop the bags at the Salvation Army in town,' said Roza, then without warning, she grabbed his head with her hands in order to examine his eyeballs. 'Josef. What's going on?'

'About what?'

'You tell me about what.'

Joe shrugged. 'Heather asked me to move out.'

'Ah. Is this for permanent?'

'Yes, it's permanent.'

'You didn't have to confess to the sex,' Roza pointed out. 'It's only that one intercourse, months ago, we're talking about. Isn't it?'

He nodded.

'The woman, Sheena – she wouldn't have told. Celia has gone away. I would never tell. So, why?'

'I felt I had no choice.'

Her son the honourable man. Josef had admitted the infidelity to his wife the very next day after the act. But it took him some weeks to summon the courage to confess to his mother that he had confessed to his wife.

Roza waggled her head. 'So, Heather has been marching you to the marriage counselling for months. Now suddenly she decides to throw you out like the garbage?'

'The decision was mutual in many ways,' said Joe, in the calm voice he used sometimes, as if his mother were a crazy woman to be handled.

'I always knew this is what she will do in the end.'

'As you made very clear.'

Roza was relieved to hear that miserable marriage was over, but even so, it annoyed her to see Heather tormenting Josef without a tiny shred of goodwill in her heart. 'Before she kicked you out, she wanted her months of watching you writhe with the guilt first.'

Joe closed his eyes and sighed. 'Mum. Please. Don't.'

'I keep my mouth shut.'

And indeed Roza's mouth did stay shut for several seconds before a question snuck its way out. 'You're not still having some kind of relations with Sheena, are you?'

'What? No. I'm not.'

Zoe and Kieran had run away together using the sister's car, leaving Sheena stranded on the farm. Desperate to transport herself far away as rapidly as possible, she arranged a lift into Narralong with a neighbour. Before she left, the sister gave Celia a piece of paper with phone numbers that might help in the search for the girl.

She also insisted on handing back the envelope of cash. She was not a charming person, that Sheena, but she was a person of honour.

Roza was convinced Josef's intercourse with the sister had been an unplanned business – foolish or selfish or a blessing, depending on a person's point of view. And she didn't believe it made any difference to the outcome of that night. The young couple would have run off together whether Josef and Sheena had kept on their underwear or not. That hour of sexual activity had other consequences, of course – precipitating the end of his marriage and brewing up a painful awkwardness between Celia and Joe.

Roza watched her beautiful son wander around the bare, chilly yard. He looked so reduced by the last months, she would have donated him some of her energy if that were possible. At the very least, she wanted to coddle and restore him, to shower him with affection and food and admiration and her boundless love. But seeing no means to do that right now, instead she said, 'Well, Josef, since you've been sufficiently tormented by your wife that she now decides to dismiss you, where will you live?'

'I've got a room at the motel near the office. Just until I find somewhere long term.'

'You are always welcome to live with me. Or you could go off on a trip somewhere in the world, now that you're a single man again. Have some fun.'

Josef looked at her pointedly.

'Of course,' said Roza. 'You don't want to be far from the children.'

'Of course I don't.'

There were men who could spend time away from their children with no great suffering but Josef was not one of them. It was strange for Roza to find herself half-wishing her son was a less deep-feeling man, more petty and selfish. But of course she was glad he was a devoted father. Even so, it was hard to see things tearing at his insides.

Joe looked out from the yard towards the rows of bare fruit trees, with their straggly unpruned branches and the ground invaded by weeds. 'The orchard's a mess.'

Roza flicked her hands in the air. 'More than four months abandoned.'

'It's a problem if the trees are left like this too long, isn't it?'

'This is why the ginger boy and his cousin should come and do the urgent work.'

'I could organise that for Celia.'

Roza shrugged. 'I suggested this.'

Joe had done his best for Celia, calling on contacts who might help in the search for Zoe and taking care of any farm business it was possible for him to do. Roza knew he fretted about whether he should telephone Celia. She might not appreciate a call from him, on account of the intercourse with the boy's sister. So he didn't call her. Instead he relied on Roza for news about Celia's wellbeing.

Roza could see her son's pudgy belly had been whittled away in the last months. This was a welcome outcome in itself, much like the end of his marriage, but, like the end of his marriage, it was sad to see the unhappiness that went along it.

'You're not eating,' Roza said. 'Stay for lunch.'

'I can't. I have to go to Hamish's athletics carnival.'

'Ah. Yes. Well, let me parcel up some food to take back to your sad little motel room of shame.'

Josef automatically responded, 'No, thanks.' But a second later, he flashed her that small smile. 'You know what, that'd be lovely, Mum. Thanks.'

Roza allowed her son to drive her back to her house and together they sorted through the bags of Heather's cast-offs on the verandah. They salvaged a few items, including expensive double-bed sheets still in their packaging. Heather had no use for them since she had recently purchased a queen-sized bed. Maybe the larger bed was more convenient for avoiding sex. Well, now she was discarding her husband, so that unnecessarily huge bed would be even more wasted.

While Joe stowed the rest of the bags back in the boot of his car, Roza ducked inside to spoon a big serving of food into a plastic container for her son to take back to town.

That evening, Roza ate the portion left over. She had just settled down to watch one of her television shows – this one featured a man with bionic body parts – when Celia phoned.

The conversation went the way it always did.

'Hello, Roza. It's me. Any news?'

She meant news about Zoe, nothing else. Soaked into every word Celia spoke was the question: *Has Zoe come home?* But she couldn't risk asking that question out loud for fear the hope for a *Yes* and the disappointment of the *No* would be more than her body could stand.

So Celia asked practical questions about mail and phone messages. Every time she rang, every time, it broke Roza's heart. 'No,' she would have to say to Celia. 'No messages or letters.'

'Oh,' Celia replied, as she always did. Then the poor woman would gather herself up again and read out the phone number of the motel where she would be staying for the next few days, so Roza could write it down. 'You can contact me here until at least Wednesday.'

The phone calls always ended this way.

'Are you okay, Roza?'

'I'm okay. And you?'

'The same. Stay well,' Celia would say and then quickly hang up.

When Roza put down the phone, and hours later lying in bed, Celia would still be in her thoughts, whether Roza liked it or not. It was easy for the mind to tune into the waves of suffering going on around the world at any moment in time. It was like owning a stupid malfunctioning radio that could only pick up wretched frequencies and then would somehow record and gather up all the miseries of the past, the cries of every childless mother, every anguished individual Roza had ever known, and transmit them into her head.

An old lady lying in her bed stewing on such things – what good would that do Celia or Josef or anyone? None. To fight off this tendency in her brain, Roza had always tried very hard to tune in to the joyful things that must surely be going on at this instant somewhere in the world. But these days such mental discipline was more difficult, so she was at the mercy of the waves of sorrowful thoughts. This was where the vodka would have come in handy.

TWELVE

Celia opened her eyes and for a few seconds was disoriented, needing to hook her gaze onto the position of the window, the light fitting and the furniture around her to locate herself on the earth's surface. Here she was in another budget motel room, with her suitcase flipped open on the luggage stand and her truck parked just outside the door.

Every morning, the shock of it hit her fresh. Her daughter was missing. It was the same when Marcus was killed, this waking up to be clobbered by the hard fact of it again, followed by the surprise of finding that her body was, unbelievably, continuing to function, blood and nerves and complex cellular physiology humming along as if nothing had changed. The daily shock of losing Marcus had been superseded by a more benign mechanism when Zoe was born, which had allowed her to persevere and then to settle and then to live with some joy.

Now, with Zoe lost, the first thing Celia did every morning, wherever she found herself, was reach for the telephone handset beside the bed, checking for a dial tone. She worried that during the three or four hours of sleep she had managed through the night, she may have accidentally knocked the receiver out of its cradle and so missed an important message. But this morning there was the strong purr of a dial tone, as there always was.

The room was much like every other motel room she'd been in. There was a television set bolted near the top of the bare brick wall, raspy carpet tiles pocked with cigarette burns, and a dark timber cupboard so battered it looked as if someone had kicked it around the bitumen car park. The bedspread was mustard-coloured quilted nylon with crusty patches, each one the dried remnant of the tears or snot or semen of a previous guest. Cigarette smoke had saturated every surface, even the brickwork, and Celia's hair stank of fags just from sleeping in the room.

Dispiriting as the joint was, Celia worried about the expense of motels, even the rank ones. She considered staying in cheap pubs (if you hunted around you could find a single for fifteen dollars a night) but pub accommodation didn't have telephones in the rooms. Celia knew she would never get any sleep at all if there wasn't a phone on the bedside table, a means for Roza or the police to reach her.

She opted for the cheapest motels she could find, but after so many nights it was adding up to a lot of cash. If that meant chewing through money, sucking up more and more through the line of credit on the property, then that was how it had to be.

Celia launched out of bed and into the shower to blast herself more usefully awake. Over the past few months, she had conducted each searching day as if she held a job with an urgent deadline.

It made no sense, but it was one of the ways to funnel the anxiety and keep going.

When Zoe first disappeared, Celia had lodged a missing-person report at the Narralong police station. The sergeant, Noel, was kind in a slightly patronising way, but unquestionably kind. As he filled out the official paperwork, the biro clamped in his meaty paw, he related stories about the many teenage runaway cases he'd encountered over the years, a dozen girls who had run off but returned home safely a few days later. His tone was steady, relentlessly calm, intended to reassure. Celia was hungry for any reassurance on offer, but as she listened to the police sergeant talk about those other runaways in his avuncular singsong, she couldn't take any comfort. If anything, Noel's stories had the effect of slapping her with the realisation that Zoe wasn't some capricious teen having a tantrum. This was something different.

Those first two weeks, Celia had stayed on the farm, never moving out of earshot of the phone. If she ever ventured from the house, it was only as far as the packing shed, where the ringer on the telephone extension was good and loud. She prowled the yard, never letting her eyes drift away from the driveway for more than half a minute, as if the fixedness of her gaze could conjure a vehicle to appear and deliver her daughter home.

Then in early February, a postcard arrived, with a photograph of a kangaroo on the front, and on the back, in Zoe's handwriting, the words *Don't worry*. The postmark was smudgy but could well have said Leeton. Celia took the kangaroo postcard as code that Zoe did not intend to show up at home anytime soon. The missing-person file would bump along through the system and police would do what they could, she assumed. But Celia knew she was the one charged with finding her daughter. That was when she left the property and set out to search.

She tried to be logical about it, mapping routes between towns where Zoe had schoolfriends, but also keeping in mind the time-table of the harvest circuit. Zoe and Kieran needed money but would want to keep moving, so picking work made sense.

Celia developed a routine: when she reached each new town, she would check in with the local police, then do the rounds of the pubs and milk bars, asking questions, showing a photo of Zoe. The only useful picture she had was a snapshot taken in a cafe on Zoe's last birthday, slightly out of focus. The other option was a school portrait photo – her daughter with plaited hair and a dutiful smile, stiffly posed against a mottled blue backdrop. Zoe had never really looked like that portrait girl, and she surely looked even less like that unworldly teenager now.

Celia would then drive around to any properties in the district that hired casual pickers, talking to the farmers. The minute she said her daughter was sixteen and missing, the farmers would generally be helpful. They were no-nonsense about it, without the sort of fuss that comes dripping in pity. Their straightforward manner suited Celia, because a direct hit of sympathy might well have cracked her apart. She would leave each farmer a copy of the photo with her home phone number written on the back, in case Zoe turned up after Celia had gone.

At the beginning of March, there was a bloke, a grape-grower, who recognised the photo. According to the guy, Zoe and Kieran had stopped by looking for work but the place already had its full team of pickers. The grower remembered them because the two kids had been smiling for no good reason he could decipher and had been 'all over each other like a rash'.

Celia quizzed the man. What exactly had the two kids said? How did they seem? Did they say where they were headed next? The grower tightened up his face against the battery of questions but he didn't take offence; he could see she was in a desperate state of mind. He was sorry he couldn't offer anything more in the way of useful information.

Through March and into April, Celia had persevered, gripping onto that one sighting and any other mention of a young couple that could have been them, or a car that could have been Sheena's old bomb. She followed the routes she guessed Zoe would have taken, chasing after the seasons, the stone fruit, the grapes, the apples.

Easter fell in the second week of April. Months back, before school broke up for the summer holidays, Zoe had been invited to spend the Easter break with her friend Mandy, whose family kept a caravan by the beach at Kiama. Celia had said yes immediately, but she had also immediately calculated the risks involved in Zoe travelling in the McAloons' car from their house in Evatt's Bridge all the way to the coast, the chance of her being swept away by a strong rip (she'd done so little ocean swimming), the odds of the symptoms of a sudden-onset illness going unnoticed by people who didn't know her daughter well. As always, she conducted this protective voodoo without saying anything to Zoe. Celia's enthusiastic 'Yes, of course you can go. How wonderful!' was genuine – she loved the idea of her daughter having a beach holiday with her friend. That was why she had given Zoe the beach towel and beach bag for Christmas. The phone calls to arrange that trip seemed inconceivably long ago now.

Mandy was the first of the friends Celia had called when Zoe disappeared. The girl insisted she hadn't spoken to Zoe since school had broken up the previous December and had no idea where she was now. Celia had believed her, if only because Mandy sounded so miffed about being neglected by her supposed best friend.

Later, on the Saturday of the Easter break, Celia replayed in her mind that phone call with Mandy, questioning her own ability to detect dishonesty in the voice of a sixteen-year-old girl. Mandy might have been hiding something. People could lie much more fluently on the phone. Face to face, it was harder to lie and easier to read a lie.

Once that doubt took hold, Celia had immediately checked out of the Batlow motel where she had slept the night. She drove out of the town, away from the apple orchards, across to the coast, then north to Kiama. She drove too fast and she drove for hours, only ever stopping to fill up the tank or buy food she could eat at the wheel. It was absurd – a few days would make no difference, but she couldn't suppress the urge to rush.

She reached the caravan park in the early evening, obeying the signs to slow down along the road that ran through the grassy area set aside for campers, with little alcoves carved out of the coastal shrubs for people to pitch their tents. The camping ground was thrumming with activity – it was the time of the day when dinners were being prepared and children were being hustled to showers – and filled with a burble of noise from pop songs on transistor radios, the clattering of cooking implements, toddlers squealing as parents chivvied them along. Half a dozen kids were playing cricket with one of the fathers on the open patch of grass. A mother herded her twin girls, maybe five years old, back from the ablution block in their matching terry-towelling ponchos. A cluster of grown-ups stood around a barbecue, cans of beer in hand, laughing and blustery.

People turned their heads to stare at Celia – curious, not hostile. A farm ute, driven by a solitary woman, was incongruous here. She kept weaving through the place until she found the section with the semi-permanent caravans, where she spotted Keith McAloon's electrician truck parked alongside one of the vans.

The van was set up for years of holidays – chocked in place on a concrete pad, hooked up to a power socket, bordered by succulent plants in pots painted bright blue. A striped annex was attached to the side and under its large awning there was room for a table and chairs.

'Oh. Hi,' said Elaine McAloon as Celia approached her. The two mothers had met at the end-of-year school concert and spoken several times on the phone.

'Hi, Elaine.'

'Keith!' Elaine called out to her husband, who was turning sausages on the barbecue on the other side of the gravel roadway. 'Keith, it's Celia. Zoe's mum.'

Celia saw the glance flicked between the two of them. The gossip mechanisms had done their work. They both knew she was the mother whose daughter had run away with a young man wanted by the police.

Keith trotted over to the caravan, tongs in hand. He smiled hello, but then exchanged another look with his wife, both unsure what to say.

Celia jumped in to save them from their awkwardness. 'Listen, I'm sorry to just turn up like this.'

'Here she is!' said Keith, pointing his tongs towards someone on the beach path.

Celia's chest lurched for one brief, excruciatingly hopeful moment. Then she looked round to see it was Mandy running up the path, holding a blow-up surfing mat on her head.

'Oh. Hello, Mrs Janson.' Mandy was straight out of the surf, her ruffled orange swimming costume still wet, shins crusted with sand, hair a salty clump, nose peeling from sunburn on top of sunburn.

Celia moved towards her. 'Mandy. Where is she? Do you know?'

'Beg yours?' the girl responded. She was flustered, looking caught out, guilty.

'You have to be honest with me. Have you talked to her? Has she told you where she is?'

'No, sorry. I mean, I haven't talked to Zoe at all for —'

'Has she sent you letters? Has she made you promise not to tell anyone? Is that what's going on?'

'No. Dead-set, Mrs Janson, I haven't even . . .'

'You must tell me the truth, Mandy.'

'Look, I think Mandy's made it clear she hasn't heard anything,' said Keith, his composed adult tone forcing Celia to hear the hectoring pitch in her own voice.

She had ended up moving intimidatingly close to Mandy, skewering the girl with her gaze. And by this point the McAloon boys, eight and ten years old, had also scooted up from the beach. The two little brothers froze, registering the tension in front of them, and glanced to their mother for explanation.

Keith shifted himself in between Celia and his daughter – a shielding move, but shielding Celia as much as Mandy, protecting this poor distressed woman from doing something foolish.

'Celia, how about you come over and sit down,' he said.

His wife chimed in, with an equally mollifying tone. 'Stay and have some dinner with us. There's plenty.'

Elaine indicated the table where she was preparing the food: a bowl of salad, a platter of waxy cheese slices, bread and margarine, tomato sauce, all waiting for the sausages. Elaine McAloon was in the process of arranging vegetables into faces on plates for the two younger kids – shredded-lettuce hair, cucumber-slice eyes with grated-carrot eyebrows, tomato cheeks and half a slice of tinned beetroot as a mouth.

Celia swivelled back to see that Mandy was fidgety, with the embarrassed grin of an adolescent who has no idea how to *be* at that moment. She suddenly struck Celia as so young. The panic she'd seen on Mandy's face was not guilt about lying. The girl had been nervous because she was just a kid, a kid afraid of Celia's ferocious questions.

'I'm so sorry, Mandy. Please forgive me.'

'Oh, that's – y'know . . .' The girl didn't know how to respond and kept silently appealing to her parents – *What do I do now?*

'Please, Celia, stay and eat with us,' urged Elaine. 'We've all been worried about Zoe but good lord, you must be —'

'No,' Celia said too abruptly, then quickly modulated her tone. 'Thank you, no. I should go. I'm sorry for barging in on your holiday. I'm sorry.'

Celia was already hurrying to the door of her ute, desperate to escape the pitying looks from these people, from their uncomprehending kindness.

Keith called after her, 'We'll let you know if we hear anything. If Zoe gets in touch with Mandy, we'll call you quick smart. That's a promise.'

Celia nodded her thanks through the windscreen, then swung the ute around and away. She drove out of the camping ground and picked up speed on the main road. She drove non-stop until the light had completely gone from the day. She wasn't heading anywhere in particular, other than far away from her own appalling behaviour. Once it was dark enough, she felt a little more comfortable, her shame unseen now that she'd sunk into the night. At the next crossroads, there were signs to Sydney and she pointed the vehicle that way. There was no future in trailing around the picking circuit any longer. Celia guessed – all she could do was guess – that Zoe would have headed for the city by now.

The first thing Celia did in Sydney was hire a private investigator, a guy she found in the yellow pages, and give him all the information she had. She suspected he was ripping her off, but she would do whatever might have some chance of working.

Several good-hearted friends had repeatedly offered Celia a place to stay in Sydney. It would make sense financially, but as a guest in a friend's spare room, she would be obliged – after some period of indulgence and sympathy – to behave normally. And she would be obliged to talk about what had happened. So she made excuses to decline the invitations. The hardest person to turn down was Freya, her husband's sister. There had always been a strong friendship between Celia and her sister-in-law, which had intensified when Marcus was killed. But that was the problem – Freya's eyes would be on her and there would be questions whirring in the air even if little was said. So Celia decided it was best to stick with motels. She found places in the outer suburbs of the city where the rooms were cheaper.

As April rolled into May and now June, the bank manager in Narralong expressed concern about the growing overdraft on the farm account, and Celia was required to call him on several occasions. She found that there was a voice she could use – this was more easily achieved on the phone – a steely tone but with a hint of crazy glinting off the edge, which, when coupled with some mention of 'my missing daughter', managed to shut someone up. However misguided people thought she was, they would step aside and let her continue on. It was an unworthy manoeuvre, that voice – cheap emotional blackmail, really – but it achieved what Celia needed to keep going without wasting time.

When the weather turned cold, she bought a knee-length sheepskin coat from the Salvation Army op shop. This wasn't about comfort – if anything, she felt a penitential urge to endure physical discomfort – but wearing that coat allowed Celia to stay outdoors for long periods of time. She was following up addresses Sheena had given her – places Kieran had lived or liked to hang out – and sometimes stationed herself outside a certain house or pub, hoping for a sighting of Zoe or the boy. Thanks to that warm coat, she could sit and wait for hours and hours.

THIRTEEN

Sheena's fingers were black up to the second joint from counting banknotes into bundles and rolling piles of coins into the paper wrappers. She would have to scrub her hands with washing-up liquid to be rid of the money grime, then slather on moisturiser so she didn't end up with dermatitis again. After a busy Friday night, La Parisienne finally closed at four a.m. but Sheena had to stay back to clear the tills and lock up.

In a narrow street off the main drag of Surfers Paradise, La Parisienne declared itself to be a nightclub but was just a bar really, seeing as there was no dance floor. The decor was red and black, with one wall sporting a shithouse mural that optimistically claimed to be a silhouette of the Paris skyline and, in the foreground, featured the outline of a French hooker with a disproportion-ately big head and one stilettoed foot up in the air at a supposedly saucy angle.

The lighting was kept dim, with red bulbs and fringed scarlet lampshades, so in the low light the place didn't look too terrible to the customers, especially through the added filter of numerous Bundy-and-Cokes. But now, with the fluorescent lights on and the chairs up on tables ready for the cleaners, the shabbiness was on display. Every surface was scuffed or gouged, the velvet upholstery on the booths saggy and tatty. By the end of the night and before the cleaners arrived, the floor was as grotty as you'd expect, with spilled drinks dried into sticky blotches that attracted a garnish of fluff, scraps of paper, human hair and cigarette butts.

To go with the chic French decor, female staff wore a uniform supplied by the management: a red off-the-shoulder peasant blouse with an elasticised neckline, a black miniskirt and fishnet stockings.

As Sheena counted the money at the end of each night, she always sat with her back to the Parisian mural, because in the merciless white glare of the fluoros, there was something truly depressing about that abysmal painting, sad beyond any joke Sheena could construct in her mind.

Sheena had left Celia's place the day after the huge mess. She didn't want to hang around Sydney, so she headed for Surfers Paradise, figuring she'd find work there. In fact, she secured a trial shift as a barmaid at La Parisienne the first afternoon she asked around. Within days she was on the full-time roster, mostly because Radenko, the owner, liked the fact that the other bar staff – all young women – were scared of Sheena and therefore less likely to fiddle the till when her eyes were on them.

Within weeks she was promoted to night manageress, probably because she was the only staff member with two neurons to rub together and smart enough to know that it would be unwise to skim money off a guy like Radenko.

Sheena might rejoice in the exalted title of 'night manageress' but the pay was shit and Radenko still expected her to wear the same slutty outfit as the rest of the staff. So, as she sat counting the night's takings, she could feel the abrasive mesh of the fishnets waffling her thighs against the chair and the nylon of the peasant blouse scratching wherever it touched her skin.

Radenko was in his fifties, dark-eyed and bulky, one of those men whose neck was as wide as his skull, so his head just sort of merged with his shoulders. He had propositioned Sheena the third night she worked there – blessedly doing so in a direct, verbal way rather than by groping her. He simply said, 'Sheena, would you like to become my mistress?' When she said, 'No, thanks,' he just shrugged and accepted her polite, equally direct refusal.

She had worried that the boss might become a nuisance, sniffing around her, but he seemed philosophical about the knockback. When he entertained business associates in the back booth – Radenko ran construction businesses and other ventures Sheena knew better than to be curious about – he insisted Sheena serve their table. She would pour the Liebfraumilch and bring over platters of oysters kilpatrick from the seafood place round the corner. The boss also liked the way she could pour cream into their glasses of Tia Maria so a layer of white sat on top of the syrupy brown liqueur. Whenever she came over to their table, Radenko would slip his chunky arm around Sheena's waist and smile seductively, giving his associates the impression she was indeed his mistress. It was no problem for Sheena to allow that impression to stand, especially if it meant keeping her job without actually having to sleep with the guy.

And anyway, Radenko wasn't the worst boss she'd ever had. He paid the lousy wages promptly and he kept the bouncer on shift during the clean-up after closing time so Sheena felt safe on the premises in the early hours of the morning. Not every boss would have done that.

La Parisienne was the kind of place where female patrons were handed a voucher for two free drinks when they walked in. The bar offered a cheap price on jugs of Slimy Maria (milk mixed with Tia Maria) and Fruit Tingle (a lurid cocktail that really did taste like the lollies). With that discount supply of infantile drinks, patrons could get themselves seriously pissed at great speed.

It attracted a lot of under-age girls, especially in the school holidays. The bouncer on the door didn't notice – he was a nice-enough Islander guy but dumb as a box of rocks. The police didn't give a flying fuck if there were minors drinking there – they were too busy counting the cash in the paper bags Radenko and other proprietors handed over on a regular basis.

If a girl came in who looked fifteen, Sheena would assess if she was the kind of kid who could take care of herself. If she was a naive little twerp likely to get herself silly-drunk and then pregnant or, worse, acquire herpes from one of the losers in the bar, Sheena would swing her intimidating gaze onto the poppet. 'How old are you, princess?' If the teenager then blanched and stammered and scurried away from the bar, well, that decided it. Sheena had probably saved the girl from getting herself into a mess. But if some chick pouted her strawberry-lip-glossed mouth, poked her padded bra defiantly through her tank top and claimed to be eighteen, Sheena would shrug and let it go. Those sharp-elbowed little molls could look after themselves.

The worst thing about the job was being awake all night and attempting to sleep in the day. Night work messed with her body, making her feel unhealthy and slightly dirty all the time, even though she showered twice a day. The uniform contributed to the dirty sensation – the cheap nylon fabric didn't breathe at all, so Sheena was trapped in there with her own sour sweat no matter how much deodorant she sprayed on beforehand.

Then again, it might have been Surfers Paradise itself that felt unhygienic to her. She'd forgotten how much she hated the place – it was as ugly as sin and harboured more arseholes per square yard than anywhere she'd ever lived. But there was always work to be had on the Gold Coast for someone like Sheena, and the streets were full of people day or night, constantly generating noise you could disappear into. Sometimes that was an advantage.

On the bus trip up to Queensland, Sheena had imagined throwing her body into the surf. It would be good to live near the beach again. But in fact she hadn't taken herself to the beach once in the four months she'd been here.

When the La Parisienne money was counted, packed and locked away in the safe – the registers had balanced tonight, thank Christ – Sheena wriggled out of the miniskirt and pulled on tracksuit pants. It was cold walking through the streets at five a.m. in June. More importantly, she didn't want any smart-mouth dickheads gawping at her legs in the fishnets.

There was still more than an hour before sunrise, but it was never properly dark in the centre of Surfers. Street lamps, neon signs and car headlights combined to pour a thin slurry of light over the buildings. Every morning, heading back to the flat at the end of her work shift, Sheena would be reminded that this was the time of day she used to start work at Celia's place.

The night Kieran and Zoe shot through, there had been an initial burst of activity. Phone calls, torchlight searches of the property, Celia driving up roads in several possible directions, more phone calls. There was fuck-all chance of finding the kids that night but everyone, including the old Hungarian lady, went along with the futile effort so they could hurl their feelings into some busy-busy action.

Just hours before, Joe and Sheena had been fucking, but for the rest of that night, while helping with the search, they didn't even make eye contact. Okay, getting sprung in a pants-down pantomime, like something out of a Benny Hill sketch, would not have been a highlight in Joe's life, but the man's discomfort was deeper than simple embarrassment. Sheena wondered if he had the secret hots for Celia and now reckoned he'd blown his chance. Or maybe he was ashamed to be caught rooting a slag like Sheena and worried his upright friend Celia would think less of him.

There was an acidic silence going on between Celia and Joe, no question. Maybe she was angry because his negligence – being sexually distracted at a crucial moment – had contributed to Zoe's slipping away. Or she was annoyed because Joe was the dimwit who'd brought Kieran there in the first place. Possibly, Celia held a candle for Joe so now she felt jealous. Or she'd simply lost respect for him because he'd chosen to have sex with Sheena. Whatever. There wasn't a lot of goodwill towards Sheena in any of the possible tunes playing under that muffled anger.

Celia was sharp when she quizzed Sheena. *What did you say to Kieran? What did he say to you? What were the words you used? Your exact words?* Even though Celia sounded stern, she couldn't bring herself to meet Sheena's gaze, because it was obvious both of them had stuffed this up. Sheena had been an idiot to go along with the plan, but it had been the mother's idea to offer the bribe in the first place.

Anyway, the kids would probably have run off together no matter what anybody had done or said. The sting for Sheena was that Kieran and Zoe had driven away believing they'd been betrayed by the people who were supposed to want the best for them. Sheena didn't like knowing that was what they would have been thinking. Then again, bugger them. And bugger Kieran especially. She'd turned herself inside fucking out to save him from his mistakes and now he'd thrown that back in her face.

'That's it. That's it,' Sheena had said aloud as she shoved Kieran's clothes into the 44-gallon drum Celia used as an incinerator for rubbish.

She wouldn't waste one more scrap of energy caring what her brother did or what he thought. She just wanted the car back, but she wouldn't hold her breath that would ever happen.

Sheena had been keen to get away from the farm but she was stranded on account of Kieran stealing her car. Joe didn't have his vehicle on the property either and there was no way Sheena was going to ask Celia for a lift. Eventually Roza suggested a solution: one of the growers down the road had a truck due to take peaches to market. Sheena could cadge a lift on the truck into Narralong.

Before she left, Sheena divided up the cash Celia had given her. She calculated the amount she and Kieran were legitimately owed for the picking work and then subtracted the money Celia had spent paying for the car. That left Sheena with a few hundred bucks – enough to get back to the city and survive until she found work. The rest of the money she handed back. She didn't want someone like Celia going around saying she was a cheat.

She wrote out a page of the names and likely addresses of Kieran's mates she could remember – any info that might help Celia find her daughter. Not that Sheena reckoned it would come to that. She was sure the girl would get a fright soon enough and scurry home to her mother.

Sheena bought a bus ticket from Narralong to Sydney and then headed to Queensland. When she arrived up in Surfers Paradise, a woman she knew, an acquaintance really, mentioned there was a room available in her flat. The bedroom was laughably small and the whole building stank of rancid cooking fat from the takeaway place on the ground floor, but the previous flatmate had left behind a mattress Sheena could use, and the place was better than nothing.

Two weeks ago, Sheena had walked in the front door to find Murray, aka The Dickless Wonder, ensconced on the couch. He was mates with the guy who lived in the front room and the two of them were putting in a productive evening of bong-smoking.

'Sheena!' Murray had said when he first saw her. 'Hey, have sex with me.'

Astonishingly, the Wonder was still single.

Murray became a frequent visitor, often hanging around the flat now he was back living in Surfers. Every time he saw Sheena, he would repeat the request: 'Have sex with me'.

This particular morning, Sheena dragged her carcass in the front door to find the Dickless Wonder sprawled on the couch, unconscious. She tried to slip quietly past him to the bathroom, but even at five-thirty a.m., his groin could detect the presence of a female and rouse him from sleep.

'Sheena. Hey, have —'

She slammed her hand in the air – *Don't bother* – and he obediently shut up. But then – she must have been in a weakened state – she flicked her head for him to follow her into the bedroom.

FOURTEEN

Celia was behaving as if she had arranged to meet someone in the foyer of the Pancake Parlour, so her presence wouldn't appear odd to the customers or staff.

She had brought her daughter to this pancake place once when she was twelve, as a special Sydney treat. Zoe had been fizzy with excitement about every detail – the flamboyant menus, the booths, the extravagant piles of gooey food.

Celia pictured the scenario of Zoe bringing Kieran to this same Pancake Parlour, the two of them laughing and relishing the nostalgic fun of it, eager to share this moment from her past. Celia could easily imagine her doing that. Of course the odds of Zoe turning up here on this particular Sunday were impossibly low – ridiculous, beyond all logic – but trying something was preferable to waiting with nothing.

A teenaged couple on an excruciatingly awkward first date ventured into the restaurant, but it was mostly families arriving for early dinners. Special-occasion dinners. The little kids were thrilled and uncomfortable to be dressed up in their scratchy best outfits as their parents wrangled them to queue up behind the *Please Wait Here to Be Seated* sign. When a hostess signalled to a family group to follow her, with a stack of oversized menus tucked under her arm, the children gasped as if they were being escorted towards some indescribably exotic wonderland.

While Celia waited, the crowd grew and she had to keep shuffling out of the way. 'Excuse me.' 'Sorry.' 'Please, you go past me.' 'No, no, I'm not in the queue.' 'I'm just waiting for someone.'

She had been maintaining her rounds of the city. In a cycle of two or three days, she would loiter outside places Kieran frequented (according to Sheena's notes), then find a chair in the waiting area of a hospital casualty department for an hour or two, then walk through areas of town the young couple might hang out. In recent weeks, she had added new locations to her search sequence, places that might draw Zoe's interest – the beach, the art gallery, movie theatres on George Street. But Celia could only guess. She couldn't be sure what kinds of things would interest Zoe now.

When Celia was in her teens, she never expected her parents to understand what went on in her head. She considered herself to be swimming along a very different channel to them, even while occupying the same house. Both her mother and father had been born at the beginning of the century, and so much in the world had changed, leaving parents and children with few shared points of reference. Her parents were formal people, reserved, slightly bewildered by the modern world, operating from a framework so old-fashioned they didn't really comprehend that it was old-fashioned.

There was love in their family, without doubt, but no assumption of understanding or common ground. Her brother, five years older, had left home straight after school, taking a job with an oil company in Scotland, and it felt as if Celia was left living in a house with two people who spoke a different language. She mostly relied on the cheerful nodding and clumsy miming gestures used to convey goodwill to foreigners. There was no chance any nuances of experience could be communicated.

That was how it had seemed to Celia at the time, anyway. Now she accepted that she couldn't have known what was going on in her parents' minds, what they did and didn't understand about their child. Chances were they perceived far more than she'd imagined and the two of them were watching her as she floundered along, observing with clear eyes, calling out to her from the shore, even if she hadn't heard them. She would love the chance, now, to ask them how that time had seemed to them. But before she'd ever understood enough to form those questions, they were both dead – her mother from cancer, her father a heart attack.

There was affection and mutual devotion during the periods of sickness and grief, but never any suggestion that her parents would tell their daughter how it felt to be dying, how it felt to lose a spouse. She wished now that she'd asked them a hundred questions.

She wanted to ask Zoe a thousand questions. But she was willing to ask nothing, content not to utter a word – whatever Zoe wanted – as long as she could know she was alive.

At each post on her searching rounds, Celia would find an unobtrusive spot to sit, in the hope that Zoe might wander past. She was convinced she would be able to pick her daughter out in a crowd of people, instantly recognise some gesture, the shape of her shoulders, the way she carried her head. Her child was so known to her, embedded in the tissues of her body, that she would identify her from the tiniest glimpse.

In the nightly phone calls to Roza, Celia didn't mention her searching routine for fear it would sound deranged. And for her part, Roza tried not to sound too worried about Celia's mental state. Roza would often pass on messages from Joe – well, always the same message. 'Joe says to please tell him if there is anything he can do to help.'

Celia tried to avoid thinking about Joe. At first she had been angry with him – he'd been too busy bonking Sheena to notice Zoe being spirited away by the boy. Later, once her head had stopped spinning, Celia accepted that was nonsense. Joe and Sheena's sexual encounter had made no difference to the outcome. But it had left Celia feeling foolish. She must've been so thick not to have noticed Joe's attraction to the woman. And she felt slighted that in all these years he'd never made a pass at her. Celia always assumed he was so staunchly faithful to Heather that he would never consider straying. But he strayed with Sheena without too much persuasion. Celia's pride was wounded a little. But then she would feel ashamed for indulging a trivial vanity. Such petty thoughts were burned away by the intensity of worry about her daughter.

Now that her relationship with Joe had been severed so abruptly, Celia was forced to recognise how important he'd become to her. For years she'd relied on him as a friend, a kind of brother really, but he'd also occupied a husbandly place in her life – without the romantic components of a marriage. She missed talking to Joe. She missed him.

Apart from the early postcard (*Don't worry*), Zoe had made no attempt to contact her mother, no message to indicate she was alive, not even through an indirect channel that would preserve the secrecy of her whereabouts. Zoe's silence was meant to punish her mother. Well, Celia hoped that was the reason – it was better than the other possible reasons for silence. And even while she suffered the sting of knowing her daughter hated her, at least it felt like a kind of connection.

Sometimes, when Celia needed to conjure up her daughter's presence, she deliberately envisaged an argument – Zoe yelling at her, excoriating, accusing her mother of betrayal and suffocation and crazy behaviour. She imagined her own bleating declarations of good intentions and love. In the imaginary scene, whatever she said only made Zoe angrier and more scornful, but at least her daughter was thumpingly alive in her mind, and there was a small consolation in that. And of course there was a self-lacerating urge, a wish to punch at herself for mistakes made.

Before, Celia had never tried to imagine the future too much. There were still two more years of school. Zoe would probably have to go away for tertiary study, but that had seemed a long way off still. And anytime she had envisioned Zoe's future out in the world, it wasn't *this*.

The next time the pancake hostess appeared to fetch another family, she glanced at Celia and raised her eyebrows. *Can I help you?*

Celia smiled and shook her head. *No, you can't help me. Not unless you happen to know where my daughter is.*

She gave up on the Pancake Parlour and headed back out into the street.

A few days later, when Celia knocked on the door at Freya's house, she must have been looking wretched, because her sister-in-law said nothing after her initial 'Celia'. Freya drew her inside and sat her on the big squashy sofa in the sunroom, shooing her two little sons out of the room.

Celia had been out all night, wandering between locations on her list. Freya's family was just waking up, eating breakfast, preparing for the day. Freya pressed a mug of tea into Celia's hands, then conducted a murmured conversation with her husband in the kitchen. A little later, Celia heard him bundle the kids out the door to school and Freya on the phone to her office, arranging to take the day off work. Celia would normally have protested, not wanting to disrupt their life, but today she was too depleted to argue.

She dozed on the sofa for hours, on and off, with Freya offering food, magazines, bath, television, never pressuring Celia to explain herself. Around midday, Celia woke to see her sister-in-law sitting in an armchair nearby, her head angled down over the big folder of work papers on her lap. Freya kept her fair hair layered short, feathered around her face. She had the same creamy colouring as Marcus and Zoe.

In the first year after her husband was killed, the grief would hit Celia in waves, forceful and unpredictable. But at the same time, there was Zoe, this creature who needed things, practical things, and who brought an astonishing amount of joy. Extraordinary, the way two such strong feelings could exist inside a person's body at the same time.

During these strange recent months, Celia discovered that the sorrow of losing Marcus was still present in her body, like a sac of poison that had never been properly absorbed. It was now leaking out, permeating every cell. She was experiencing it freshly, recalling the exact flavour of the pain from all those years ago.

Celia had come to her sister-in-law's house today out of the need to be with someone who had known her husband, who had cared about the man as much as she did. She trusted Freya would understand that without needing to discuss it.

In fact, the two women had only one conversation of any significance during the day.

'She hasn't contacted you, has she?' Celia asked. She knew Zoe loved Freya.

'No.'

'If she rang and swore you to secrecy . . .'

'If she rang me, I would tell you,' said Freya firmly.

When Freya went out in the mid-afternoon to collect her kids from school, Celia put her shoes on and left before they came back.

From then on, her day/night cycle was permanently inverted. She would sleep in a motel room for a few hours in the middle of the day so she could stay out until the next morning. Night was when she needed to concentrate, because night-time was when bad things happened to people. Celia couldn't bear the idea of being sunk into mindless sleep at the exact moment Zoe was facing some monster. She needed to summon up images of what might be happening to Zoe and run through the scenes of danger in her head, to create a force field around her.

And through the night, she scanned the streams of people hopping on buses, eating hamburgers, meeting friends on street corners, and she would have to fight the impulse to roar at them. The earth's crust had split open and sucked her daughter down where she couldn't find her, while all these people were scurrying around on the surface as if nothing had changed.

FIFTEEN

It had been a heavy-duty night at La Parisienne. The cash register had been a bastard to sort out and the new waitress possessed the mathematical ability of a house brick. Sheena didn't make it back to the flat until six a.m.

She eased the bedroom door open to see Murray asleep on the mattress. A month ago he was kicked out of his share house and she'd let him move his stuff into her room for a while. He'd been there ever since.

Sheena was well aware she was a bad-tempered scrag, intolerant of other people's habits, bodily noises and the stupid thoughts she knew were buzzing through their heads. But the truth was, she hated being alone more than she hated the irritating proximity of other human beings. This was a pathetic way to be. She wished she could hack being on her own. It was one of the things she admired about Celia – running that farm single-handed, handling so many solitary hours during the day and then every night in her bed alone.

Anyway, Sheena had meandered into a live-in relationship with The Dickless Wonder again – a situation that turned out to be pretty ordinary. Exactly as she would have predicted it would be. Which made her angry with herself and even more pissed off with the world.

Murray had two part-time jobs when he moved in, but both of those evaporated. There was then a lot of yappety-yap about well-paid work coming up, dudes who would be calling, excellent opportunities on the horizon. But of course no dudes called and the horizon was unobscured by any opportunities. Sheena couldn't kid herself any more: she was supporting a guy whose only contribution to her life, other than his pretty average cock, was the bong water he spilled on the carpet of the flat for which she paid the rent.

Murray wasn't a *bad* guy. He could be funny sometimes and he wasn't nasty or violent or criminal (apart from dealing a small amount of weed). He put up with Sheena's sour moods – her snarky comments just slid off his Teflon-coated surface. That placid demeanour was another facet of his profound laziness. He wouldn't waste energy reacting to stuff she said to him, especially if there was a risk she would be less likely to buy the milk and cereal that sustained him. Opportunistic sloth was his gift, like a moss growing on other plants to suck up their nutrients.

Sheena lay on the mattress, too exhausted to strip off her work uniform, let alone have a shower. Murray, flaked out in the bed, flopped his sleepy arm heavily across her belly and then his fingers gradually woke up, snaking inside the top of her fishnets, like a parasitic organism burrowing its way into the host animal.

Sheena sighed, poised to slap his hand away, but then she changed her mind, yanked the wretched fishnets down her thighs and tossed them on the floor. Murray would be easier to handle all day if he scored a root. And she was in such a low mood, she wanted to feel someone touching her.

Moments later he was humping away on top of her. (His dick was the least lazy part of him.) With his neck pressed against Sheena's face, he smelled of dope and the coloured popcorn he liked to buy in jumbo packets. Lying under him now, she recalled a stupid conversation they'd had a few days before. She had been watching him as he sat in front of the TV with a big plastic bowl of the sugar-encrusted kiddie popcorn, selecting one colour at a time – the bright-red ones or the electric-blue ones – to pop into his gob.

'What's the colour thing in aid of?' she had asked. 'Why do you do that?'

'I don't want to mix the flavours up in my mouth,' explained Murray, The Genius.

'That's just artificial colouring, not actual flavour, you moron. What flavour do you reckon the red ones are?'

'Strawberry?' Murray shrugged. 'Some kind of fruit.'

'Fruit? Do you honestly believe a piece of fruit has been within two miles of that piece of crap?'

He didn't respond, just kept staring at the screen and chewing with his stupid mouth slightly open. He started to pick out the blue bits of candied popcorn.

She knew it was crazy to persist but she couldn't help it. 'What flavour can you detect in the blue ones you're eating now? *Blue* flavour? Try eating them blindfolded, you monumental tool. They all taste the fucking same. They taste of sugar.'

'How come you care so much about the way I eat popcorn?' he asked.

'I don't care. I don't care. I don't fucking care,' she had snarled and forced herself to walk away into the bedroom.

She didn't like the person she was with him. He might be a gormless slob but when she was with him, she became a carping witch.

Now, in bed, Murray was emitting the little gasping grunts he made when he was working for his orgasm. She fantasised they were the choking noises of him getting popcorn stuck in his throat.

In the past, there had always been some variety of Kieran crisis that would allow Sheena to extricate herself from a substandard situation. These were never phoney excuses – they were real messes that required a rescue mission by Sheena. But now she didn't even have the excuse of Kieran, seeing as she had cut dead all feeling for her brother.

After the sex, Murray flopped over to his side of the bed and was snuffling back to unconsciousness. Sheena should have done the same, but she was too scratchy and antsy to sleep. She jumped out of bed, pulled on jeans and a clean T-shirt, and headed out the door, intending to get her ears re-pierced. She'd taken out the hoops during her stint picking fruit, and the holes had closed over since the summer. Now, suddenly, today, she was seized by the need to get them re-pierced as soon as possible.

It was once she was out on the street that she realised it was still only six-thirty, too early for any piercing place to be open. Even the tattoo parlours shut for a few hours after four a.m.

There was a chemist shop on Surfers Paradise Boulevard that might open fairly soon. She'd seen a lady in there doing ear-piercing at a little set-up in the corner, wearing a white zip-up uniform to give the impression she was some kind of medical professional.

In fact she was just a lady who worked in a shop, selling tampons and tinea cream.

Sheena headed in the direction of that chemist, which meant walking past shopfronts. In the plate-glass windows, she caught her reflection at an unexpected angle that made her suddenly see herself. She was surprised how young she looked. Sheena had only just turned twenty-eight but she felt so much older than that.

She turned away from the shop windows and walked out to the Esplanade. She was just crossing to the grassy part when a young guy swung round the corner on a motorbike. Kieran. Riding without a helmet, which was the kind of stupid shit he would do. So Kieran had stumbled his way up to Queensland, which wasn't surprising. But a second later, the motorcyclist turned his head and he wasn't Kieran.

From the age of five, Sheena had been lumped with looking after her younger brothers as each baby came home from hospital to whichever house they were living in and whichever bloke her mother was shacked up with at the time. Even as a little kid, she knew her mother couldn't be relied on to take care of her own babies, not for every single moment babies needed looking after. Sheena didn't know when she acquired this awareness of her mother's inadequacies – it was just knowledge there in her head before conscious memory. So Sheena had to do it – look after her brothers – because she didn't want to be responsible for them starving to death or falling off the landing and cracking their baby skulls open. But she resented it fiercely. Those babies stank and shat and cried so fucking loudly it was like someone punching her constantly in the temple. Her mother's boyfriends were never much use, even when the bawling, shitting baby in question was the fruit of their particular loins. And the babies themselves never took into account who did the looking-after – they were just as likely to puke up on Sheena and then smile at some random loser who'd never done anything for them.

By the time Kieran, the fourth brother, was born, Sheena was nine years old and already an angry, dark girl with low expectations of the adults assembled around her and suspicions about the world beyond them. From the day Kieran came home from the hospital, he was different from the other brothers. He looked up at Sheena from the crib and they locked eyes. She loved him passionately, furiously.

He didn't sleep much. When he was so full of twitchy beans that he was driving everyone else in the house mental, Sheena would chuck him in the pram and wheel him around the neighbourhood. He'd be cheerful little fucker then, squealing and laughing and yabbering to every person, dog or rubbish bin they passed. His smile was one of the few things on earth that could spark joy in cranky little Sheena. She knew she wasn't being singled out for those smiles – Kieran loved everyone – but that didn't matter to her. It was her job to protect this brother. In return, she was able to tap into the positive energy source he had brought into their house.

Taking care of this brother as he grew up wasn't easy, once their hopeless family and the messed-up world were stirred in with Kieran's own dizzy personality. Especially once he started getting himself entangled with a poisonous type like Mick.

Over the last couple of years, there had been many times Sheena vowed to give up on Kieran and keep her distance from the family. Even so, whenever there was a crisis involving her youngest brother, she would go back.

But that last time would be the last time. She had driven him away from Sydney, with clean pillowcases wrapped round his bleeding, cut-up feet, while he slept on the back seat. Driving through the night and the next morning, she kept twisting round to look at his sleeping face, checking he was breathing, as she had when he was a toddler with bronchitis. On that trip out west, she had doubted she could bear it anymore – that is, the desperate business of hoping Kieran would stay alive.

She should have realised that whole trip was pointless. She couldn't drive him away from risky situations. She couldn't transport Kieran beyond his own capacity to get into trouble. And then when he ran off with that girl, he had pissed all over every attempt she'd ever made to help him. So, fuck him.

At times in the past five months, Sheena had had an urge to ring Celia or the old lady. She kept both their phone numbers on a piece of paper in the leather pouch she used for her jewellery. She could ring and ask if they'd heard anything, had seen Kieran, whatever. But she must resist that urge. She couldn't be drawn back into caring, or even wondering, what happened to him.

By now she had walked down close to the beach. There were only a few surfers and people walking their dogs. An overtanned old dude in Speedos, leathery skin puckered across his chest, jogged along the sand in front of her.

Sheena took a few steps closer to the water and angled her gaze away from the surf break, so no one was in her eye line. From the spot she was standing, with an unobstructed view of the ocean and the morning sky, you would have no idea Surfers Paradise was right behind you. You could kid yourself none of that shit existed.

Sheena kicked off her sneakers and slipped the money from her pocket into the toe of one shoe. Then she walked straight into the water, pausing to allow each breaking wave to bash against her jeans before wading further out. This was better than a shower. Once she was out deep enough, she dived under again and again. She flicked her head around underwater, rinsing the smell of Murray and

Tia Maria and other people's cigarettes out of her hair. She let the clean salt water flush out all the accumulated crap in her head and the sand scour away any last bits of filth.

When she stepped out of the water, she carried her shoes and walked barefoot back to the flat, her sodden jeans and T-shirt sticking to her and the fine crust of salt drying on her face.

Murray was still asleep, so she thumped the door jamb a couple of times. He sat up, squinting, confused to see Sheena's wet hair dripping on the carpet.

'I'm leaving,' she said.

'To go where?'

'Not sure. Maybe Sydney to start with.'

'Cool. If you lend me enough for the bus, I'll come with you.'

'No. No, you moron. I'm leaving you. I'm breaking up with you. That's the whole point of going to – well, that's part of why I'm going to Sydney.'

'To do what?'

'I don't know. But not this.'

*

In late July, Roza saw the headlights of the ute pass by her house just before dawn. By the time Roza had walked up the path to Celia's house, Celia had already put herself into bed.

She never explained why she had abandoned the search in the city, but from what Roza could see, her beloved friend was worn out beyond a person's ability to function in the world, and sleep-deprived to the point of delirium. It had been an act of foolishness for Celia to drive a vehicle all the way back to the district in such a state, and a piece of luck there had not been an accident.

Perhaps she planned to recuperate a while and then head back out on her searching. She didn't say and Roza didn't ask.

Joe rushed out to the property the moment Roza told him Celia was home. He brought bags and bags of food to stock Celia's fridge. He insisted his mother point out little jobs that needed doing around Celia's house so he had an excuse to linger for some hours, until she emerged from the bedroom.

'Hello, Joe,' she said as she padded out to the kitchen in socks. Wearing baggy track pants and a voluminous Aran sweater that had belonged to her husband, Celia's body barely seemed to be present inside the loose folds of fabric.

'Hi,' said Joe.

Roza watched him take a step forward, arms lifting slightly, ready to fold Celia in to him, but then, suddenly not sure his embrace would be welcome, he dropped his hands and slid them down the side of his suit pants. Maybe she was radiating a don't-touch-me signal that Joe detected. Maybe she seemed too fragile to engage with another person, even if it was just the engagement required to receive a comforting embrace. Or perhaps what Celia really wanted was for Joe to shred all those doubts and cautions so he could reach across and grab her firmly. Either way, he stood awkwardly in the middle of the kitchen and she remained in the doorway.

'Mum's filled me in on the latest,' he said. 'I'll let you know if I hear anything.'

Celia nodded. An anaemic smile.

'I hope you'll tell me if there's anything I can do,' said Joe.

Now she was back home, Celia stayed indoors, much of the time in bed. If anyone came to the door, she pretended to be asleep.

After a while, local friends understood she didn't want visitors, so they kept away and just rang Roza from time to time to check up.

Roza cooked food that might tempt Celia to eat, walking up every day to collect the used-up dish from the kitchen bench and put a fresh meal in the fridge. From what she could see, Celia wasn't eating a great amount – just enough to live.

SIXTEEN

Sheena hadn't spent time inside many men's toilets in her life, but she'd seen a few. Enough to reckon that the front bar of this pub, with its insipid green tiles, yellow linoleum floor and mirrors eaten away at the edges like leprosy, looked a lot like a gents'.

As she walked in, she regretted suggesting it as a meeting place. There were a couple of other hotels around Parramatta that had been revamped, done up like a Spanish hacienda or filled with fake Tudor shit. Maybe she should have picked one of those. She wouldn't want anyone thinking this kind of grotty old-blokes bar was her natural habitat. But the location of this pub was easy to explain, and anyway, people always thought whatever they wanted to think, no matter what she did.

She spotted Joe at one of the window tables. He'd probably got there dead-set early – he was that kind of guy. He stood as she walked over and they said 'Hi' simultaneously. There was an awkward little manoeuvre on approach, with Joe presumably unsure about the etiquette for greeting a younger woman he'd fucked once, a woman whose drug-addled brother had run off with his sort-of-niece and torn out the heart of the girl's mother. Sheena wasn't too sure about the etiquette from her end, either. So they both froze for a second until Joe lurched forward to give her a peck on the cheek.

'Thanks for meeting me,' he said. 'Let me get you a drink.'

'Sure. Ta. A middy.'

While Joe stood at the bar getting them both beers, Sheena had a chance to observe him for a moment. He was an attractive man, even though she'd never gone for older guys as a rule. She remembered what his body looked like under that suit. It was weird to dwell on her intimate knowledge of the body of a person she'd shagged, but a person she didn't know very well and certainly had no claim on.

After Sheena had broken up with The Dickless Wonder for the last time, she'd returned to Sydney and collected her mail that was supposed to have been forwarded. Most of the envelopes had little holes where snails had chewed the paper while the mail sat in the letterbox for too long. There was nothing from Kieran – not that she had any reason to expect he'd suddenly take up letter-writing. Or that he'd want to make contact with his bitch sister at all.

She had landed a factory job in Blacktown, filling shampoo bottles. It was as boring as batshit, but then again it was probably wise to take a break from dealing with the public. Sheena had always been good at reeling in work and earning her own money. This time she was determined not to repeat past patterns by also reeling in a boyfriend who would happily sponge off her earnings.

Then two days ago, she received word that some guy was trying to track her down, phoning various places she'd lived, leaving
messages. When she rang back the number, it turned out the guy
looking for her was Joe.

'How are you, Sheena?' he said, putting the beers on the table
between them.

'Okay. I was up the Gold Coast for a few months. Back here
now.'

Joe drew breath to ask Sheena a follow-up question. She didn't
want him to feel obliged to make chat and show some phoney
interest in her life, so she quickly said, 'How's Celia going?'

'Not good.'

That poor woman must be going mental. Joe had explained on
the phone that Zoe was still missing, with no calls, no messages,
nothing.

'Have you had any contact with Kieran?' Joe asked.

'No.'

'If he does contact you, I hope you'll —'

Sheena jumped in, 'Yeah, der – course I'd let Celia know straight
away.' She was offended he thought she was the kind of low-life
who didn't care enough about people to do the right thing.

'Yes, yes, I know you would,' said Joe. 'I was going to say, I hope
you'll let me know if I can help. If Kieran needs legal advice, call me.'

'Oh. Right.' Sheena could feel herself stuck in guarded mode
and her voice came out sharper than it should. 'Don't feel like you
owe me anything.'

'Your brother might need help. I'm able to offer some. That's all.'

'Okay. Thanks.' Sheena felt like an idiot. She'd forgotten about
Joe's nice-guy manners and she had slapped his kindness away
ungraciously. She should stop doing that.

There was an awkward silence, which Joe filled by saying something even more awkward. 'Heather – my wife – she and I have separated. I've moved out.'

'Oh.'

'It was a long time coming, really.'

'Fair enough. Still, I'm sorry if the thing with you and me – y'know . . .'

'Please don't worry. It wasn't your fault in any way. I would say the thing that galvanised my decision to let the marriage go was – well, part of it was listening to the mean-spirited way Heather spoke about Celia. She was *gloating* about her suffering, you know? Being judgemental and uncharitable about it. I couldn't stand hearing it. And I couldn't stand being married to someone who speaks like that about people.'

'Sure, I get you,' said Sheena. She took a punt that a sly comment might be allowed at this point. 'Roza would be stoked to know you share her opinion – about Heather being a hard-hearted witch.'

Joe laughed. 'Ooh yeah, Mum would love to hear me say that.'

They both smiled and it suddenly felt intimate between them, there in that grotty pub. It struck Sheena that he'd asked to meet because he wanted to pursue something with her. She was thrown off balance, trying to decipher her own feelings about this prospect. But before she had a chance to think, Joe changed gear, getting down to the real reason he was here.

'Anyway,' he said, 'I'm planning to stay in Sydney for a while. See if I can find any trace of Zoe. Any information is going make things easier – easier for Celia.'

She heard the way he said the name, concentrating all his energy and yearning into the word 'Celia', and it was instantly clear he had no interest in Sheena beyond a kind regard. She registered a flicker of disappointment in herself. Surprising. In some pathetic back pocket of her mind, she must have nursed a fantasy about being with someone like this man. But a second later any soppy disappointment was cauterised – Sheena knew how the world worked and her place in it.

Looking at Joe sitting in front of her now, Sheena was sure the guy was helplessly in love with Celia. He loved that woman without any expectation she would ever love him back. And he would do anything to save her from suffering. Someone in the world looking out for you – everyone wanted that.

'I wouldn't get your hopes up about finding Zoe,' Sheena said. 'Seems like she doesn't want to be found. But look, I can check out the palaces my brother crashes in.'

'Thanks, Sheena. I really appreciate it. I'm working out of an office in town for a while.' Joe passed her a card with a Sydney phone number on it. 'You can always leave a message for me here and I'll call you back.'

It took Sheena a few days, several annoying phone calls, two trains and one bus trip to track her mother down. When she found the place, she had to check the address on the piece of paper. No way her scrag of a mother could be living in this posh suburban pile with its ostentatious portico. It was in a cul-de-sac of equally grandiose, recently built houses, all the construction so new and fake, you could smell the concrete and glue and paint.

When Sheena's mother opened the front door, she appeared startled to see her eldest child and only daughter standing there. 'Oh . . . uh . . . oh,' she mumbled. The woman had never had a lot going on in the social-skills department.

'G'day, Dawn,' said Sheena. From the age of six, Sheena had called her mother by her first name. She'd never acted like a 'mum', so there was no way Sheena was going to offer up that word.

The two women didn't hug or kiss. Dawn had always been keen to paw and be pawed by whichever man she was with at the time, but she'd not been much of a cuddler of her children. And Sheena figured it would be hypocritical to introduce physical affection into the equation now.

'Can I come in?' Sheena asked.

Dawn laughed nervously and wiggled her head in a little display of *I've forgotten my manners*. 'Yeah, yeah, come inside. Just a shock to see you here. Come in.'

Sheena was surprised Dawn looked so pulled together. Her hair was bleached to a brittle frost but with no dark roots showing, and it was smoothly brushed. She was wearing make-up – even home alone in the daytime. Sure, the foundation was too thick, slapped on with a trowel, and someone should've told her to go easy on the clumpy coats of mascara and shiny pale lipstick. But still, she was making an effort.

Sheena followed her mother into the house. Dawn was wearing mauve velour pants that snugly packaged her bum, and a tight embroidered top that showed off the fact that she had a neat little waist. Sheena knew Dawn's figure was more or less identical to the body shape Sheena herself walked around in. It was upsetting to face the biological link to this person. She hated the idea there was shared genetic code ticking away in her body.

Inside, there was a lot of reproduction French-polished furniture, gilt-framed mirrors, stiffly upholstered chairs, velvet curtains with tassels. The kind of interior design that says, *Did you not know I'm a duchess?* Hanging over the main living room was a chandelier. A chande-fucking-lier.

Sheena would hate to live in a place like this but even so, it annoyed the shit out of her that Dawn had scored this house. How was it right that her mother had stumbled her way to a cosy deal after creating so much havoc and populating the world with her screwed-up children?

'Let's not sit in here. When I'm in here I always feel . . .' Dawn shrugged. She was never good at retrieving words, on account of marinating her brain in booze for too many years.

Sheena finished the thought for her. 'You always feel like you've got a stick up your bum.'

Dawn giggled at that. A woman of forty-six, mother of five, giggling like a brainless schoolgirl.

She led the way through the vast new kitchen and waved her hand at the fridge. 'Can I get you anything?'

How about a decent childhood? Sheena thought, but she didn't say it aloud.

'Nothing for me, thanks,' she said.

Dawn ushered Sheena into the casual living room at the rear of the house, where the decor suddenly morphed into modern and space-agey with a white leather sofa, chrome-and-glass tables, white shag rugs and huge sliding doors opening onto a patio and a lawn so newly laid you could still see the squares of turf.

'Fuck me dead, Dawn. You landed on your feet here.'

Dawn giggled. 'I know! Oh, but probably won't be here long. Sal says – oh, Sal's the guy I'm . . .'

'The latest guy you've found to make all your dreams come true?'

Dawn registered the sour note in Sheena's voice – the woman was dim, but not that dim – but she ignored it, to avoid getting more of a mouthful from her daughter. 'Sal's in the building trade. Once he gets the right price for this place, we'll be moving.'

Sheena nodded and scanned the property, as if doing her own quick real-estate valuation. Dawn was looking over at her through mascara-clumped eyelashes, wary. Sheena knew her mother was worried she was going to blame her for something or ask something of her. And it was true that Sheena's guts were clenched for a fight. She could envisage how the scene would go: her snarling abuse about Dawn's selfishness, while her mother spluttered out justifications, scrunching up her face tightly, as if that could stop Sheena's words going into her brain.

For the moment, Sheena controlled her tongue and asked, 'Do you know where Kieran is?'

'No clue. You'd be more likely to know than anyone else in this family.'

'And why would that be, do you reckon?' snapped Sheena.

'Yes, okay, Sheena. Oh . . . but there's something here I should . . .'

Dawn moved across the room to a buffet where there was a pile of loose papers and mail. She stumbled a little in her rainbow-stripe heeled slippers, maybe because the tiles were polished to a treacherous gloss. But then Sheena saw her mother reach out to steady herself on the edge of the buffet – the kind of fake casual manoeuvre people use to hide their pissed condition. It was eleven in the morning and the woman had already been into the Bacardi or whatever was her current drink of choice.

Then Sheena noticed the marks on her mother's upper arm – finger marks from being yanked around by a big builder's paw. And there was bruising across her cheek, which explained why Dawn was wearing so much foundation.

Traditionally, Sheena would have used the bruises as a cue to lay into Dawn about her stupid life management. But she felt too tired to crank up that speech, so tired she even felt a glimmer of pity for this floundering woman who happened to have given birth to her. Sheena decided to give herself and Dawn a break by not launching into that argument today.

Dawn waved a piece of notepaper with a cartoon kitten on the top. 'A cop rang here looking for you.'

'For me?'

'The police found your car. Out Dural way, where those five-acre places are. The guy said it'd been stripped.'

'Well, Kieran had my car. Did the cops say what happened?'

'No. They asked me a lot of questions about Kieran, but said they want to talk to him. He's in some trouble, I think.' Dawn did an apologetic wince, as if the duty to do something helpful about her son's fucked-up life was a minor task she had naughtily neglected.

In that moment, Sheena could easily have reached across to grab one of the glass-and-chrome side-tables and smash it over Dawn's head until her mother's blood spattered out all over the white tiles. But what would be the point.

Dawn held out the notepaper. 'There's the number of the cop, anyway. I suppose you should ring them. Oh, wait, let me just . . .' She scribbled something next to the cartoon kitten. 'And this is our number at this place. Oh, but, y'know . . . I don't know how long we're gonna be here.'

Sheena took the notepaper with her mother's temporary phone number, and the number of the policeman searching for her brother. That was the nearest the woman could come to maintaining connection with her offspring.

'Ta,' said Sheena, as she pushed the note into her pocket.

SEVENTEEN

Roza walked along a corridor of sunlight on her way up to Celia's house. The way the light fell between the trees around midday at this time of year, this section of the path was always a warm patch. She was carrying a paprika-chicken dish in a round earthenware pot covered with aluminium foil. It felt heavy and she looked down at the loose skin on her chickeny wrists. She did not enjoy being so woefully old.

Passing close by the cabin in the orchard, Roza heard a small clunk, followed by a louder clunk. She stopped still, to hush the crunching of her shoes on the winter-dry grass. She waited, listening for more odd sounds, but it was quiet except for the swish of the windbreak pines. 'The dementia is getting you now, old chicken,' she said to herself.

Then, as she reached the garden of Celia's house, Roza looked behind her and caught a flash of blue in the orchard, near the shack.

Either someone was down there or her mind had slipped off the rails. She put the earthenware pot down on the edge of the verandah and yelled towards the window.

'Celia! You should come! Someone is here, I think. By the cabin.'

Roza hurried back towards the orchard, calling out, 'Hello? Are you there, someone? Or are you an animal?'

If someone was there, they made no response.

Celia was squinting against the daylight as she walked down from the house. 'What's going on?'

Roza pointed to the cabin.

'Who's there?' Celia called out. 'Zoe? Is that you?'

Celia ventured close enough to push open the door of the shack. Roza could see how much she was hoping. Sometimes it was dangerous to hope so much.

The cabin was empty, and Celia let the door swing shut again. 'Both of us are imagining things that aren't there.'

Celia turned to walk away, but then a thumping noise from behind the shack made her spin round. 'Who's there?'

She picked up a lump of wood from the ground as a weapon. Roza wasn't sure a lump of wood would be much protection if there was a treacherous individual behind the shack. But Celia looked fierce as she held it out from her body, like a woman who would at least put up a fight. 'If someone is there, come out now!'

There was a rustle in the weeds around the footings of the building and then Kieran stepped into view.

Celia demanded, 'Is she with you? Is she with you? Is she with you?'

The boy shook his head. He was filthy, the sleeve of his blue sweatshirt torn open to reveal an ugly gash on his shoulder, but it was the face that shocked Roza. Two dozen or more small wounds sprayed across his neck and face, some of them scabbed over, others with the scabs torn off and freshly bleeding. Would a person do this to themselves? Would an animal shred a man's face like that?

'Is Zoe here?' he asked.

'Don't you bullshit me. Tell me where she is.'

'I don't know,' Kieran said feebly. 'I thought she'd come home. Is she here?'

'No, she's not. When did you last see her? Did she tell you she was coming home?'

He was shaking his head – saying no, but also trying to shake things clear inside his skull. 'I don't know where she is. That's why I came back here. Fuck. Fuck.'

Celia took a step closer to him, still holding the wood like a weapon. 'Listen to me, you piece of shit, you tell me right now where I can find her.'

Kieran scrunched up his face, afraid she would clobber him. 'I don't know. Really.' Blood was beading on his forehead and temples where the face-scrunching had torn open the little cuts.

'Where did you last see her?'

'Sydney. Well, near Sydney,' he said. 'But then we lost each other.'

'Give me a list of places I can look.'

Kieran was shaking his head. 'I already looked every place I could think. If I knew where she was I wouldn't be here.'

He whimpered, then rallied a little and fixed Celia with a desperate look. 'Wait. Wait. You're trying to trick me – asking me . . . She's really inside, isn't she. She's in there and you won't let me see her.'

He shouted up towards the house, 'Zoe! Zoe! It's me!'

But a moment later, he crumpled back to a pleading mode. 'I just wanna talk to her. Please. Let me talk to her. She's inside. She's asleep in bed, tucked up in bed in her old room, isn't she.'

'No.'

This time, he heard the misery soaking through Celia's voice and he understood she was telling the truth. 'Oh. She's not here.'

Celia didn't answer, so Roza said, 'No, she's not. The last time you saw Zoe, she was okay? She was in one piece?'

'Yes. Yes. But now I don't know. I'll wait for her. She'll come back home. I'll wait.'

Celia growled at the boy, 'You get off my property. I don't want you anywhere near this place.'

Kieran was agitated, his limbs overtaken by the fidgety movements Roza had noted the first day he appeared in the packing yard. 'You hate me,' he said to Celia. 'I get that. Fair enough. But I can't go. I have to see her.'

'If you don't get off my property right now, I'll ring the police.'

'That might make trouble with the cops for Zoe,' Kieran countered. 'I know you don't want that.'

Celia stabbed the hunk of wood in the air towards the young man and Roza thought she might really hit him this time. 'Bugger off, you little shit. I don't want to look at you. Get away from here!'

Kieran moved backwards, towards the road. 'Okay. I'll stay off your property. But I can't go away. She'll come back here. I'm sorry to be a shit. But I'll do whatever I have to do to see her. You can't make me go away.'

Celia roared at him and he turned, running through the orchard, over the fence and off the property.

Once Kieran was out of her line of sight, Celia dropped the lump of wood. 'I should go to Sydney. Find her.'

'Where? The boy can't give you any useful information,' Roza pointed out. 'You saw how he was. And what if he's right? What if Zoe comes back here?'

'He seems so sure she's coming home.'

'He does.'

Later in the afternoon, when the sun was almost gone and the cold was seeping through the ground, Roza walked from her cottage along the public roadway to where the boy was waiting. From the spot he'd chosen, he would see any person driving through Celia's farm gate and could see the very edge of the garden around the house.

'Are you planning to stay out here all night?' Roza asked. 'This is a stupid thing. There is a bed for you in my house and hot food too.'

'Thank you,' he said, 'but no thanks.'

For the next two nights and days, Kieran waited in his spot on the roadside near Celia's front gate. There was some rain during this time, enough to soak the boy's clothes through to the skin. And in the mornings, there was frost over the ground that must have bitten through to his bones. But he did not budge himself.

Celia patrolled the orchard and the driveway to make sure the boy stayed off the place. She yelled 'Piss off!' like someone snarling at a stray dog. Kieran did not budge himself. He was afraid that if he moved from his watching spot, he would miss Zoe coming home. Roza could also see that the bitter conditions, his poor battered face, Celia's vicious shouting – the young man thought he deserved such punishment.

Late on the third day, Roza walked up to find Celia in the yard of the packing shed.

'I think you need to talk to the boy,' said Roza. 'Two nights he's been out there.'

Celia shrugged. 'If I could get the police to drag him away, I would.'

'But all he wants —'

'If he can't help me find her, he's no use to me,' snapped Celia and walked inside the shed.

Some people might consider Roza was being an interfering mad old lady when she walked down the driveway and signalled to Kieran, beckoning him towards her. But it was Roza's opinion that sometimes mad old ladies should interfere.

A few moments later, when Celia emerged from the shed, the young man was standing right in front of her. Taken by surprise, Celia stopped, silent. Kieran, too, was speechless, unsure he had any right to request anything from this woman. Roza had to gesture to him – *Speak*.

'I was wondering if . . . Has Zoe called you? You don't have to tell me if she's called. I mean, that's your right.'

'She hasn't called.'

'I tried to get her to ring you heaps of times. I should've tried harder. I should've made her do it. I'm really sorry.'

'Are you?' Celia's stared at him, harsh.

'Yes. Yes. I'm so sorry. I messed everything up. I know that.'

She watched him, her body rigid, determined to feel nothing for this boy.

Kieran was shaking, from hunger or injury or distress – probably from all of these. He rubbed both his hands over his face, as if he could clear his mind that way. 'I don't mean to, but I make dumb, dumb, dumb mistakes and . . . everything gets stuffed up.'

The roughness of his hands was tearing off the scabs.

'Don't do that,' said Celia, firmly. 'You're making yourself bleed.'

Kieran didn't seem to notice and kept rubbing his hand back and forth across his ravaged skin. 'I want you to know . . . please know I'm sorry . . . I'm really sorry.'

'Hey. Look what you're doing.' Celia took a step towards him and grabbed one of his wrists to pull it away from his face. 'Don't do that to yourself.'

Kieran looked down at his hands, the palms bloody from the reopened cuts.

'What happened to your face?' she asked him.

'Oh . . . uh . . . I fell.'

'Your shoulder should have had stitches.'

Kieran swayed a little, groggy on his feet.

'Sit down a minute. Don't fall over.' Celia kept her tone hard and unyielding, as if her main concern was not wanting him to bleed inconveniently on her property.

Roza ducked into the shed and by the time she came back out, Kieran had managed to stumble across a few steps to sit on a pile of wooden pallets.

Roza held out the first-aid box she'd fetched from inside. 'My old-lady hands are too shaky for this job.'

Celia flashed a dirty look at Roza but then she took the first-aid kit and propped it open on the pallets. Steadfastly avoiding eye contact with Kieran, she began to methodically clean up the wounds on his face and shoulder.

'Keep still,' she said and the boy obeyed. She soaked cotton wool in antiseptic to dab on the broken skin. 'This will sting.'

'No worries. Thanks. Already hurts anyway. Thanks.'

Maybe Celia enjoyed inflicting the little stabs of pain on him, but she was also doing a careful job of cleaning the cuts and taping gauze over the worst ones. Roza was of the belief that it was possible for a person to sustain two strong and apparently conflicting impulses at the same time – a desire, for example, to slice this young man into small agonised pieces and an inclination to care for the injured creature in front of her.

'When you last saw Zoe, how was she?' Celia asked him.

'I want you to know, things were great. I mean, to begin with, things were great. Me and Zoe looked after each other. And I was trying to fix things. But then everything got messed around. We ended up getting separated.'

Celia stepped away from Kieran in order to throw the used cotton wool in an empty box but also, Roza suspected, in order to move away from this boy she was tempted to smash.

Kieran was full of tears now, too distressed to speak clearly. 'You've gotta believe I would never do anything to hurt Zoe. I thought we could look after each other. Please believe me. I'm sorry. I'm sorry.'

When Celia turned round, she was startled to see the boy had slid himself off the pallets and onto the ground right at her feet. He grabbed onto her legs, like a small child in the supermarket mistaking a stranger's legs for their mother's. But this wasn't a confused toddler. This was the young man who had stolen away her daughter.

Kieran wept, big sobs tearing out from his belly. Celia stood there, paralysed. Eventually, she lifted her hand and Roza wondered if she was going to punch him in the head. But, in fact, she just touched his hair. The boy cried for a long time, and Celia realised she couldn't ask him any more questions in this state.

Finally, she extricated herself from Kieran and walked away, speaking to Roza in a voice as dry and flat as she could manage. 'I suppose he can sleep in the cabin tonight.'

'Yes,' said Roza. 'Yes. I'll bring blankets and food from my house. Don't you worry about it, Celia.'

EIGHTEEN

In the morning, Celia stirred several teaspoons of sugar into a thermos of milky tea, knowing that Kieran liked to drink things sweet. She put the thermos in a string bag, along with a cheese sandwich, an apple, a clean shirt and a warm sweater.

Walking down through the orchard, she was surprised to see the cabin door wide open. Maybe he had scarpered during the night. Celia wasn't sure whether she would be relieved or disappointed to find Kieran gone. His appearance on the property was maddening, but he was also, in his frustrating, hopeless way, the only connection she had to her daughter.

Closer, she could see he was still inside the cabin, asleep on one of the lower bunks. He must have wedged the door open to get rid of the fusty smell inside, left to go mouldy during that damp winter with no one around to air the place out.

Celia stood outside for a moment and watched the sleeping

young man tucked inside a nest of blankets and eiderdowns Roza had brought him. The small cuts on his face were scabbed over again and the deeper ones had only bled through the gauze a little. The wounds looked okay, not infected. Apart from the injuries, Kieran's face looked different, possibly transforming into his adult face, or maybe just temporarily showing the strain of recent ordeals.

When he eventually woke and saw Celia watching him through the doorway, he jerked his body upright as far as he could in the limited space of the bunk. 'Oh . . . Sorry, sorry.'

Was he sorry for waking up, or for not waking up sooner? Maybe he was stung with remorse simply for being in Celia's field of vision, apologising for his very existence. And so he should, the little shit.

'I brought you some food, clothes,' she said, and slid the string bag through the door of the cabin without stepping inside.

'Thanks. Sorry. Far out, you don't need to do anything for me. Sorry you have to put up with – fuck – sorry . . . Thanks. Thank you.'

To stop him blathering out thanks and apologies, Celia nodded briskly and left.

At the house, she made phone calls – the police, hospitals, the private investigator she was still paying too much money – but without mentioning Kieran. Several times, she lifted the phone to ring the cops back and dob him in, have the bastard arrested. Each time, as she listened to the dial tone, a flare of anger burned along her sternum. But each time, she hesitated, then dropped the receiver back in the cradle. She didn't want to cause trouble for Zoe.

Later in the morning, Celia headed back to the cabin with a new plan. She would stay calm, quiz Kieran further, extract whatever useful information she could and then demand he leave. His injuries were healing, he had been fed and then slept the night in a warm bed, so it would not be too callous to ask him to move on now.

When Celia reached the yard and looked out into the orchard, she couldn't miss the vivid shape of Roza in her red jumper and gaudy mirrored skirt. Roza was strolling between the rows of peach trees, supervising Kieran, putting him to work clearing the ground around the trunks.

'Something is better than nothing, don't you think?' Roza called out to Celia, flapping her hands at the straggly trees, choked with weeds.

Kieran kept his head down, intent on the task, as if dealing with an emergency. He was throwing his body at the work, so vigorous and relentless he must surely have been hurting his injured shoulder.

Celia spent an hour in the shed working on the tractor, to coax the thing into running again after its long hibernation. She enjoyed the methodical sequence of chores – changing the oil, cleaning the spark plugs and carburettor – and when the engine rumbled into life, there was an unexpectedly intense level of satisfaction.

She drove the tractor along the track between the fruit trees, pushing the jumble of slashed grass, weeds and brittle branches down the slope, into a huge pile outside the orchard. As she chugged through, Kieran avoided eye contact with her. Maybe he could sense the fantasy that was dancing across Celia's mind as she passed him: it would just take a swing of the steering wheel to slam Kieran against the trunk of a tree with the tractor blade, squelching him. She allowed herself to relish that image – satisfying in a dumb, childish way. And then, as she repeated the brutal images in her mind, there was a purgative effect, draining away some of her anger towards the boy, like drawing pus from an abscess.

At midday, Roza spread a rug on top of the stack of pallets in the yard and laid out lunch, including small chicken pies she'd baked. Celia had not had an appetite for months. She'd taken enough sustenance to keep herself functioning, but any food had been flavourless, like a mouthful of nothing or sometimes, worse, like a mouthful of sandy nothing that she had to chew in her dry mouth and force her throat to swallow. But the smell of those pies, still warm from the oven, made her feel a twinge of hunger.

'Thank you, Roza. They look delicious,' Celia said, and sat on the edge of the pallets to eat. 'This is very kind.'

'It's always a good idea to eat,' said Roza, then signalled to Kieran to come and get himself some of the food.

He walked up to the yard from the orchard and ventured close enough to take one of the pies, and then, with a nod of thanks, retreated a few steps. He reminded Celia of her old kelpie-collie cross who would snatch meat scraps out of his food bowl and take them away to eat in a corner.

Celia reckoned the boy wasn't afraid of *her* exactly. If he was submissive, careful not to get in her face too much, it was out of fear she would send him away. He still hoped Zoe would show up here and didn't want to risk missing her.

Roza was muttering to herself in Hungarian and then, indicating that she'd forgotten something, she headed down towards her own house, leaving Celia and Kieran alone in the yard.

The boy was uneasy, sitting close to her, without Roza or work or any other distractions in between. He stayed very still, tackling the pie with small apologetic bites.

Eventually, Celia broke the silence. 'When you and Zoe first left here, where did you go?'

Kieran jerked, surprised she was addressing him.

'I know you didn't go straight to Sydney,' Celia added.

'Okay, look, the thing is, when me and Zoe left, we stayed away from trouble. I want you to know that. No trouble.'

Celia set her face hard. She didn't want to listen to snivelling or excuses from Kieran. She just wanted to hear what had happened to her daughter. 'You needed to find work, I suppose.'

'To start with, we had some money for food and petrol and stuff,' he explained. 'I mean, money Zoe brought with her.'

Celia already knew that. On her dressing table, Zoe had kept a moneybox – a little china cottage with a pixie perched on the roof in a jaunty pose – which held the cash she was saving for a car. The pixie was face down now, with the black rubber plug on the under-side of the cottage removed when Zoe had hooked out the cash.

'And Zoe was dead-set to chew up some miles, y'know . . .'

'A road trip.'

'Exactly, yeah. And she wanted to do half the driving. I said no way, because she doesn't have a licence. I mean, I know she drives the vehicles on this farm but that's not the same as driving on the highway. I went, "What if we get pulled over by the cops?" And she went, "If the cops pull us over, me not having a licence is the least of our worries." But I said, "How about you just drive on the side roads, not the main ones." And she went along with that until she worked out – sorry, you won't like this part . . .'

Why would the boy imagine she 'liked' any part of this story?

'Me and Zoe tell each other everything, okay, so I had to tell her I didn't have a licence either. I mean, I used to have one. Got cancelled. Speeding fines.' He flinched as he looked over at Celia. 'I thought Zoe would crack the shits, but she laughed. I mean, she whacked me around the head a bit but she was laughing when she did it. She reckoned, "My mum would go berserk if she knew that."'

Celia wasn't delighted to know that her daughter had been driven around the country by an unlicensed speeding idiot. But much more than that, she was stung by the image of those two sharing laughter about her.

Kieran started to yabber with a trace of his old enthusiastic energy. 'But yeah, anyway, then we went after the picking work. Zoe knew the places we should try. Like, she worked out the circuit we could go on. No matter where we went, Zoe could suss people out really quick. She's excellent at dealing with people, isn't she. She's so fucking smart.'

Talking about Zoe made the boy happy and he smiled at Celia.

Celia didn't smile back.

'So, you found picking work?' she asked.

'Yeah, heaps. Enough for what we needed.'

'And, what, you two stayed in pubs or bunkhouses on the properties?'

'No, she didn't want to do that.'

No, thought Celia, because Zoe would have known her mother could more easily find them if they stayed on the farms.

'We bought camping stuff from a disposal store,' Kieran explained.

He seemed proud of their self-reliant purchases. And he grinned as he went on to describe their routine. At the end of each work day, he and Zoe would buy food and then drive around until they found a pretty spot by a creek or a river to set up camp. That way, they could wash their clothes in the creek and wash the sweat off themselves. They'd make a fire to cook on or just because it was lovely to have a fire. The evening light lasted long enough for them to eat a meal and stay up a while, with the car windows wound down so they could hear music from the radio. It was warm enough, at least in the early weeks, for the two of them to sleep outside in their swags. Zoe had brought a small alarm clock to wake them up early enough to have a swim before another day of picking.

'You could've kept going like that,' said Celia.

'Yeah, yeah, we could've. But Zoe said we should go to Sydney. I went, "Why? This is good. Let's keep doing this for a bit longer." But she really wanted to go to Sydney and I wanted her to be happy, so you know . . . Oh, but I'm not making excuses. I should've known it was a bad idea.'

'Why a bad idea?'

Kieran kept talking as if he hadn't heard that. 'Sydney can be a top place. We stayed with mates of mine and that was, most of the time, that was – I mean, to start with, things were good. I tried to make everything good for Zoe. I want you to know that.'

Celia said nothing and waited until Kieran felt obliged to fill the silence.

'Zoe started getting really down sometimes. Not all the time. But some days. I should've worked out what to do so she'd never ever have to feel so – but oh, man . . . she could get dark. "Everything is stuffed. I'm a bad person. Everyone dies, so what's the point. I deserve to die because I'm a bad person." I'd go, "Come on, Zoe, don't be so down, baby. We're the lucky ones." I've seen people be slack or straight-out cruel to the exact people they're sup-posed to be looking after. I knew what me and Zoe had was good, because I've seen the other ways it can be. And most of the time I could goof around, make her laugh, or we'd have some fun and she'd cheer up. But some days, far out, she'd sink into a hole so deep you couldn't even yell down to her.'

Celia could hear Kieran's voice rasp as the tears came. But she said nothing.

She had seen Zoe sink into the occasional sad funk, but she hadn't thought her daughter had the capacity for such black moods. Now Celia found herself replaying scenes from the last year, wondering if Zoe had been struggling, wretched, but keeping it to herself.

Marcus, Zoe's father, had generally been a buoyant man, but sometimes he'd tumbled down into a gloomy state, sluggish, hopeless. He wouldn't discuss it with anyone – even with Celia only a little – and he would keep going, doing whatever he was obliged to do, but only by pushing himself. Celia would determinedly interrogate everything that had happened, everything she'd said, anything that could explain his misery. If you could understand the cause of something, you could fix it or at least avoid being vulnerable to it in the future. But Marcus always assured her there was no use searching for a reason – at least, not a reason commensurate with the level of his melancholy. 'Wait it out,' he would say. But Celia would always continue to fret and question and analyse, until her husband's regular upbeat, energetic self came back to her.

'I didn't know what to do for Zoe,' said Kieran. 'And I thought if we could drive up north, where it's warm, Zoe could get . . . we'd get back to the way it was. Put ourselves back into a proper rhythm. A person's gotta have some sunlight on their body. And Zoe was up for it. So we could make things good again. But we needed money – for petrol and maybe a better car than Sheena's bomb, if we were going to drive right up to north Queensland. I was so desperate to get Zoe somewhere better, I didn't think straight. My mate Mick always knows how to get money together fast. So, I asked him. I thought it'd be okay. But Mick, he's not a good person.'

Kieran was crying, contorting his face so much, some of the cuts reopened and blood was beading on his forehead again.

'What happened?' asked Celia.

'Mick knew where some guy kept big rolls of cash in his house. Massive house, on this five-acre place near Dural. Mick reckoned the owners were away, so it'd be snack easy. I never wanted Zoe to be there. "No way are you coming," I said. But she said, "I want to make sure things don't get out of hand." She didn't trust me not to be a dickhead when I was around Mick.'

'So, she went with you and Mick to the place?'

'Yeah. I mean, I knew that was probably a mistake. It was a mistake.'

The boy hesitated for a moment but Celia gestured – *Keep going.*

'Okay, so we drove out to the house in Sheena's car,' he went on. 'No one home – Mick was right about that part. But he didn't know they had guard dogs. Big black vicious rottweilers, two of them. They were barking like crazy and giving Mick the shits. And then Zoe got upset because Mick hurt the dogs. She got so upset, she took the car and pissed off. Which was good. Because Mick was going spare, especially when it turned out there was no money. He started smashing stuff up. Pushed my face into the broken glass on the floor and then there was so much blood in my eyes I couldn't see properly. I just ran out the door, up to the main road. Anyway, I was glad Zoe was safely out of that place.'

'The last you saw of her she was okay?'

'She got bitten on the hand by one of the dogs. Mostly she was shaken up. About Mick hurting the dogs. And she was mad with me. But she was okay, yeah. Then later on, I couldn't find her. I figured she'd driven home. That's why I came here. She'll come home. That's why I'm here.'

NINETEEN

Zoe floated just below the surface, trying to push upwards to be fully awake, but at the same time she was so very tired, limbs aching, head heavy with fatigue, it was easier to sink back down into sleep again. She was in her own room at home – no need to open her eyes to know the position of the bed under the window and the location of every object on the white-painted desk, the posters on the blue walls, treasures on the windowsill.

She rolled onto her side and became aware of dampness on the mattress. The smell, a sharp ammonia smell, disturbed her enough to register she must've wet herself, and then to recall she wasn't in her own bed.

The bare mattress was on a linoleum floor, alongside milk crates full of empty bottles and old newspapers. She wasn't clear-headed enough to remember where this room was, but she definitely wasn't home. And she knew she was alone and ill – febrile, shivering, heart tapping out a rapid, tinny beat. She should get up off the mattress, wash herself, but she was too feeble to stand up.

She wanted to be home. She could never face going home. She wanted Kieran to walk through the door. She wanted the door to be bolted shut so she could hide from everyone. She wanted her mother to appear and nurse her back to health. She wanted to die in this place, unseen, so she would never have to be seen by anyone and it would all be over.

Sinking back down into the fever-sleep, she found more noxious dreams waiting there for her.

One night, months ago, not long after she and Kieran had first arrived in Sydney, Zoe had woken up, shaken by a dream.

Kieran had scooped her in against him. 'You okay, baby? Having a nightmare? Tell me about it. That's the trick. That way you can get the nightmare out of your head and gone.'

Zoe murmured 'No' but Kieran held her tight, urged her to tell him. So she described the dream, in which she'd been walking through some kind of car park.

'The other people wandering around the car park – I knew they were dead . . . the way you can just know stuff in a dream?'

'Yeah, I get you.'

'I recognised faces,' Zoe explained. 'The lady who used to run the kiosk at the pool, this kid from primary school who died. My father was there too.'

Zoe had often looked at photos of Marcus – dead before she was born – but she never imagined her father as a dead person.

'Maybe it's a beautiful thing,' Kieran suggested, 'you seeing your dad like that.'

Zoe could tell Kieran didn't get it. Nothing about the dream was beautiful.

'There were others,' she said. 'People who aren't dead yet – only, in the dream they were. Everyone's internal organs were turning liquid, like soup. Then I saw you and me sprawled out.'

Zoe didn't give Kieran any detail, didn't tell him that she'd seen their bodies rotting in front of her like a sped-up movie, like time-lapse photography on a nature program. The two of them decomposing, liquefying, until there was nothing except a greasy slick staining the concrete.

Kieran ran his hands up and down Zoe's warm flesh. 'We're not dead. Look at us.'

'But we will die. That's the truth of it.'

'We won't die.'

'One day.'

'But not now,' Kieran said. 'Here we are.'

He wrapped his arms around her, as if he would hold her in life with him that way. 'Don't have dreams like that. Wake me up next time. I'll stop that horrible stuff filling up your head.' He peppered Zoe's forehead with a dozen kisses.

She had stopped sharing her bad dreams and her bad thoughts with Kieran. He didn't understand and it would just upset him if she pushed to make him understand. There were occasions when she would be feeling low and Kieran would be so bouncy, so perky, it annoyed the shit out of her. She'd snap at him and then a second later feel lousy about letting her misery infect his beautiful spirit. Then she would be even more disgusted by herself.

She was a repulsive and stupid person, so stupid she was dangerous. It would be just as well if she decomposed into a gelatinous pile that could seep into this mattress and disappear.

'Zoe.'

Someone was saying her name repeatedly, nudging her shoulder.

Zoe opened her eyes to see Sheena crouching beside her.

'What have you taken?' Sheena asked.

'Nothing.'

That was true. For weeks now, Zoe had steered clear of any substances, even booze.

When they were on the picking circuit, camping out, Kieran and Zoe had got pissed a few times on port. Zoe tried smoking joints but because she'd never been a cigarette smoker, she just coughed and that was a waste of good weed.

In Sydney, Kieran had been anxious about the drugs floating around, wanting her to be cautious, but Zoe had a list, a list of things to try. To begin with, she had enjoyed the way speed fizzed through her veins and the warm, cushiony, boneless torpor from the downers. Her one go at a hallucinogen was too frightening to repeat – she was afraid the distortion might never wear off, as if mechanisms inside her could twist permanently out of shape.

She wasn't like Kieran. He could get wasted but he always bounced back. For Zoe the come-down was too harsh, her disposition too unsteady, her capacity for darkness unknowable. The risk was there that she might never come back from one of those black moods.

She couldn't explain this to Kieran, so she just tried to laugh about it with him. 'I want to be a wild girl but I'm no good at it!'

Kieran said he didn't care, that she was his spectacular girl no matter what.

But then Zoe felt guilty. Wouldn't he prefer to get wasted with his friends, rather than sit around nursing the hangovers or managing the freak-outs of his piss-weak girlfriend?

'No way. I'd rather be with you anytime, anywhere. We don't need anything else.'

Kieran was right – when the two of them were together and it was good, they hadn't needed anyone else. But now everything was messed up. Suddenly Zoe was swamped by that sensation that she had unbuckled inside and might never be able to reassemble herself into one coherent piece.

'Cold!'

The shock of the cold water was like a blow to the head. Sheena had stripped off Zoe's fever-sweated clothes and put her under the shower.

*

Sheena hadn't planned to shove Zoe under a dead-cold shower, but the electricity had been cut off to this house, so, cold it was. She couldn't deny there was a scrap of satisfaction in subjecting the stupid girl to a blast of icy water.

As she'd promised Joe, Sheena had gone looking for Kieran. She asked around, quizzing the losers her brother called his friends, but those guys had no useful information to offer. No one had seen Kieran or his pretty blonde girlfriend for a couple of weeks, to the extent that those morons could be expected to have an accurate sense of the passage of time.

Sheena checked out various places Kieran had lived, hoping to track him down. As a last resort she tried this huge old Darlinghurst terrace – Kieran and her second-youngest brother had lived here for a while way back when their mother was shacked up with a truck driver who wanted to live near the depot. Sheena knew that Kieran and Mick had sometimes squatted in the house when they needed to stay off the radar.

The place was empty now, any squatters turfed out, because the house was due to be gutted and then transformed into one of the dolled-up renovated terraces appearing along this street.

Sheena had almost walked away without bothering to look inside, but then she spotted a side window wedged open, and she climbed in. Pushing open the door to each room, she felt queasy with the fear she was about to confront the sight of her brother's dead body.

In an upstairs bedroom, tucked behind crates of rubbish, she saw Zoe. There was a sting of disappointment to find her and not Kieran. Then again, it was a fucking relief she was alive. Sheena wouldn't want to be lumbered with the responsibility that her brother had contributed to the silly girl's death.

Slicing through the musty fug in the room was the stink of piss. The kid had wet herself. Sheena's first thought was that Zoe was off her face on something, but when she knelt down, she saw the girl shivering violently and her forehead was hot to touch, like a child with tonsillitis that no one had been taking care of. Sheena then saw the reason for the infection burning through the girl – dog bites on her right hand, infected so the skin was red and swollen shiny-tight, with pus oozing from the puncture wounds.

She needed to strip off Zoe's scungy clothes, haul her into the bathroom along the corridor and bring her temperature down quickly.

There were a couple of batik sarongs tacked up as curtaining in the front bedroom of the terrace. The fabric was dusty but cleaner than anything else to hand, so Sheena ripped the sarongs down and used one as a towel to dry Zoe off after the shower. The girl stood naked on the tiles, shivering with cold as much as the fever. Limp, compliant, she allowed Sheena to turn her, lift her arms, rub the sarong over her legs and buttocks and breasts, too ill or wretched to care, beyond any modesty. Sheena bound Zoe's long hair in the damp sarong, then twisted it up on top of her head.

Sheena took off her own shirt – she was wearing a T-shirt underneath – and eased Zoe's arms into the shirtsleeves, careful not to touch her poor infected hand. She tied the other dry sarong around Zoe's lower half.

She had sluiced the bite wounds a little bit cleaner in the water but they were still lurid red and weeping pus. She had nothing hygienic enough to bandage them and figured it was best to leave them to air-dry until she could get proper medical treatment.

'Is Kieran here?' Sheena asked.

Zoe shook her head.

'Do you know where he is?'

Zoe shook her head again, then she murmured, 'I don't understand.'

'I was looking for Kieran. Found you.'

'I don't understand why you're helping me. You hate me. You think I'm some . . .'

'I think you're a selfish little bitch who doesn't have any clue how lucky she is.'

Sheena sat Zoe on top of the toilet seat and unwrapped the sarong on her head. She used her own brush to smooth the knots out of the girl's long, wet hair. That was when she copped a proper look at Zoe's neck – the mottled plum-coloured marks staining the milky skin of her throat.

Sheena hated asking, but she had to ask, 'Did Kieran do that?'

'Mick.'

'Is Mick hanging around here too?'

'No.'

'And your hand – those are dog bites?'

'Yes. Dogs.'

Zoe refused to go to the police or a hospital. When Sheena pushed the idea, the girl started to cry, gulping for breath between sobs and pleading.

'Okay. Okay. Settle down,' Sheena relented. 'But we have to get your hand fixed up. Stay there a sec. Don't fucking move.'

She ran downstairs to the kitchen and fetched an old teacup, then found Zoe's sneakers lying on the lino floor of the small bedroom. She filled the teacup with water and handed it to Zoe, who was still sitting on the toilet seat, obedient, or maybe just too feeble to move.

'Keep taking little sips. Don't guzzle it or you might chuck up,' Sheena instructed.

She eased Zoe's bare feet into the sneakers and tied up the laces. It was awkward, tying up the shoelaces on another person, and she was hit by the memory of putting on Kieran's school shoes when he was a little boy.

Fucking Kieran. If he hadn't pinched her car, Sheena would have had transport to cart his stupid girlfriend to medical attention. As it was, the best she could do was drape her own padded nylon jacket around the girl's shoulders and steer her down the stairs.

There was no way Zoe had the strength to climb out the side window, so Sheena forced open the boarded-up front door – the wood on the doorframe was so termite-chewed and crumbly that the nails gave way easily with two sharp kicks. Sheena let herself relish the satisfying burst of violence it required.

She was hoping to hail a cab on the street but, typical of her shit luck, there were no cabs in sight. As they walked along the footpath, Sheena held Zoe upright and steady, with an arm round her waist, making sure not to brush against her injured hand. People were staring at the two of them – the scrawny woman with bottle-black hair, just wearing jeans and a T-shirt despite the cold day, supporting the teenage girl in a grubby sarong, with wet hair dripping down the back of a nylon jacket, a string of neck bruises and lurid puncture wounds on one hand. Let those fuckers stare and think whatever they liked. Sheena didn't care.

Luckily, the medical practice Sheena remembered was still on this street, two blocks down. And luckily, it wasn't the kind of GP surgery with responsible, cosy family doctors who might ask questions. This was the kind of walk-in-off-the-street clinic where the dozy quacks didn't remember one patient from the next and would write a prescription for valium or pethidine without even looking up from the prescription pad to eyeball the loser they were giving the drugs to.

Sheena spoke to the woman at the front desk and then parked Zoe on a chair in the waiting area. There were several individuals already sitting there – unsanitary types who looked as if they had germy spores flaking off their skin and were exhaling bacteria through their mouths into the shared air and straight into the open wounds of a teenage girl who shouldn't be in such a shithole in the first place. Sheena realised she was instinctively leaning forward and sideways, as if she could use her body to shield the sick girl from being infected by these people.

When it was Zoe's turn, Sheena steered her into the consulting room, trying to devise a plausible story for the doctor. She need not have bothered. The GP was an old dude, obviously over the job, and possibly without a complete set of marbles rolling around in his head. The doc didn't care why this teenager had choke marks round her neck and untreated dog bites. He squinted at Zoe's hand as if he were half-blind, then he yanked her arm closer, making the kid gasp with the pain of his clumsy fingers on her poor swollen hand.

'They're dog bites,' Sheena said sharply. 'Need to be flushed out and disinfected, yeah?'

'Yes – uh – yes, that would be . . .'

'How about I do that part myself later.' Sheena didn't want this incompetent codger hurting Zoe any more than was necessary. 'But I need you to write us a prescription for whichever antibiotic you give a person who's been bitten by a dog.'

The guy eventually scrawled what was needed on a script pad and then the practice nurse – very pleased with herself in her white zip-up uniform – took Zoe into a side cubicle to do the dressings on her hand. Just as well. Sheena had bandaged plenty of cuts and burns and injuries over the years, but better if the job was done by a qualified person who knew what they were doing.

TWENTY

Zoe was strapped down, tied to the bed. But twisting sideways, she realised there weren't any ties – it was just the sheets tucked neatly around her. Crisp, white, citrus-scented sheets on a huge bed. She lifted her head enough to see she was in a posh hotel room, with wood panelling, caramel fabric on the armchair and curtains, glossy brown ceramic table lamps, framed botanical prints.

She had no idea how long she'd been sleeping, but she felt stronger for it. She was bundled up in a soft towelling bathrobe and her hand was bandaged, still aching but not burning up like before. It was a relief to be somewhere quiet and clean. It was a relief not to have to answer any questions or make any decisions.

When they first came to Sydney, Kieran had tried to make it good for her, as if he was the one who had persuaded her to dive into the city. In fact, it had been Zoe's idea. Kieran had wanted to stay away from his old mates, keep travelling, doing the picking work.

They started out couch-surfing at houses where his friends lived – a couple of crumbly old terraces close to the city, but mostly places in the suburbs out west. Their car – well, Sheena's car, really – felt more like their home, their own little piece of the world, than any house they stayed in. The bomby car had been handling all those road miles fairly well, especially once Kieran found a guy to replace the barrel on the ignition so they didn't need to wire-start it every time.

As Kieran drove them from one house to another, Zoe gave up trying to keep the map of those endlessly spreading distant suburbs clear in her head.

The place they finally ended up was a shabby fibro house in Toongabbie, with half a dozen cars parked across the front lawn and the back yard choked with waist-high summer weeds that died off in the winter and flattened into a dry, grey carpet around the Hills hoist. At some point in the past, many of the paintable surfaces had been slathered with thick coats of matte black paint – kitchen cupboards, bathroom tiles, bedroom wallpaper, doors and window frames. The black was now scratched and in some places scraped off, revealing the pastel kitchen cupboards, swirly laminex benchtop and mint-green tiling underneath.

Zoe never understood who owned the house or which people officially lived in it. But there was always at least one person sprawled on the nubbly beige nylon sofa, watching the TV set resting on a milk crate. Anytime day or night, an occupant of the house would squawk at whoever was playing music too loud on the cassette player in the kitchen.

From the start, she was curious about Kieran's mates as well as the small number of girlfriends who drifted in and out of that house. She wanted to know their stories, to inhale every detail of their experiences, to discover how it would feel on her skin to enter their magnetic field. Trouble was, she didn't dare ask questions of anyone in case she revealed herself as naive and stupid. But if she kept quiet, no one noticed she was younger, a soft creature with no streetwise gristle to her; or if they noticed, they didn't care.

She had to acknowledge that she had been harbouring fantasies of being sucked into a darkly glamorous bohemian underworld, as if she might walk into a 1930s Berlin bordello or be ushered through a secret entrance to an intoxicating New York nightclub. She had always relied too much on novels to picture the world. This fibro house, these guys with their flannel shirts and home-made bongs, their girlfriends with overplucked eyebrows and cheesecloth tops, vomiting into the laundry sink – these people were not the occupants of the dangerous but seductive demimonde Zoe had been carrying in her silly head.

She did hear stories about a chick they all knew who had died of a heroin overdose last Christmas. There was something shivery-thrilling about that. And she did overhear talk about drug deals and warehouse robberies, but Kieran was adamant – as adamant as a person like him could be – that they should steer way, way, way clear of that kind of trouble.

Even so, even if the life here was far from what she'd imagined, it still felt authentic and unfiltered and exciting compared to the anodyne city she'd been allowed to know on trips to Sydney with her mother to visit her aunt Freya.

For months – from the day after they ran off together from the farm until the day they were separated – Kieran had pestered Zoe to ring her mother. She wouldn't need to say where she was. She could just leave a message with Roza. But apart from that one postcard at the start, Zoe never did make contact and she forbade Kieran to do it either.

At the beginning, she hung onto an urge to punish, to scream in her mother's face about the price to be paid for manipulation and mistrust. Silence was her most powerful weapon for doing that. Later, Zoe became wary, almost superstitious, about making contact. Even in Sydney, she constantly felt her mother's gaze on her, heard Celia's voice judging everything. Zoe struggled to drown it out with the loudness of this new life, and that worked sometimes. But if there was to be any chance of properly hushing the voice in her head, she couldn't contact Celia. Not yet.

Zoe had been finding it harder and harder to pull herself out of black moods, which was another reason she couldn't risk speaking to her mother. Celia would know – she would be able to detect in any word Zoe uttered – that things were bad.

And then the longer the silence went on, the heavier the shameful load became, the sheer weight of the not-ringing. She should've just left some simple phone message early on and then she could be clear of it. She hadn't thought about it coherently, and now it was too late.

But then there were times Zoe was busting to know what Celia would make of the characters her daughter was hanging out with now. She pictured the conversations the two of them would have together – speculating about people, laughing, gossiping, fretting over possible outcomes – and she could enjoy that imaginary scene.

More than anything, and more urgently, Zoe wished she could hear her mother's take on Mick.

Kieran's other mates were fun to hang out with, sometimes at least. It was true some of them were guys who *used* other people. Zoe was proud that Kieran always operated from a nice-guy impulse, but then she hated seeing friends take advantage of him, always bludging lifts from him, cadging money from his cash fund – the remains of Zoe's moneybox plus their savings from picking fruit. She would get cranky on Kieran's behalf, protective, urging him not to let his supposed mates exploit him.

He would laugh, flap his hands. 'Don't worry about it. Gaz'll pay me back. And you and me'll be sweet no matter what.'

But Mick was different from the other friends.

Zoe first met him in a Granville pub, and the air had shifted the moment he stepped into the back bar. She was thankful it was a room full of bodies and noise that could soak up some of the force of this man. His dark buzz cut had a rat's tail at the back, his face bloodlessly pale like a nocturnal creature. Mick was older than Kieran – some people said twenty, other people reckoned twenty-five – but his heavy eyebrows and the smudgy discoloration around his eyes, like permanent grey eyeshadow, made him look way older. He wasn't especially beefed up but you could tell from the hard lines of his forearms and his sinewy neck that he had the physical power to do whatever came into his mind. He scanned the bar as he walked in, passing his reptilian eyes over every breathing person in the place.

Kieran jumped to his feet the minute he saw Mick and threw one arm up in the air to grab his attention, like a fanatical soldier eager to receive his orders. Zoe had never seen him react like this to anyone else. Kieran then grabbed her elbow and steered her – well, almost pushed her – across the floor to present her to Mick.

As Kieran approached, Mick yelled out, 'Where you been lurking, dickwad?'

'Ha. Yeah, well, sorry. I was out in the bush for a while.'

'Yup, I heard,' Mick said, with a dismissive flick of the head. He was the kind of guy who liked to know things already.

Kieran grinned and did a little hopping dance, a dog eager to win favour. 'So, anyway, Mick, been busting for you to meet my girlfriend. Zoe.'

Mick puckered his mouth and pushed her name through his lips with an exaggerated drawl. 'Zoe.'

'Hi,' she said, but very little voice came out.

Mick scanned her body, down to her thighs and then up again to her face. 'I heard about you. You're the one who's got my mate Kieran pussy-whipped.'

Kieran laughed a bit too loud. 'Steady on. Zoe's incredible.'

'If you say so, mate. I better keep an eye on this little skank, but.'

Kieran pulled Zoe closer to him, with that same nervous laugh. 'He's just teasing, being a dickhead.'

Mick leaned forward, putting his mouth right up close to Zoe's face. 'I am. A dickhead. Who's just teasing ya.'

Kieran relaxed a bit after the introductions had been made. Beers were bought, stories were told, bullshit was spun and, blessedly, Mick seemed to lose interest in her.

After that first meeting in the pub, Mick started turning up at the Toongabbie house. Zoe worked out early on that he liked to be regarded as unpredictable – no one was ever sure when he would show up, where he was living, how he sourced his money, which girl he might bring with him to fuck in whichever bedroom he commandeered for the night.

At first Zoe was intimidated by the girls Mick brought round, assuming they must be tough and cluey if they could handle a man like him. But it turned out they were mostly stupid-drunk or wasted or super-young, even younger than she was.

Everyone reckoned Mick was the man to talk to if you wanted drugs or a cheap TV set or a gun, not that Zoe ever saw a gun at the house. Rumours about him buzzed through all the houses and pubs – mutterings about big-time criminal connections and different versions of a story about him breaking a guy's neck with the roof rack Mick had ripped off the bloke's own car.

'You don't want to believe half that shit,' Kieran said. 'People like telling stories about him.'

But even Kieran agreed when people said Mick overdid the speed.

'Yeah look, he's a wound-up customer even when he's straight, so doing so much crank isn't the best idea,' Kieran acknowledged.

Mick ignored Zoe anytime he appeared at the house to hang out with Kieran, and that suited her. But unexpectedly – for no reason that Zoe could decipher – she would find him watching her. He might be lying on the carpet, sleeping off a big night, but then, with no sound, he would open his lizard eyes and aim them at her.

'You don't wanna pay attention to the shit he goes on with,' Kieran said. 'He's all noise.'

The two guys had been friends since they were kids, and Mick had helped Kieran out of shitty situations more than once. There hadn't been many people Kieran could count on back then, especially in the time before he found Zoe. So Kieran owed Mick his loyalty and wanted to be a staunch friend – she got that. But even so, how could he make excuses when he saw Mick bash one of their mates or treat his girlfriends like garbage? Nothing she said seemed to shake the spell Mick had over him, and that scared her.

Whenever it was Zoe and Kieran alone together, everything was better. They could retreat to their small bedroom and Kieran would wedge a chair under the door handle to ensure no out-of-it dickhead could come barging in looking for a soft corner to crash.

And after they had sex in the narrow bed against the black-painted wall, Zoe could handle anything, even Mick.

There was a time – just a few weeks ago – when Zoe hadn't been able to sleep for several nights in a row. She would leave Kieran in bed while she wandered the house until morning. So the next evening, she tried swallowing a few gulps of Bundy, hoping it would help her drift into sleep once she flaked out in bed. It didn't help, and the inside of her skull was even more glutinous by the time Mick showed up at the Toongabbie house.

One of the girls said Mick had sourced some PCP. Zoe didn't know if that was true but it didn't matter. Mick was cranked up, lying on the floor, stretching his hands over his face and staring incessantly at Zoe through the gaps in his fingers, terrifying her. For once, thankfully, Kieran could see it for himself. He grabbed her hand and led her into their room.

As Kieran wedged the chair under the door, Zoe stood there, swaying, dizzy. The floor was rolling under her feet, folding in on itself like boiling water.

'The ground keeps moving,' she murmured.

Kieran took her hands and eased her down to sit on the floor. 'It's not moving. It's solid, see?' He grabbed a jumper off the bed to drape around her shoulders in case she was cold. 'You need to sleep. Awake too many days at a stretch. It does your head in. And yeah, look, Mick's being a spaz tonight. I know that. I don't know what's wrong with him. I mean, you're right, baby – he's a worry, that guy.'

Zoe couldn't handle talking about Mick right now. If she could just sleep, she might be able to think clearly.

Then Kieran said, 'I should've never brought you to Sydney.'

'What? Don't make it sound like I'm a little girl you led astray.'

'No, no, I never said that.'

Zoe flared at him, 'I wanted to come here, didn't I?'

'You did.'

'So, what are you saying?'

'I'm saying this place isn't right for us. We should've kept it just you and me. We never had fights before we came here.'

That was true. Not a single argument when they were on the road, but now there were more and more fights that could fly out of control until there was crying and shouting. They argued about Kieran letting people scrounge off him. They argued about Mick. They argued about Zoe's unfathomable moods. Kieran complained that she didn't confide in him anymore, which made him feel paranoid and distant from her. Usually, any bad temper between them would crumble quickly – they'd end up having a weepy, passionate fuck and it would be good again.

This night – maybe it was the ugly vibe Mick had brought into the house with him – the tension was spun up higher than usual. Zoe hated hearing the shrill edge in her own voice but she couldn't stop.

'Don't make it sound like I'm some silly girl who can't handle the big nasty world.'

'Zoe, I'm not doing that. Why are you saying this stuff?'

'That's what you think, isn't it? You reckon I'm some hopeless —'

'No.'

'You think I've wrecked everything. You're saying —'

'No! What do you want me to say? Fuck, Zoe. Fuck.'

Kieran's spark of anger, the way he slammed the words at her, landed like a slap across the face.

'You hate me,' she said.

'Don't talk shit. I don't hate you.'

'Yeah. You hate me.'

'I don't know what you want me to do.' His anger was gone as quickly as it had flared, and now his voice was thick with tears. 'Should I take you back home?'

'I knew it. You want to get rid of me. You wish you'd never laid eyes on me.'

Kieran grabbed her face in his hands. 'No, no. The day I laid eyes on you was the most perfect day – the day I realised something could be so good.'

And suddenly, like an unexpected rescue, Zoe was able to grab hold of how much she loved him. 'I'm sorry,' she said. She kissed him gently, again and again.

'You're not sorry you ever came with me?' Kieran asked.

She would never be sorry. She had to make him understand that. 'No, no, no. I wouldn't want to miss out on anything.'

'I dragged you down.'

'Don't say that. You didn't.'

That was the night they decided to leave the house, just the two of them, plan a trip north, somewhere warm, and make things good again.

Now, lying on the clean white hotel sheets, Zoe had no clue if Kieran was even still alive. She started to cry, which made her bruised throat hurt even more.

A moment later, the door into the hotel bedroom eased open.

'You're awake,' said Sheena, who must have heard the crying. She walked over to Zoe and refilled a glass on the bedside table from a bottle of Lucozade. 'You look terrible. Keep drinking this stuff.'

'Have you called my mother?' Zoe asked.

'Well, I phoned Joe. He booked this room so you could have a sleep.'

'Do you know where Kieran is?'

'No.'

'Would you tell me if you knew?'

'Look, I have zero idea. All I know is the cops found my car.'

Zoe nodded. She felt Sheena's eyes on her.

'They mentioned what police officers like to call "serious matters",' said Sheena. 'But they wouldn't say more than that.'

Zoe hauled herself up onto the pillows and took a sip of Lucozade. The syrupy yellow stuff was soothing, even if swallowing was painful.

'I know you blame me,' said Zoe. 'And you're right. It's because of me everything got messed up.'

'Don't flatter yourself, sweetheart. My brother would've got himself into major shit without any inspiration from you.'

'It's my fault we even went to the Dural house. Kieran only came up with the plan to travel north because he was worried about me.'

Money would be no problem when they got themselves up the coast – there'd be picking work to earn what they needed. But Kieran reckoned they needed an escape fund to start them off and extra money to buy a more reliable car.

'He said Mick would know a way we could get some quick cash.'

Sheena groaned, 'Jesus fucking Christ.'

The three of them had driven in Sheena's car beyond the edge of the proper suburbs, into an area where the few remaining market gardens were giving way to five-acre blocks with sprawling, show-offy houses. Mick directed them up the driveway of a property with elaborate but still raw landscaping and an enormous new house built to look like a French chateau.

'When the guard dogs started barking, Mick went ballistic. Kieran kept saying to me, "Don't worry. He's just a bit amped up. It'll be okay." Mick was smashing the glass panels around the

246

front door with a sledgehammer, but the whole time, the dogs kept barking. To shut them up, he started hitting them with the sledge-hammer. I tried to pull the dogs away so they wouldn't get hurt.'

'That's how you got bitten.'

Zoe nodded. 'I couldn't help them anyway.'

Shaken by the bites, Zoe had retreated into the garden and Kieran rushed over to her. That was when Mick clobbered the rottweilers until they went down, then continued swinging the sledgehammer until their heads were pulpy masses of fur and brain and fragments of bone spread across the sandstone porch. One of the dogs was convulsing, the hind legs twitching with its few last spasms. Zoe reached down to hold the leg, with some ridicu-lous impulse to soothe the poor animal. Too angry to cry, she kept screaming at Kieran, 'Look what he's done!'

Mick went inside the house, yelling for Kieran to follow him.

'Let's go, Kieran! Let's just go!' Zoe hissed.

Kieran was jittery, in shock about Mick killing the dogs. 'Let me just think. Let me just think a sec.'

'What? Think about what? We have to go!'

He held the car keys out to her. 'You go. You take the car. That's safer. And your poor hand – you should go.'

Mick was calling 'Kieran! Kieran!' in drawn-out yowling sounds, yelling the name over and over. Kieran scrunched up his face, trying to shut out that howling voice, trying to think clearly.

'Look, I reckon I should stay. Better make sure Mick doesn't do anything else. I mean, someone has to – I just need to think . . .'

'Fuck you, Kieran. Are you crazy? Are you an idiot?'

'Shut up a sec. Shut up and let me think!'

'No. I'm the idiot. For coming here. For believing the shit you say. For ever being with a moron like you.'

Zoe snatched the keys from Kieran's hand and hurried to the car. She thought he might follow her but he didn't. She would take care of herself.

She drove back down the driveway and turned onto the road that would eventually take her to the highway. But she'd only travelled a short distance when the car conked out. She clung to the steering wheel and gave in to fit of sobbing – about the dogs, the horrible things she'd said to Kieran, the whole mess she should never have allowed to happen. She was a terrible person to leave Kieran stranded with Mick.

She tried to start the engine one more time but it just gave up a guttural scraping noise. She jumped out of the vehicle and ran back along the road to the big house, but by the time she reached the big house, Kieran had disappeared.

TWENTY-ONE

S heena selected a face cloth from the absurd array of lush white towels in the hotel bathroom. How many towels did people need? How many showers were the rich wankers who stayed in these places having per day?

She wet the cloth and used it to wipe and cool Zoe's face. Talking about that night at the Dural house, the girl had whipped herself up into a weeping, trembling state, and she needed to settle down.

Sheena left Zoe to rest and returned to the lounge room, thinking she'd kill time flipping through the fashion mags fanned out on the coffee table. She wanted to fix her eyes on the glossy pictures and fill her head with that rubbish rather than dwell on the repugnant scene the girl had described, rather than imagine Kieran being out there somewhere with a monster like Mick.

Earlier that afternoon, while the nurse was tending to the girl's dressings, Sheena had taken the opportunity to use the red payphone in the waiting room and ring the office number Joe had given her. She heard the hitch in his breathing when she told him Zoe was found.

'How is she? Is she all right?'

'Not pregnant, not addicted to heroin, alive,' Sheena had replied and then given him a quick report on Zoe's physical state.

Even over the phone line, she could hear Joe immediately quarantine his feelings and gather himself to take on the Mr Responsible role. 'Okay, I'll ring Celia. Sort out a few things and then come to you. Where are you now?'

'Darlinghurst. Listen, the kid's temperature is still high and she's pretty shredded. She needs to have a lie-down.'

'Yes. Yes, of course. If I book a hotel near where you are, can you take her there in a cab?'

'Sure.'

The hotel was tucked next to Rushcutters Bay, a protected curve of the harbour filled with chinking sounds from the rigging of rich blokes' yachts. Approaching the sleek reception desk, Sheena and Zoe must have looked a ropy pair – a teenage girl so feverish she appeared drunk, with a bandaged hand, dressed in a grubby sarong and a cheap jacket, accompanied by an older female who was clearly not a creature who belonged in this luxurious habitat. Sheena had tensed up, ready to be hassled by the reception staff. But it turned out Joe had phoned ahead and paid with his Bankcard, so check-in was a smooth process, lubricated with smiling, as all transactions must be for the folks who stayed in such hotels without even thinking about it.

The unctuous young man behind the desk handed Sheena the room key and offered to have someone help with their luggage.

'No luggage,' Sheena responded, with a defiant look. She didn't want these people to think she was impressed or intimidated or pretending to be someone she wasn't.

It was the plushest room Sheena had ever been inside – well, not even a room, it was a fucking *suite*, done up in chocolatey and creamy decor with a few discreet golden touches. While Zoe slept in the gigantic bedroom, Sheena could ponce around in the whole other room – a lounge with sofas, teak coffee tables and slim side-tables that didn't seem to have any purpose other than supporting the bronzed lamps sitting on them. Along one wall was a long timber unit with a desk, a minibar, a TV set and whatever else a travelling Important Guy might need. Broad windows looked out over the city, but so high up and insulated that there was no sound from the traffic below – it was like being wrapped in foam casing.

Joe was kidding himself if he thought he could miraculously make everything right by booking a suite in this fancy-pants hotel. As if that could undo all the shit that had happened. But then Sheena checked herself for being a cynical bitch. Joe had probably just booked the one hotel he knew was nearby. And oddly, this did feel like the right place to be now – a quiet, orderly waiting room between the world Zoe had been inhabiting and what would pre-sumably be her return journey home.

Sheena had been babysitting Zoe in the suite for a couple of hours when there was a gentle knock and then Joe's voice through the door. 'It's just me.'

As soon as Sheena opened the door, he kissed her on the cheek. 'Thank you, Sheena. Thanks for taking care of her.'

She shrugged, 'I just found her,' and indicated the door to the bedroom.

Zoe was awake, and when she saw Joe, she sat up in the bed, anxious about what to expect from him. He smiled broadly, but at the same instant Sheena heard him breathe in sharply to see the girl so ill.

Joe embraced Zoe, but carefully, handling a fragile thing. She let her weight fall against him, her forehead flopped against his chest, as if she could sink into the safety of this man. He rested his cheek against the top of Zoe's head and struggled not to cry. It struck Sheena that there was something compelling – something that could undo her – about watching a guy trying not to cry.

Eventually Joe said, 'I left a message for your mother on her answering machine. I imagine she'll phone as soon as she gets the message. She'll be desperate to talk to you.'

Zoe answered in a frayed whisper, 'I don't think I can talk to her.'

Joe took a step back, puffed out a breath and looked at Zoe.

'I tried to ring her,' she said. 'Couldn't ever do it.'

Sheena was surprised to hear the hard edge from Joe. 'It was cruel, Zoe.'

Zoe opened her mouth to respond but nothing came out.

'It was cruel,' he said again.

'I'm sorry.'

'It's going to be difficult for me to forgive you. If you weren't so sick right now, I'd shake you hard. I'd shake the teeth right out of your stupid head.'

The girl crumpled into tears and he softened immediately, holding her tightly again as she wept. 'It's okay, sweetheart. I'm so happy to see you. It's okay.'

He had a way of saying *It's okay* that made every fucking thing on earth feel okay – at least inside this soundproofed executive hotel suite.

*

Joe and Sheena went back into the lounge room, leaving Zoe to sleep. He was restless – possibly unsettled to be here with Sheena, but most likely he was just anxious for Celia to call.

'Have you eaten?' he asked. 'I could order some room-service food or something.'

Sheena shook her head. She should go now. There was no need for her to hang around now Joe was here to take care of things.

'Look, one thing I was thinking,' she said, 'Zoe needs some clean clothes to put on. It might freak Celia out a bit less when she sees her.'

'Oh yes . . . that's a good idea. I wouldn't know what —'

'I could go and buy her some stuff.'

'Thank you. Would you? Thanks.'

Sheena had to walk a long way from the hotel towards the centre of town to find a street with clothing shops. Even though she was physically tired, the lengthy walk turned out to be a relief, an opportunity just to be a person walking along the footpath, a respite from the business of thinking about Kieran and the girl and any of that. It was a chance to breathe, like stepping out of the hospital room of a dying person for a brief stroll.

Once she found the right kind of shop, Sheena made a pretty good guess at the sizes, but it was still weird buying clothes for another person. With a wad of Joe's twenty-dollar notes, Sheena bought Zoe a bra and undies, a nightie, jeans and a cotton top with loose sleeves that would be easy to put on over the bandages. She found a warm sweater in the shade of blue she'd noticed Zoe liked to wear, which had a loose polo neck to cover the bruising without being tight enough to hurt.

Anyone who saw Sheena walking along with shopping bags hanging off her arms would assume she'd been on a jolly shopping expedition. The regular people she passed on the footpath had no notion of the drama going on in the hotel room one suburb away. They were just going about their normal lives.

Sheena's normal life – such as it was – would resume soon, and she would have to squeeze herself back into some kind of realistic accommodation of the shitty way the world worked. She would like to know if Kieran was okay. She would like to know. But whatever. The cops would find him eventually, maybe dead, and the news would filter through to their mother and finally to Sheena.

Sheena suddenly realised people in the street were staring at her – something about the expression on her face must have looked stricken or anguished, and folks didn't want to be dealing with that when they were strolling past clothing boutiques. She scowled back at one bloke for no particular reason – just to get a fucking grip on herself – and then headed back to Rushcutters Bay.

When Sheena let herself back into the hotel room, Joe was sitting at the desk, talking to his sons on the phone. He signalled hello to Sheena as she draped the clothes on the arm of the sofa and put the leftover cash on the coffee table. Joe mouthed, *Thank you.*

Sheena moved across to the window and stared down at the yachts in the bay, as if she'd suddenly developed a fanatical interest in boating. She didn't want Joe to think she was eavesdropping on his phone call, the last part of which was a terse exchange with his estranged wife. Sheena could hear the distinctive truncated sentences, his resolute attempts to be civil, his final sigh of capitulation.

When Joe put down the receiver, he took a moment to shake off the chill of the call and then turned to smile at Sheena. 'Thanks for getting the clothes. I really appreciate it. Zoe's sleeping again, which is good, I think.'

'Yep. Listen, she's got to keep on the antibiotics. She could easily get blood poisoning from the bites.'

'Right. Yes. Thanks.'

'I'll get out of your way now.'

'Stay, please. Celia just rang from a service station on the highway. On her way here.'

'Right. Did Zoe talk to her?'

'No, she was asleep.'

'Ah. But hey, I'm sure it's going to be sweet – well, maybe not sweet but not too shithouse in the end. Anyway, I'll leave you to it. No one needs me to hang around for the big family reunion, so I'll head off.'

'You really should stay, Sheena. Celia has Kieran in the car with her.'

'What?'

'Apparently he showed up at the farm. I had no idea.'

Sheena felt her chest, her belly, her throat, clench tight. So the little fuckwit was alive. 'What's the story?'

'Celia didn't say. She was keen to get back on the road.'

Sheena had a good crack at being acerbic. Hard-boiled. 'Maybe she's got my brother trussed up in the tray of her truck. Hopefully sticking pins into the stupid bastard every few miles.'

A second later, she took a huge involuntary intake of breath, as if she'd been underwater a long time, and then the tears came. Joe grabbed the shiny tissue-box holder off the desk and pushed it across the coffee table towards her.

'Ta,' said Sheena. It was the second time the guy had handed her tissues, but this time she made sure to keep her distance, leaving the sofa between them as a barrier. Another weepy consolation fuck would not be a helpful complication to throw into the mix.

Instead of having sex, the two of them sat on opposite plush brown sofas and gave the minibar a good walloping. They talked, both of them exhausted, about Zoe and Kieran and the last months, and it was gentle, like a brief lull in battle.

'I've known Zoe since she was a baby,' said Joe. 'I loved her before I had kids of my own. There's a chance, even now, that I love that child more than my own kids. Is that terrible?'

Sheena shrugged. 'Your mother always said that was so. You're in agreement with Roza yet again.'

They laughed and selected two more tiny bottles from the minibar.

The day was fading into evening by the time Celia knocked on the hotel-room door. Sheena was shocked when she first laid eyes on her. So much thinner, skin dulled and papery, the light leached out of her eyes. She was breathless from rushing up from the car park, from rushing hundreds of miles to get here. She nodded a quick acknowledgement to Sheena but then looked to Joe.

'Don't panic when you see her,' Joe said. 'She's sick, but she's all right.'

Zoe, having heard the voices outside, was already out of bed, standing barefoot on the bedroom carpet, wearing the hotel bath-robe. Celia threw herself forward like a person running downhill and wrapped her arms around her daughter, chanting her love for the girl and how wonderful it was to find her safe. Celia's face was lit up – Sheena had never seen a human being's face transform so utterly in a moment.

Celia and Zoe clung to each other for a long time, both of them crying, sometimes laughing, shaking their heads in disbelief. Every now and then, Celia would lean back at a slight angle so she could take a proper look at the girl, soaking up the sight of her, then she would fold her daughter close again.

TWENTY-TWO

Celia had attempted to prepare herself to see Zoe, silently rehearsing during the drive to Sydney, assembling and reworking the lines to say, the things she must be careful not to say.

But the electric charge of seeing her, the physical blast of it, pushed words out of the way. She thought her legs would give way under her. She wasn't sure her body was strong enough to handle that much feeling going through it without disintegrating.

Then, as she held her daughter, Celia felt strength flood back, as if all the cells and blood and fibres in her body could now settle and restore her power. There was also – of course – anger in there, self-reproach, accusation, those bitter notes, but not for now. Those things might be churning away, but right now, all were overtaken completely by joy.

Celia never wanted to break that embrace, but she could feel Zoe was exhausted and would need to lie down. There would be time later for the two of them to talk, to sit with Zoe's head in her lap and talk. And at this stage, there was something else Celia needed to do.

'Kieran's here,' she said, checking to see Zoe's response.

'What?' Zoe was thrown, but she was smiling, bright-eyed.

Kieran had suggested he wait in the corridor, anxious not to impose himself or cause any more damage.

'Come in here!' Celia called out.

He rushed into the hotel suite and straight through to where Zoe was waiting for him. Celia could see he was awkward – desperate to sweep Zoe up but trying not to be boisterous with the sick girl.

The two of them kissed and wept, tumbling out apologies and explanations – how each had searched for the other across the city, how they must have just missed each other at every place they looked – talking over each other, neither making much sense.

Celia stepped away, into the lounge room, to give Kieran and Zoe time alone. She exchanged a quick smile with Joe, who was over by the desk speaking quietly on the phone.

Sheena was perched on the back of one of the sofas, observing the weepy reunion going on in the other room.

'Thank you, Sheena,' Celia said. 'For finding her, taking care of her.'

Sheena twisted her mouth and shrugged, uncomfortable, as if any kind word was a slap in her face. But bugger that – Celia wanted this woman to receive the thanks and feel at least some of the warmth she offered.

'I mean it, Sheena. Thank you so much.'

This time Sheena looked directly at her and nodded. 'You're welcome.'

'I'm sorry you didn't know your brother was okay,' Celia said. 'Even if I'd known how to contact you, Kieran didn't want me to tell anyone where he was.'

'Fair enough.'

By now, Zoe and Kieran were sitting side by side on the end of the bed. He was kissing her wrist, kissing the tender skin just above the bandage.

'You'll be okay now,' he was saying to Zoe. 'You'll be looked after now.'

*

Sheena figured she'd stay out of the histrionics and let Kieran paw at his girlfriend for as long as he needed to paw. After the pair of them had blubbed and gushed at each other for a while, Zoe expressed a desire to have a soak in the voluminous hotel bathtub. Celia was only too happy to hurry back in there to run a bath for the girl and fuss over her.

When Kieran came out of the bedroom to face his sister, his eyes were puffy from bawling, but he was beaming like a gormless fool.

'Sheena, it's so great to see you!'

He bounded over, close enough that Sheena didn't have to stretch far to slap his face hard.

Kieran was startled, but only for a second. 'Yeah. Yeah. Fair enough. I deserve that. Have you been good? Have you been okay?'

Sheena slapped him hard again.

'Okay, Sheena. I reckon you've got a right to do that. You got every right to be mad.'

She raised her hand to whack him again, but this time Kieran ducked away and grinned at her from a safe distance. Sheena couldn't deny that it was good to see him. Separate from the relief to know he was alive, she had really missed the annoying deadhead.

'I'm sorry if you were worried about me,' he said in an un-expectedly grown-up voice.

'I wasn't worried.'

'Yeah? Good. Great.'

'I decided months ago not to give a flying fuck about you anymore,' Sheena explained.

'Yep. I can see why. Excellent decision. Good one.'

'I should've let you get yourself arrested last year.'

Kieran nodded firmly. 'You probably should've.'

'I should've left you to clean up your own filthy messes.'

'Maybe that's right.'

'I should've walked away three years ago when you were frying your brain with chemicals.'

'Maybe.'

'I should've left you to kill yourself.'

'I'm glad you didn't,' he said.

Sheena shrugged and looked out the window, not wanting to sob like a wet fool in front of him.

Kieran risked moving closer to her again. 'How are you, Sheena? Be happy. I want you to be happy. I wish I could give you that.'

'Well, you can't.'

'No, that's beyond even the powers of a legend like me.'

He grinned and Sheena let him see her smile.

'A smile!' he said with mock triumph. 'I can do that. Which is not much. Not a tiny fucking scrap of what you deserve, Sheena.'

'Just shut up for a second, Kieran. Can you do that?'

'I can do that,' he said and leaned against the window ledge beside her for several minutes in silence. Which was a record for Sheena's motor-mouth little brother.

*

'Mum?'

Celia hurried back into the bathroom to help her daughter out of the bath. She held open one of the large white towels and cupped Zoe's elbow to steady her as she stepped over the bath edge, still so weak she could easily slip on the wet tiles.

'My hand . . . I might need your help drying myself,' said Zoe.

Celia dropped her gaze, wanting to give her daughter some privacy even while she was drying her off with the towel. It was hard to look at the bruising on her daughter's neck and not burst into furious tears.

Sheena had told Celia what she knew about the break-in, the guard dogs, Zoe's failed search for Kieran. But whenever Zoe talked about any of it, she became so distressed that Celia decided it was better to leave it until she was stronger.

Meanwhile, Joe had booked a twin room down the hall where Kieran and Sheena could stay the night.

'Everyone's exhausted,' Joe reasoned. 'Let's all of us get some sleep and in the morning we can think more clearly.'

Sheena argued a bit but when Joe was gently insistent, she accepted the offer. 'Okay. Ta. It's a long way back to my place in Parramatta,' she said.

Joe went out and brought back generous piles of food from Una's on Victoria Street: schnitzels, potatoes, coleslaw and slabs of cherry strudel, along with two bottles of wine. It made Celia smile to think of this evening as one of those occasions – the last night of a holiday or the day of a house-move or some family event – when everyone mucks in together. She realised it *was* an occasion, a family reunion of a sort.

Kieran took a plate of food in to Zoe and sat on the edge of the bed, coaxing her to eat a few little bits.

When dinner was finished – Celia was surprised at the amount of food they'd all consumed – Sheena excused herself.

'I might go and have the longest shower in human history. Use three towels doing it. Then maybe veg out in front of the telly,' she said. 'Not many times in my life I'll get to stay in a high-class joint like this.'

With Sheena down the hall in another room and Kieran in the bedroom talking quietly with Zoe, Joe and Celia were left alone in the lounge room. She wondered if it would feel strained between them, too loaded, but all of that awkwardness seemed to have been blasted away. In fact, it was blessedly peaceful to sit here with this man who knew her so well.

They sat in companionable silence for a while until anxious thoughts started to buzz in Celia's head. Should they go to the police? Was Zoe well enough for that? What should their next move be?

Joe must have detected the shift in her mood. 'Don't worry about police and any of that tonight,' he said, answering her unspoken concerns. 'I'll find out more. Find out where we stand.'

'You're such a good friend to us, Joe. I don't even know how to measure the amount of gratitude I owe you. And Roza.'

Joe shrugged and poured them both another glass of wine.

'Maybe I should've locked Zoe in her room for a few years,' Celia said. 'There are parents who do that. Until social workers break into the house years later and find the children squinting against daylight.'

Joe was staring at her.

'I'm joking,' she said.

'I realise that.'

Celia flopped her head from side to side against the sofa and laughed with exasperation at herself.

Joe was watching her, smiling. 'Oh, Celia. I'm glad to see you so happy. It's torn me up to see you unhappy.'

She was surprised by his tone – it was intimate, as if he was asking something from her.

The moment was broken when they heard Kieran calling Celia into the bedroom.

She hurried in to find Zoe hunched up in a ball on the bed, wearing the nightie Sheena had bought her. Her breathing was shuddery after a bout of crying and Kieran was stroking her back.

'She really needs to sleep,' he said. 'She needs her mum right now, I reckon.'

Kieran kissed Zoe gently on the shoulder, then stepped away. He said goodnight to Joe before heading off to join his sister in the other hotel room.

Celia kicked off her shoes, climbed onto the bed and curled herself around Zoe's back. She smoothed the hair back from the girl's forehead and tucked it behind her ear, repeating this gesture in a steady rhythm until Zoe's breathing settled. Eventually, the two of them fell asleep.

TWENTY-THREE

It was too dim in the room for Sheena to see her watch. She was prepared to admit it was morning, sort of, but it was still very fucking early – too early for Kieran to be stumbling around the carpeted floor putting on his jeans.

She growled at him.

'Sorry, sorry,' he whispered. 'Go back to sleep, Sheena.'

Too late for that. She was awake now whether she wanted to be or not.

She dragged herself to sit up against the upholstered bedhead. 'Don't go in there and wake up that girl this early.'

'I'm not.'

'Where are you going?'

Kieran ignored her and finished putting on his shoes. Sheena could see he was wired up, fixed on some notion.

'What's going on?' she asked.

'She's so beautiful. None of that muck should've ever touched her. You know what I should do?'

'Crawl back into bed, grab a few more hours sleep, then ask Joe for proper advice on how we can handle the legal mess.'

'No. No,' Kieran insisted. 'I have to fix it so Zoe isn't dragged down into any of this. I'm going to the cops and handing myself in.'

'Well . . . hold on . . . talk to Joe about the best way to do this.'

'I'll take myself to a cop shop far away from here – in Penrith or Windsor or wherever. I can say it was just me and Mick went to that house.'

Sheena tried her stern voice with him. He mustn't rush and do something dumb. She pointed out that the police might not get hold of Mick, which meant Kieran would need Zoe as a witness. Otherwise, he could end up taking the blame for a shit-load of heavy-duty charges – malicious damage, those poor dogs, all of it.

Kieran came back at her, unwavering. 'No, don't you get it? I can't let Zoe be tangled up in it. The cops don't ever have to know she was there. This is the right thing to do.'

'But you gotta make sure it's the right thing for you, mate.'

'I have to go, before anyone talks me out of it.'

Sheena sighed. 'If this is a mistake, don't expect me to bail you out or feel bad for you.'

'I won't.'

'Hang on. Shit . . . should I come with you to the police station?'

'No. I'll call you later.'

Sheena clambered across the bed in T-shirt and undies to reach the desk. She tore a piece off the hotel notepaper and scribbled numbers.

'This is the phone number of the house I'm living in. The other one is the place I'm working. But no, wait. Give me a sec to get dressed. I should go with you,' Sheena said and reached for her jeans.

'No. I'm going on my own. Thanks for offering, though.' Kieran slid the notepaper with the phone numbers into his pocket. 'I can ring and let you know where they've put me.'

He grinned, trying to look cheeky, maybe even bold, but she could tell he was pretty fucking scared, too.

'See ya, Sheena.'

*

The heavy drapes in the hotel room blocked most of the morning sun, but there was enough light leaking in around the borders. Celia sat on the edge of the bed and watched Zoe sleep. She was stronger, fever gone, colour in her face again. Lost in sleep and with the sheets covering the bruises on her neck, she looked serene, as if she were home in bed.

Celia hadn't heard any noise to suggest Sheena or Kieran were up – they must still be asleep down the hall. She was glad. Let everyone keep sleeping as long as possible. Once awake, they would have to deal with the practical questions, the police, the accumulated toxins of the last months.

She peeked out the bedroom door. At some point during the night, Joe had fallen asleep on the sofa in the other room. She winced to see how uncomfortable he looked, with his neck cricked forward and legs bunched up, because the sofa wasn't long enough. She leaned in the doorway and watched him sleep. This lovely man.

Even though Celia stayed completely still and silent for those few moments, Joe opened his eyes. He must've sensed she was there, or maybe he'd been awake the whole time. Celia felt self-conscious, caught out.

Then he smiled and she smiled back.

Joe made a little show of trying to unfold his cramped limbs to sit upright. Celia mouthed 'sorry' and he shrugged, grinned – *it's fine*.

There was a knock on the door and he jumped up to let Sheena into the suite. Sheena only took a few steps inside, signalling she didn't intend to stay long. Joe didn't seem to notice the woman's strained manner and cheerfully asked her how she'd slept, offered to order breakfast for everyone, wondered if Kieran was awake too.

'My brother left a couple of hours ago.'

'Where's he gone?' Celia asked.

'He's gone to hand himself into the police.'

'He went on his own?' asked Joe.

For a moment, all Celia could think about was that boy, on his own, in a police lock-up.

Then Zoe, still warm and rumpled from bed, appeared in the bedroom doorway. 'Who told Kieran to go to the police on his own?' she demanded.

'No one told him,' Sheena replied. 'He wants to protect you. He's going to say it was just him and Mick. He decided it's the right thing to do.'

'It's a stupid thing to do! Why didn't you make him wait until . . . Shit, shit . . .' Zoe was agitated, breathless, as if someone had suddenly trapped her in this hotel room.

'You know, it's not a stupid idea.' Sheena addressed Celia now, trying to make this sound as matter-of-fact as any regular decision. 'Kieran's in deep shit anyway. He was always likely to end up in jail.

Doesn't mean your daughter has to get her life ruined too. Explain to her why this is a reasonable idea.'

Celia glanced round at Joe but he was staring at the floor, his hands pressed together. He must be at least entertaining the notion of going along with this. Celia and Zoe could just drive back to the farm now, as if Zoe had never been anywhere near the Dural house on that night.

'Tell Sheena that's bullshit!' said Zoe. 'Mum, you don't think this is right, do you?'

'What I think,' Celia said slowly, 'I think there is a lot for Kieran to deal with all on his own and we should see if we can —'

Sheena fired up then, her tone fierce. 'Look, look, my brother doesn't want to wreck Zoe's life and that's – that's a decent thing, isn't it? That's fucking honourable. It's what he wants to do. Let him do this.'

'No,' Zoe insisted. 'I was there. I have to say what happened.'

'You don't need to worry,' Sheena argued. 'The cops'll round up Mick – maybe have already. The guy's not an intellectual giant. So, they'll catch Mick and charge him with all the serious shit from that night.'

'You don't understand,' said Zoe flatly.

*

On that night, after Zoe had dumped the conked-out car, she had hurried back along the road on foot, then up the long driveway of the Dural house to find Kieran. By then, she was out of breath and her painful hand throbbed with every pulse.

She made a wide arc around the bodies of the poor dogs, as if their deadness might touch her if she went too close.

Even from outside, she could hear Mick — smashing the place up, yabbering, shouting abuse at Kieran, and every now and then letting rip with a howl of frustration. Zoe didn't want to go anywhere near him. At that moment all she wanted to do was persuade Kieran to leave. Afterwards, once they were well away from Mick, there would be time to apologise for running off, apologise for the things she'd said.

The front door was wide open, so Zoe could walk straight into the marble-tiled foyer. To the right was a formal sitting room. Mick had already been through there — two huge peacock-blue ceramic pots were smashed apart, paintings pulled off the walls with the canvases torn open, cupboard doors splintered where he'd gone hunting for the cash he'd been promised was in the house. It was the same in the dining room, the polished-wood cabinets fractured and gouged by the sledgehammer.

She moved further inside, down a central corridor, until she heard Mick in the study. He was ripping the place apart, yanking every drawer out of the massive rosewood desk carved with Chinese dragons.

Zoe was wearing soft-soled shoes, and with Mick making so much noise smashing things and cursing at Kieran, she figured he wouldn't hear her approach. She could find Kieran and signal to him to follow her out while Mick was occupied with the money search. But somehow, even with all the racket, Mick knew she was there.

'Did you bring back the car, you skanky bitch?'

Zoe backed away, towards the front door. A second later, Mick was out in the corridor, his clothes ripped and bloody, his body jerking as if the only thing holding it together was twitching ligaments.

'Where's Kieran?' Zoe asked.

'Your boyfriend fucked off. Ran up the road looking for you. The useless dickwad.'

There was a chance Mick would just let her go – he was there for the money – so Zoe turned her back on him to head towards the door.

'Where's the car? What did you do with the fucking car?'

She ran then, trying not to lose her footing on the polished floor. As she reached the doorway, Mick lunged after her, hooked his hand round her belly and slammed her down onto the marble.

He flipped her over onto her back and pinned her there with his knees. He was muttering about the car, yanking at her clothes, shoving his hands into the pockets of her jeans to scrabble for the car keys.

When Mick realised she didn't have the keys, he grunted, even angrier, and stared down at her. She could smell his breath, rasping out of his wet mouth. His pupils were so dilated that his eyeballs were just dark shiny stones in the eye sockets.

Zoe didn't make a sound, but just the sight of her riled him up. He grabbed the side of her neck with one hand, digging his fingers into the flesh, then shoved the heel of his other hand down hard on her throat.

She couldn't breathe with the weight of him on her neck. He pushed harder and Zoe realised he wasn't going to release the pressure until she was dead. She couldn't see properly, vision clouded, pain searing down her gullet, light-headed from lack of air. *I'm going to die. This is it.*

Mick had pinned her injured arm to the floor, but her other arm was free. She stretched out her hand as if she could miraculously grab hold of a rope to pull herself out of this moment and stay alive. Her fingertips hit something cold.

It was a cast-iron doorstop in the shape of an owl, with a sharper protruding piece of metal that formed the stand. The thing was heavy and Zoe wasn't sure where the strength came from for her to lift it. She swung the metal owl up until it slammed into the side of Mick's head. He lurched sideways and his hold on her weakened sufficiently that she could roll out from under him. She got up on her knees and smashed the doorstop down on his temple twice more.

Holding the cast-iron owl against her belly, she dragged herself across the tiles, out of Mick's reach, and gulped air back into her lungs. He lay completely still, and there was a lot of blood. She watched his chest move with a few meagre breaths and then stop entirely. The lizard eyes were open but opaque, dulled.

Once Zoe was certain he was dead and couldn't come after her, she got to her feet and ran out of the house. Her throat was scalded by every intake of breath, but she kept running until she reached a big enough road to hitch a lift.

*

Sheena had always figured there was a high likelihood someone would bash Mick's skull in one day. She hadn't expected it to be a sixteen-year-old princess.

The girl was shaking, holding her hands in front of her to make the others back off, not wanting Joe or her mother to touch her, not wanting them to come too close and be contaminated by the story she'd just told them.

'Does Kieran know what happened to Mick?' Sheena asked her.

'He didn't know. But I told him last night.'

So when Kieran left this morning to hand himself in, he knew this. He knew the police had found a dead man in the house, as well as the slaughtered dogs. Sheena sank onto the sofa and considered the full weight of the load her little brother had decided to take on. She had to respect it – he was a crazy fucker, but she had to respect it.

Zoe's voice was surprisingly steady. 'I didn't know Kieran would do this . . . try to take the blame, I mean. I have to go to the police now and say what really happened.'

Sheena watched Celia, who stared at the floor, pale and silent, not even looking at Joe. Maybe the woman was contemplating allowing Kieran to take responsibility for this. It occurred to Sheena that the way things usually went, he could tell some plausible provocation story and it wouldn't go too badly for him in court. Celia could be weighing that prospect, tempted to let her daughter slip away from this trouble.

'Mum. Listen to me, I need to go to the police straight away and tell them.'

Sheena waited for Celia to argue against the plan, but instead she looked at Zoe and nodded.

'I'll come with you,' Celia said. 'If you want me to.'

'Yes. Please.'

TWENTY-FOUR

Roza was relieved the summer of 1977–78 had been blessedly mild all through December and most of January. Today was the first baking-hot day and her limbs felt heavy, like wading through molasses.

She was absurdly old to be still working as a fruit packer and the job was becoming burdensome – the early starts, the walk up from her house to Celia's place, long days in the packing shed – although she would just laugh and wave her hands airily if anyone else mentioned it.

For this harvest, the old picking team was in the orchard and moving through the pick at a good speed. Mind you, Roza observed that Roy, the team boss, was being cautious with his crumbly spine and she hoped the poor man would manage through the weeks of hard work ahead of them.

Not so many peaches to pick this season, because the trees had been left to go almost into ruin during the winter. Even so, there would be enough fruit to pay off some debt and begin to pull the business back onto its feet. No one could deny that Celia had worked tremendously hard since she came home – first making up for the neglect around the property and now throwing her effort into the harvest.

Celia steered the tractor with full bins of fruit up to the shed just as Josef drove his air-conditioned car into the yard. The two of them smiled hello and did a little pantomime to each other about the heat.

Joe kissed Roza. 'Hi, Mum. I dropped another carload of boxes on your back porch.'

He was moving into his mother's place, just for the months it would take to restump and then renovate the house he had bought in town.

'Have you laid your eyes on the ugly hovel Josef has purchased?' Roza asked Celia.

Celia laughed. 'Yes.'

'What can you say when you discover your child has no taste?' Roza asked. Sandor had brought Josef up looking at books about the great cities and their fine buildings, appreciating what was well proportioned and elegant. 'I had always thought Josef was a man of good taste.'

Celia shook her head with mock disbelief. 'And yet now he buys an ugly house.'

'We are talking make-you-want-to-slit-your-throat ugly,' Roza added.

She saw Celia exchange a smile with Joe. She knew the two of them talked about how to handle her. She knew this very well.

'Mum, I explained to you. It's a matter of finding a place I can afford that's near the boys, where I'll have room when they stay over.'

'None of my business.' Roza put her hands in the air, surrendering.

Roza then saw Celia's gaze shift to the orchard. Zoe was walking between the rows of trees, up to the yard. The girl filled her water bottle from the big container, then sploshed water over her face and neck to cool off. She was filthy, sweaty clothes stuck to her, face greasy with sun-cream, hair squashed under a cap, but no one with eyes in their head would say she was not a gorgeous creature.

There had been many talks with police officers and lawyers, explanations given, allowances made, charges answered in the court. Zoe received what is called a suspended sentence, but not for killing the fellow. In the end, no one thought that should be on her head. The judge warned Zoe that she must be of good behaviour. (Roza wasn't convinced many people in the world would last long if they were supposed always to have good behaviour.) Because of Zoe's age, none of the criminal matters would stay on her record.

Of course, there were matters that would stay in a person's mind for a long, long time, and no court rules could change that.

Joe had organised legal help for Kieran. Roza suspected he paid the young man's costs without telling Heather, who would most surely have disapproved. Kieran spent some months in prison and when they released him two weeks ago, he travelled up north to find work on a prawn trawler, wanting to stay away from unhelpful influences and earn himself some money.

Zoe and the young man wrote letters to each other while he was in jail and had pledged to keep in contact. Roza wasn't sure if it counted as a romance anymore. Nobody would say it aloud, but Zoe's future and that young man's future were likely to be very different. But there was a love between the two of them, a loyalty, a bond, whatever somebody might want to call it, and there was surely a chance that would last in some fashion.

And who could say what would happen to Kieran in the long run? Roza sometimes pictured bad things for a boy like that – rolling his car on a dirt road, stumbling into the path of some angry man at the worst moment. But no one can see into the future. Roza hoped that anyone hearing the boy's story might join her in wishing the best for him.

Celia was still in contact with the sister, that Sheena. At first the two women needed to speak about legal matters and such. But since then, Celia had made a point of ringing Sheena every few weeks for a chat – if you could call a conversation with that sharp creature a 'chat'. Celia persevered, believing the young woman appreciated their connection deep down. It was not for Roza to judge this or offer any comment.

Apparently, Sheena was doing well. She had moved to Melbourne for a fresh start and had been quickly promoted to manager of a bar there. She had recently acquired a new boyfriend who, as far as Celia could assess from the phone calls, was not a bad fellow and was in no way a dickless wonder.

Roza looked out into the orchard to see that the sun had started its swing down from the midday point and there was now a ribbon of shade alongside the fruit trees. Zoe was standing half in shade and half in sun, with the light flaring off her fair hair as she tipped her head back to drink from the water bottle. Celia's eyes were fixed on her daughter, soaking in the sight of her, hoping to make it last for the months they would be apart.

'Zoe's all packed,' Celia said to Joe. 'Her suitcase is just inside the kitchen door.'

'Right. We'll need to head off in half an hour or so.'

Joe was giving Zoe a lift into town to catch the Sydney bus. During the remainder of the past year – after all the trouble – Zoe had attended a high school in the city, living with her aunt Freya. She had returned home for the summer holidays but today she must leave again and Celia would have to do without her for the school terms.

'Zoe!' Celia called out. 'Time to go soon. Better hop in the shower. Which means you can stop working now.'

Zoe stretched with exaggerated relief, miming that her back was aching from all this slave labour. She peeled off the sweaty cap, tipped the rest of the water over her head and shook her wet hair from side to side. Celia laughed, adoring her.

So. It seemed there was to be no vodka for Roza this coming winter, since she would have her son living with her. This wouldn't be such a bad thing. Josef could help around the place, and more importantly, he could keep Celia company when Zoe went back to the city for the next months.

Of course, when Celia and Zoe were separated, they had regular phone calls. The girl was stronger, no doubt about that, but Celia said she only needed to hear two syllables over the phone line to detect the blackness in her daughter's voice, if Zoe was in one of her wretched moods. Other times she would sense a distance and know Zoe wasn't telling her something. But Celia couldn't drive down to Sydney and demand answers, take over. She would have to let the phone call end and just sit with it. Some problems could be solved by throwing effort at them, but some necessary things – like letting your child go out into the world, the beautiful, perilous world – required you just to sit with things gnawing in your belly and learn not to do anything.

Roza knew that Celia still had some sleepless nights, hours in which she would imagine and catalogue all the possible dangers.

But now, according to Celia, she made the effort to add extra moments to the conjured scenes, envisaging how Zoe might escape trouble by her good judgement, quick wits, strong heart. There was comfort in that – urging her daughter to be strong – as if all the hours of worrying and urging would distil and harden into a small amulet Zoe could wear around her neck, wherever she might be.

ACKNOWLEDGEMENTS

Debra Oswald would like to thank Michael Wynne, Kerrie Laurence, Annabelle Sheehan, Karen Oswald, Michele Franks, Les Langlands, Anthony Blair, Shelley Eves, Dale Druhan and Noel Franks for their help. Thanks to Currency Press who published *The Peach Season* in 2007 and to Rodney Seaborn, Christopher Hurrell, Stephen Collins, David Berthold, the cast and creative team of the Griffin Theatre production; Ben Ball, Rachel Scully and the team at Penguin Random House. Huge thanks, even more than usual this time, are owed to Richard Glover.